"I am grateful for my father, who keeps me good and sweet. I am grateful for my mother, who keeps her own heart guarded and safe. I am grateful for my adviser, who keeps me protected. I am grateful for the Path, which keeps me pure. Ever after."

ELISSA SUSSMAN

Stray

A FOUR SISTERS NOVEL

Greenwillow Books
An Imprint of HarperCollinsPublishers

Stray
Copyright © 2014 by Elissa Sussman

All rights reserved. No part of this book may be used or reproduced in any manner whatsoever without written permission except in the case of brief quotations embodied in critical articles and reviews. Printed in the United States of America. For information address HarperCollins Children's Books, a division of HarperCollins Publishers, 195 Broadway, New York, NY 10007.
www.epicreads.com

First published in hardcover by Greenwillow Books in 2014; first paperback publication, 2016.

The text of this book is set in Horley Old Style MT Standard
Book design by Sylvie Le Floc'h
Maps illustrated by Betsy Peterschmidt

Library of Congress Cataloging-in-Publication Data
Sussman, Elissa, author. Stray / by Elissa Sussman.   pages cm—(Four Sisters)
"Greenwillow Books."
Summary: Princess Aislynn's magical ability is powerful and uncontrollable, so she is "redirected" into the order of Fairy Godmothers, where her heart is removed and stored in a hidden cabinet, and she must spend the rest of her life devoted to serving another royal family—but her growing friendship with a palace gardener causes Aislynn to question the vows she has taken, and the motives of those who would prevent her from "straying" from the path.
ISBN 978-0-06-227455-7 (hardback)— ISBN 978-0-06-227456-4 (pbk ed.)
1. Fairy godmothers—Juvenile fiction. 2. Magic—Juvenile fiction. 3. Princesses—Juvenile fiction. 4. Gardeners—Juvenile fiction. 5. Choice (Psychology)—Juvenile fiction.
6. Identity (Psychology)—Juvenile fiction. 7. Friendship—Juvenile fiction. [1. Fairy tales.
2. Fairy godmothers—Fiction. 3. Magic—Fiction. 4. Princesses—Fiction. 5. Choice—Fiction.
6. Identity—Fiction. 7. Friendship—Fiction.] I. Title.
PZ8.S88St 2014 [Fic]—dc23 2014028779

15 16 17 18 19 20 CG/RRDH 10 9 8 7 6 5 4 3 2 1
First Edition
Greenwillow Books

For my family,
both given and found

N

E

Eremurus
(Home of the
Eastern
Monarch.)

S

1 week/carriage
1 Month/foot
3 Days/horseback

North
Nerine
Manor

North
Nerine
Township

Nerine

Nerine
Lake

Nerine
Castle

Nerine
Academy

Nyssa
Manor

Muriel

South
Elderwood
Township

Border between The Northern Kingdom
& The Eastern Kingdom.

Detail of
Inset Map

North Nepeta Township
Nepeta Academy
East Erysimum Township
Nepeta Castle
Nepeta Lake
West Nepeta Manor
Nepeta
Erysimum
Erysimum Manor
Erysimum Castle
South Nepeta Township
South Erysimum Township
Nyssa Castle
Nyssa Township
Erysimum Academy
Nyssa
North Elderwood Township
East Elderwood Township
North Elderwood Manor
Elderwood
Elderwood Academy
Elderwood Castle
1 Day by Foot
1 Day by Carriage
1/2 Day by Horseback

Stray

There once were four sisters

Who were exceptionally ordinary,

But desired more than a maiden should desire

Ravaged by their shameful wants

Their loving hearts never bloomed

Instead four wicked brambles

Grew in their place

Each tainted

With poisonous magic

—*The Four Sisters 2:16*

Chapter 1

Aislynn's hands were bleeding. Her dress was stained with dirt and muck, her hair unraveling with each heaving breath. The scent of dampness, of mud and sweat, filled her nose. She was alone in the cold, dark garden, with a ruined dress and bloodied palms.

Through the nighttime came the muffled sounds of the spring ball, of laughter and dancing and people falling in love. Aislynn felt so very far away and wished that this was just another nightmare. That this was something she could be awakened from.

All of it was her fault. She should have tried harder, should have controlled the curse, should have remained on the

Path. But there was no use wishing to change what could not be changed.

Soon they would come looking for her. With a trembling hand, Aislynn brushed the dust from her gown, careful not to bloody the material, and tucked a loose strand of hair behind her ear. Glancing at the destroyed rosebushes strewn across the dirt, Aislynn went though the gate, up the stairs, and back to the ball.

That morning she had woken tangled in sheets and nightmares. The linens were easily discarded, but the dreams lingered like smoke. In them she was always alone. Alone in an unknown forest, with sharp branches and a round, waxen moon above her.

But last night had been different.

Last night there had been footsteps. They had echoed in the dark, and Aislynn had searched the shadows, turning round and round until a pair of yellow eyes appeared in front of her, as if they had been there all along. Above her, the clouds had shifted, and the moonlight revealed the creature. A long snout and wet, wide mouth. A wolf.

No matter how many times Aislynn prayed for a chaste heart, no matter how often she vowed to keep her desires pure, every evening her wild wishes followed her to bed, sprawling across her pillow and tangling in her hair. Jealous, prideful wishes. And as she slept, they wrapped themselves around her and twisted into nightmares.

Aislynn knew she was to blame. No good girl had such dreams, of darkness and moonlight and now of wolves. Of animals so fierce that they lived off brambles sharp enough to cut their pink tongues. The dream was a warning, a reminder that a maiden's heart was capable of growing both roses and thorns. That if she was not careful, if she was not diligent, her step along the Path would falter.

Aislynn stood and faced the wall. Crossing her wrists over her chest, she could feel the warmth of her heavy gold locket against her palm. She dropped to her knees and, in a sleep-sore murmur, recited the words inscribed on the pendant.

"I will accept the Path I am taking. I will not stray. I will not yearn for what I cannot have. I will heed the words of my advisers and guard my loving heart against cursed magic. Ever after."

As Aislynn's heartbeat settled back into a slow, steady rhythm, she heard the soft patter of footsteps and the rustle of uniforms in the hallway. Her bedroom door opened, letting in Tahlia, tea, and the beginning of the day.

Aislynn would not mention last night's dream. She forced a smile and sat back on her bed, smoothing her nightgown tightly around her stockinged feet and legs. Just another secret to keep.

"Good morning," said Tahlia as she set the tray down on the vanity and pulled back the curtains, inviting bright spring sunlight into the bedroom. From behind, the fairy godmother barely looked like a person, more like a soft triangle in her wimple and loose robes. As was traditional, her uniform hid all but her hands and face. She returned Aislynn's smile, only hers was easy and sweet, the corners of her green eyes crinkling.

"What would my lady like to wear today?" Tahlia asked, dropping sugar cubes into the tea with two soft *plinks* before opening the massive wardrobe to reveal the dozens of blue dresses inside. Without waiting for a response, the fairy godmother retrieved two gowns. The one she passed to Aislynn was a cotton periwinkle dress that had been worn dozens of times. Pretty and simple.

The other dress Tahlia hung carefully next to the mirror. It was exquisite. Made of a rich satin, the vibrant sapphire color was slightly muted by a layer of organza across the massive skirt. Blue lace and delicate beading decorated the long sleeves and high collar that were customary for a young lady from the Northern Kingdom.

But it wasn't the sleeves or the neckline that had Aislynn's attention. It was the rose. Now that she was sixteen, it would be embroidered on each of her gowns: a rose in perfect bloom over her heart.

Disappointed that she had to wait until the evening to wear the beautiful gown, Aislynn stepped into the cotton day dress. Tahlia tended to the endless line of buttons down its back, and Aislynn did her best not to flinch each time her fairy godmother's fingers brushed against bare skin. No matter the warmth of the room, or the heat of the season, Tahlia's hands, like all fairy godmothers', were frigid.

The morning bell rang just as the last button was fastened. Slipping into her shoes, Aislynn followed Tahlia out of the bedroom and down the stairs to breakfast.

Four years at Nerine Academy, but to Aislynn it had never felt anything like a home. Until a girl was settled into her married life, everything else was only temporary. It was best not to get attached, and the academy made it easy. Everything was stone, hard and bleak. Though Northerners were fond of embellishments, the only decorations the headmistress tolerated were the enormous tapestries. The one outside the dining hall portrayed a young woman with her head arched back, her mouth open in a silent scream. Between the hands crossed over her heart was a tangle of briars tearing through her chest, bloodying her fingers. She had black hair like Aislynn's.

The familiar sounds of gossip and laughter floated into the corridor as Aislynn made her way into the dining hall. At the sight of the lone figure seated at the farthest corner table, she walked a little faster.

Maris didn't look up when Aislynn approached, her attention focused on the blond curl she was twisting between her fingers. Her other hand was tracing the embroidered rose on her yellow dress.

"Morning," Aislynn said as she took the seat opposite her friend.

"Morning" was the sullen response.

There was a burst of laughter from across the room where the other, more favored girls were seated. Maris cast an envious look in their direction.

Guilt filled Aislynn's chest. Someone should have told Maris, when she had arrived at Nerine last season, that offering friendship and kindness to someone like Aislynn meant sacrificing her own social standing within the academy.

Selfishly, Aislynn was glad for Maris's misstep. At least now they had each other. She cast a covert look behind her, where half a dozen girls were seated separately, their heads down, trying not to draw any attention to themselves.

The room grew silent as the headmistress entered the

dining hall, followed by a line of equally stern-faced teachers. Their robes were nearly identical to the ones fairy godmothers wore, except for the embroidery over their hearts.

Aislynn crossed her wrists over her chest as Madame Odette led them all in the morning prayer. "May our hearts be modest and our steps unwavering. Ever after."

Both Aislynn and Maris were silent as breakfast was set in front of them, a bowl of porridge for each, accompanied by a dish of brown sugar and a platter of fruit. Adding large scoops of sugar, Aislynn stirred her food until it was nearly the same shade as her skin.

"You're going to eat that?" Maris asked as Aislynn took her first bite. The porridge was too hot and burned her throat as she swallowed. "You know it's a bad idea to eat on the day of a ball," Maris said.

"Of course." Aislynn quickly pushed her food away. "Thank you."

"Someone ought to remind Sariah." Maris was looking over Aislynn's shoulder with a smirk. Aislynn glanced back. The girl in question had already finished her breakfast and was now eating from the platter of fruit. "I still can't believe she'll be Contained before me. Maybe if *my* father was a lord . . ." Maris pressed her spoon hard against the table. "*You'll* probably be Contained within the season."

"Do you think so?" Aislynn said, surprised. To become engaged, let alone marry, soon after being Introduced was quite unusual.

"Of course." Maris laughed, the noise empty and forced. "Truth and honesty, Aislynn, whomever you marry will get to be king. It doesn't matter what you look like."

Aislynn's father was one of the handful of kings in the North. Like all kingdoms, the North had one first-class monarch, who ruled over the entirety of his country. Under him were the second-class kings, who oversaw several provinces, each in turn run by third-class dukes. And below those were the fourth-class royals, like Maris's family, who managed their own lands and servants. Once her father died, Aislynn's husband would take on the responsibilities of king and manage Nepeta and its surrounding provinces.

Aislynn knew that Maris was right, that it was her status that would be tempting to suitors, but she couldn't help wishing there were other reasons she could be Contained so quickly. A dangerous heat began to flicker in her chest, and Aislynn took a deep breath, willing away her vain and wicked thoughts.

"At least no one can tell I'm from the West," Maris said, pushing blond strands back from her pale face. Indeed, of the two of them, it would be easy to mistake Maris for being northern born, where her coloring was more common. "The last thing I'd want is to look too . . . exotic." She eyed Aislynn's dark hair, but there was a hint of jealousy in her gaze.

"I'm sure you'll be Contained soon."

Her friend glared at her. "Of course I will," Maris said. "Have I told you about the shoes I'll be wearing this evening?" There was nothing Maris liked to talk about more than her small feet and delicate shoes, so even though Aislynn had already heard about them, she shook her head and let the other girl launch into a detailed description.

"Well, they have tiny stitching across the heels, and each toe is embroidered with a single perfect yellow rose, so when anyone bows to greet me, they will see the rose and be reminded that I am in bloom." Maris had previously mentioned that her gloves would also be embroidered with yellow roses, so the added embellishment to her shoes seemed like a rather desperate indication of her status.

But Aislynn said nothing. She supposed that being so close to turning seventeen without a proposal of marriage would make someone very desperate indeed.

On any other day, the time between breakfast and lunch would be occupied by lessons in needlepoint and calligraphy, both of which had been canceled due to the evening's events.

As Aislynn was an artless student of both, she was grateful for the respite. Since the ball was to be hosted at Nerine Academy, time that would usually be spent traveling could now be used for reflection and contemplation.

Aislynn had hoped to spend this time with Maris talking more about their dresses for the evening, but the other girl claimed sleepiness and retreated upstairs to nap. So Aislynn went to the library, which was blessedly empty. From the window seat, she could see the enormous hedges that wrapped around the ballroom, its balcony, and the small gardens below.

The layout of Nerine Academy was not unlike a person lying down with her arms spread out and her feet together. With the kitchen at the head, the classrooms and the second-floor dormitories occupied what would be the body and legs, while the dining hall was one arm and the ballroom the other. The library was in one of the feet.

Aislynn's stomach growled. She was disappointed that Maris had gone to her room. For several weeks now, she had been searching for the courage to suggest to her that they become each other's lady-in-waiting. It was a title reserved for only the most loyal and loving of friends, someone who would be completely truthful and honest. Young maidens were encouraged to find such a companion so they would refrain from annoying their husbands with the silly topics of conversation that women preferred. Occasionally there were rumors of friendships that had developed further than was appropriate, but advisers were quick to extinguish any such entanglements.

Aislynn would ask Maris tonight after the ball. Or before that, when they were getting ready. Maybe during lunch. Yes, during lunch, she decided as she watched the sun climb in the sky.

Their table was empty when she entered the dining hall hours later, so Aislynn took her usual seat and waited. It wasn't long before the room filled with girls and giggling as her classmates made their way to their places.

"Eating alone, Ashy-linn?"

Shoulders tensing, Aislynn stared straight ahead, refusing to meet the amethyst eyes she knew were watching her. Violaine had not bothered her for weeks, harassing other students instead, but it had been foolish to imagine that such luck would last.

"Is your lady-in-waiting keeping you waiting?" Violaine moved closer, her cotton day dress brushing against Aislynn's back. She sighed loudly. "I just heard her crying in her room. Probably about having to eat with you again." There was a ripple of laughter, but Aislynn clenched her jaw and said nothing. "Truth and honesty, you know Maris only tolerates you because your status is higher than hers," Violaine sneered. "It's not as if she actually likes you."

Aislynn knew the other girl wanted to make her cry. She had done it before. When she first arrived at the academy, Violaine's favorite activity had been stepping on the hem of Aislynn's gown whenever they walked past the headmistress or other teachers. She never got caught. Instead, it was Aislynn who was always punished, since a proper lady never stumbles.

One time, though, Aislynn had turned just as Violaine was lowering her foot. Aislynn's toes got caught under Violaine's sharp heel, and as pain shot through her, she grabbed Violaine's shoulders. With a gasp, the other girl shoved her to the floor, but not before Aislynn felt magic surge through her palms, faster than she could control.

"What happened?" the teacher who had rushed to the scene demanded.

With a smug look on her face, Violaine had opened her mouth to answer, but instead of words, a tiny frog slipped from her lips. It hit the floor next to Aislynn before quickly hopping away. Violaine's shriek had shattered the silence.

Aislynn had been confined to her room for over a week. By the time she was allowed back in the dining hall, the story had been respun, and the tiny frog had become a nearly endless stream of toads and snakes and Aislynn had become someone to fear. For good reason, she supposed.

When a proper young lady had an occurrence, she might change the color of her hair ribbon or slam a door that she wasn't touching. When Aislynn had an occurrence, she made girls spit toads or worse. She could still picture her first time, when she had lit a pile of books on fire.

"I suppose it's not your fault," Violaine said now. "Wasn't your father a Westerner? Wasn't he one of *hers*?"

Aislynn didn't want to hear any more. Uncurling her fingers, she lifted her hand from her lap and raised her eyes to meet Violaine's.

"Ribbit," Aislynn murmured.

Violaine jerked back, her skin so fair that it seemed translucent. Her companions shrieked and scattered.

A throat cleared. Glancing up, Aislynn realized that the entire room had gone still. All eyes were on Madame Odette, who was watching the events with a displeased tilt of her head. The headmistress beckoned, and Aislynn walked to the front of the room on shaky legs. As she passed Violaine and the other girls, they cowered away from her. Aislynn allowed herself the tiniest sliver of satisfaction.

But as she curtsied in front of the teachers, that satisfaction was quickly replaced by shame, and she did her best not to flinch when Madame Odette rose from her seat.

Her words were as withering as her gaze. "I think it would be best for you to take your lunch in your room."

"But I didn't . . . ," Aislynn blurted out, regretting the words instantly. Talking back to a teacher was nearly unheard of, but contradicting the headmistress was unthinkable. The entire dining hall seemed to gasp.

"'Journeys,' chapter fourteen, verse twenty-four." Madame Odette's words were loud enough for everyone to hear. "Now remove yourself from my presence, or your punishment will be even more severe."

Aislynn could hear the other girls snickering as she curtsied again. The distance from the teachers' table to the door felt longer than her sixteen years. As soon as she was out of sight, even though it was against the rules, Aislynn raced all the way up the stairs as if she could outrun her humiliation and impudence. Slamming the door of her bedroom behind her, she struggled to calm her uneven breathing and *rat-tat-tat* pulse.

Sitting on the dresser was her copy of *The Path*. She didn't need to look up the passage the headmistress had recommended. She knew it by heart.

"'The flowers farthest from the Path have the sharpest barbs,'" she murmured to herself. Curling her fingers around the book, Aislynn willed the words to calm her. They didn't. Instead she felt her chest tighten with anger and frustration. Sucking in a breath, she drew back her arm.

"Thorns!" she swore. With a tremendous heave, she sent the sacred text flying.

As it hit the wall and tumbled down, the reality of what she had done, the wickedness of her actions, jolted Aislynn out of her self-pity. She rushed to the fallen book and scooped it from the floor. Some of the pages were bent. As she smoothed them down, Aislynn reminded herself that she was the one to blame. She wouldn't be treated this way if she didn't deserve it.

Her entire room served as a reminder of that. The headmistress had forbidden Tahlia to perform any permanent fixes, but her fairy godmother had done her best to hide the worst of it. From where she sat on the floor, Aislynn could see under her bed, where the cream carpet was stained with uneven splotches of color, as though someone had spilled purple and yellow ink all over it. The wallpaper, once blue, was now streaked with green and covered in scorch marks.

Aislynn hated her room.

There was a soft knock at the door, and Tahlia entered with a tray of cheese and fruit. "I thought you might want some lunch," she said.

Avoiding Tahlia's gaze, Aislynn pressed *The Path* against her chest. "Thank you."

"I'll start your bath," the fairy godmother said, piling a robe and dressing gown into her arms before disappearing into the bathing room. In a few moments the bathwater would be heated just right, and it would remain at the perfect temperature until Aislynn was ready to get out.

Her stomach grumbling, Aislynn sat down at the vanity and reached for one of the strawberries Tahlia had brought her. Most of the girls regarded their meals in the same way they regarded their fairy godmothers: as a displeasing necessity. That was Aislynn's problem. One of her many problems. She was overly fond of both.

It would be easier if Tahlia were more like the others—distant and detached—like the fairy godmother Aislynn had been given when she first arrived at Nerine.

Returning the strawberry to the tray, Aislynn opened *The Path* and turned the thin pages carefully until she found the chapter on fairy godmothers: "Servants of Purity."

> "Embrace her heart, but do not hold her close.
> Though she is pruned of all desires but devotion,
> her thorns can still draw blood."

Gently resting her fingers on her chest, Aislynn imagined a copper kettle there, between her ribs. When she was lucky, when her thoughts were pure and good, the kettle remained cool and still. But there were times when wickedness would overcome her, and she would begin to simmer, her terrible desires churning and boiling until her kettle heart cracked, magic spilling from her like scalding water.

Aislynn felt Tahlia's hand on her shoulder. This time she welcomed the cold—it pulled her away from her unpleasant thoughts. Once submerged in her bath, Aislynn rested her head against the smooth porcelain and slid down beneath the bubbles. Filling her ears with the soft, round sound of water, Aislynn calmed her mind with fantasies of the night ahead.

She tried to imagine the suitors Adviser Hull would present to her father. It was commonly said that men married up for power, down for beauty. Aislynn's husband would be the future king of Nepeta, and a man could forgive a lot to be king. Or so Aislynn's teachers had told her.

With the fragrant water embracing her, Aislynn imagined herself a beau who was handsome and tall, who gazed down on her with such love and affection that the entire room would stare. She imagined his cheek warm against hers.

It would have been nice to stay in the bath all day, floating among her fantasies, but there was too much to be done. Aislynn wrapped herself in her long dressing gown and stepped into her bedroom. Tahlia had cleared the untouched tray of food. She had also set out clean undergarments and stockings, which Aislynn quickly put on. It had been a long time since her fairy godmother had seen Aislynn's legs, and like the walls of her room, they were something that could not be fixed.

Spread out across the bed was the blue satin gown Adviser Hull had chosen for her. Everything followed his design, from her hairstyle to the length of her sleeves and the height of her heels. Next to the dress was the original sketch, in Adviser Hull's formal, linear style, which portrayed Aislynn with a tiny waist and hips in equal balance to her shoulders.

The corset would help, but she shuddered as she glanced at the stiff boning and silken ties draped over a chair. Next to the corset was a full underskirt so sturdy that it could stand on its own. Smoothing her hand over the dress's slippery soft fabric, Aislynn pictured a suitor taking her waist and imagined how his fingers would feel through the layers of satin and linen.

Tahlia returned. It was time to prepare. The corset was first. Taking her last deep breath of the evening, Aislynn allowed her fairy godmother to begin lacing up the stiff contraption. With each tug, she reminded herself that a smaller waist might garner more dance requests.

Those who were kind would say that, in looks, Aislynn

was the perfect combination of her parents. While she didn't have her mother's Northern complexion, they shared the same long fingers and eggcup chin, a chin that seemed far too small for Aislynn's face. Her wavy hair and large brown eyes were an inheritance from her Western father, along with skin the color of toasted bread. But while his was lovely and smooth, her cheeks turned a splotchy red when she blushed. So while she appreciated these gifts, she couldn't help wishing that she could also have been given her mother's thinly shaped nose and her father's easy smile. Or Maris's delicate feet and Violaine's arresting eyes.

Before arriving at the academy, Aislynn had not given much thought to her looks. But students were expected to help one another recognize their flaws, both to maintain their humility and to encourage self-improvement. Aislynn's fellow classmates had been quick to point out the areas in which she was lacking.

Watching herself in the mirror as Tahlia made the final adjustments to her unruly hair, Aislynn tried to clear her mind of jealous, covetous thoughts, the same desires that undoubtedly conjured last night's dreams. She didn't need to be beautiful to get married. Maris was right. It was her royal rank that would secure her future, not her looks. And it was wrong to want what she did not need.

Chapter 2

There was a sumptuous spread of food in the waiting room, but Aislynn knew it would go untouched. Her stomach rumbled traitorously, but she ignored it, searching the crowd for Maris.

Something soft danced across her nose. "Well, don't you look nice, Ashy-linn." Violaine wore a green feather in her hair, and brandished another like a weapon. She flicked it once more across Aislynn's cheek and gave a slow *tsk*, tongue against teeth, her eyes sweeping over Aislynn's blue gown. "Well, nice for *you*, I suppose." This caused a flurry of giggles to pass through the group of girls gathered around her, their dresses creating a cage of crinoline and satin. "However, if you ask me—"

"I didn't," Aislynn muttered.

"If you ask me, I think you'd look much better in purple." Violaine glanced across the room to where the fairy godmothers were standing in a silent sea of lavender.

This set off a new round of laughter, one that was cut short by the second bell, indicating that the ball was about to begin. Deep within her chest, Aislynn's kettle heart had begun to heat, so she took a slow breath and willed the magic to go away. Once it settled into a quiet hum, she joined the other girls who had just turned sixteen, keeping a good distance from Violaine and her feather.

"Ladies." The headmistress waited for silence. Behind her was a pair of open doors leading to a staircase. At the bottom of that staircase was a silk curtain, and on the other side of that curtain was a crowded ballroom—and Aislynn's future.

Madame Odette gave the girls a smile as thin as thread. "Please join me in the prayer of gratitude."

Crossing her wrists over her chest, Aislynn recited the familiar words.

"I am grateful for my father, who keeps me good and sweet. I am grateful for my mother, who keeps her own heart guarded and safe. I am grateful for my adviser, who keeps me protected. I am grateful for the Path, which keeps me pure. Ever after."

"Very good." The headmistress's grimace was almost an expression of approval. "Step forward and accept the Path's gifts."

The first to go were the newly engaged, like Lady Sariah, who would be escorted for the first time not by her father, but by her future husband. Aislynn looked longingly at the silver band surrounding the rose on her gown.

Next were the girls who were approaching the end of their sixteenth year, most of them wearing similar expressions of anxiety and desperation. Aislynn glanced over at the fairy godmothers and balked, truly seeing for the first time how young some of them were.

Finally it was Aislynn's turn, and she obediently took what was offered to her. The glass of pure melted snow was icy against her teeth, and the sugared flower petal dissolved quickly on her tongue. She curtsied and made her way through the doors.

As she headed down the steps, she realized she could not remember what she was supposed do with her hands when she was announced. Should they be in front of her or behind? Should her fingers be linked or clasped? The curtain parted.

"Now presenting . . . Princess Aislynn of Nepeta."

She left her hands at her sides, though they felt as awkward and stiff as branches on a barren tree. The ballroom was magnificent and imposing, candlelight flickering in time with Aislynn's pulse as hundreds of eyes turned toward her.

Her father stood waiting. She had seen him only last season but was surprised to find his hair had grayed, mostly at the temples. Aislynn thought it suited him. He wore a small smile, his mustache curving upward, but he did not look directly at her. She didn't expect him to. Taking his arm, Aislynn followed him into the ballroom.

"How are you, my dear?" His voice was quiet, and his attention seemed focused on the tapestry against the wall in front of them. It depicted the first adviser in a regal white suit, his hands gently resting on the heads of the two women who were kneeling in front of him. The fairy godmother on his right and the noblewoman on his left had their hands outstretched, their fingers just barely touching.

"I'm well," Aislynn responded, noticing, for the first time, the serene smiles stitched on the women's faces. A chill ran up her spine, and she shuddered.

Her father glanced at her. "You look well," he said.

"Thank you."

Next to the tapestry was an ornately decorated map of the four kingdoms, the geography carefully detailed in colorful ink. Quickly Aislynn's eyes found her family's castle in Nepeta. Barely a hand's length away was Nerine Academy, surrounded by townships and kingdoms she knew only by name. Aislynn's entire world, it seemed, could be contained within a few inches.

Across the center of the drawing was an angry tangle of briar bushes. They cut across the mountains that touched all four kingdoms and dangerously darkened the West. This was the Midlands, ruled by the Wicked Queen, Josetta.

"Let's join your mother, shall we?" the king said, pulling Aislynn away from the map.

Everything in the ballroom was decorated for the season. At the center of each table was a wide glass bowl, filled with waxy lily pads and their spiky cream flowers. Delicate daisy garlands and pastel curtains hung corner to corner. The room was as fresh as the bright butter daffodils firmly fastened in each gentleman's lapel. Aislynn resisted the urge to adjust her father's boutonniere, which was just slightly crooked.

As Aislynn watched the swirling, colorful couples on the dance floor, her heart leaping with anticipation, Violaine crossed suddenly in front of them, her arm linked with a woman who had matching eyes.

"Truth and honesty, Violaine, you may not be as beautiful or clever as your sister, but look at these girls," Aislynn heard the woman say. "If they're your competition, why aren't you Contained yet?"

"I'm sorry, Mother." Violaine's head was bowed, her cheeks flushed.

"Your dance card is shrinking with each season. I don't understand. Are you being purposefully disappointing or just incompetent?" Both women looked wan in their green dresses.

"Hello, darling," said Aislynn's mother, coming through the crowd to greet them. As Violaine and her mother moved away, the queen gave them a pitying glance. "Thank the glass slipper you look so fetching in blue."

"Hello, Mama." Aislynn accepted her mother's embrace, lighter than a spiderweb.

"It really is a shame when the colors of your status do nothing to elevate . . . your status." The queen beamed at her clever turn of phrase.

"Very well said, my dear." The king patted her hand. Glancing around the room, Aislynn was grateful not just for the flattering color she wore but also the ease with which she could determine the exact rank of the guests. Those who were second class, like her parents, wore blue; the third class dressed in green and the fourth class, like Maris, in yellow. The handful of first-class royalty wore red.

"Are you nervous?" the queen asked.

"No," Aislynn lied. She wanted to ask her father who Adviser Hull had included on his list of suitors, but she knew her dance card would only be revealed after she was Introduced.

"Your Majesties." Madame Odette joined their small party. She was accompanied by another woman in an identical uniform, whose face was stern and angular. They both bowed to the king and queen. For the second time that evening, a chill darted up Aislynn's spine.

"Madame Odette," the queen said, taking the older woman's hand. "What a pleasure to see you."

"The pleasure is all mine," the headmistress replied, though her tone was devoid of any. "I was hoping for the opportunity to talk with your adviser. Has he arrived?"

"We haven't seen him yet. I assume he's preparing for the many Introductions he'll be facilitating tonight." The king gave his daughter a small smile. "Including Aislynn's, of course."

"Of course." But the headmistress seemed doubtful. Aislynn's stomach turned.

"Is there something we need to be aware of?" the queen asked, glancing at her daughter with concern.

"There are some . . ." Madame Odette cleared her throat as she turned her cold gaze toward the portraits across the room. ". . . incidents that need to be brought to his attention." Her gaze swung back to Aislynn, and she smiled unpleasantly. "Adviser . . . Hull, isn't it?"

Fear stuck in Aislynn's throat like an unswallowed piece of bread. She had been so good, so careful, for months now. Was she being punished for her foolishness this afternoon? Would the headmistress delay her Introduction for such a small infraction?

"I'm sure it won't take me long to find him," the headmistress continued, running a thin finger along the edge of her wimple. "Your Majesties." Madame Odette and her silent companion curtsied before disappearing into the crowd.

"Aislynn?" her mother's voice was shrill. Inside her chest, Aislynn's kettle heart began to shake.

"What is she talking about?" her father asked.

Why had she allowed herself to get angry today, of all days? If the headmistress delayed her Introduction and made her wait for the next ball to be presented, Aislynn had only herself to blame. She took a deep breath, trying to calm the magic now burning hot inside of her.

"I have to . . . I need . . ." Throwing her apologies over her shoulder, she pushed past her parents. "I need some air. I'm sorry."

Aislynn darted to the open doors, practically spilling out onto the terrace that wrapped around the side of the ballroom. The wide row of steps that led down into the quiet moonlit garden was deserted, but Aislynn didn't dare risk being seen, so she crossed the flagstones to where a small bench sat near the top of the steps, hidden behind a rose arbor. She dropped herself onto the cold seat and gathered the skirt of her dress over her knees.

With a shaking hand, she rolled down one of her stockings, exposing a bare leg. Marking her skin were at least a dozen welts, ugly and pink.

Placing her hand on her lower thigh, Aislynn gritted her teeth, bracing herself. For a moment, there was nothing but the relief of expelling the magic, like the release of a long-held breath. Then pain slammed into her. It was an agony worse than the tightest corset, worse than the prick of a spindle, and worse than the sting of a hot oven door.

She could feel her skin pucker and knew that the scar would be as large as a peach pit and just as jagged. Aislynn was ashamed of her inability to control her magic, but at least she had learned how to manage it. Though it burned, there was a sense of relief.

She waited a minute for the pain to lessen, and when it faded into an ache, she gently rolled her stocking back up her leg, folding it just beneath the new mark. Carefully, she lowered her dress, wincing as the fabric brushed against the raw skin.

"I knew it!" A voice shrieked from the darkness, and

Aislynn sprang to her feet. A girl, dressed in yellow, emerged from the gardens below and rushed up the steps toward Aislynn with a shaking, outstretched arm. Tiny bare feet peered out from under a muddied hem; black hair draped across her shoulders like skeins of uncarded wool. Hair that was usually as yellow as corn.

"This is your fault." Maris grabbed a fistful of her ruined hair. "You did this to me, you witch . . . you stray!"

Chapter 3

It was not the first time Aislynn had been called a stray. The slur seemed to follow her wherever she went. It was a favorite of Violaine's, and even the teachers looked the other way when they heard it whispered in the hallways. It was an awful word, and it felt even worse coming from someone Aislynn considered a friend.

But a friend would never look at her the way Maris was looking at her now.

"What happened?"

"You know what happened," Maris spat.

Aislynn didn't understand. "Can't your fairy godmother fix it?" If Tahlia were here, Aislynn knew she would help, but Maris laughed.

"Have my fairy godmother fix it? Who do you think reported me?" Her face crumpled. "The headmistress forbade me from coming tonight. But I won't let them Redirect me. I won't."

Aislynn knew the fate that awaited a royal woman who failed to find a husband before the end of her sixteenth year. They all did. To remain unmarried would leave a girl's heart untended, unguarded, and so, for her own safety, she was Redirected to the Order of Fairy Godmothers, her loving heart forfeited for a life of purity and devotion.

"We'll figure something out." Aislynn reached out to comfort Maris but was rewarded with a stinging slap across her face.

"Don't touch me!" said Maris. "This is your fault. Everyone knows what you did to Violaine."

Aislynn put a hand to her burning cheek and remembered how Maris had looked longingly at her black hair that very morning. How envious she had seemed.

"You wanted to have hair like mine," she murmured, raising her eyes to meet Maris's. "You were vain. You were covetous."

"How dare you!" Maris stepped forward, her face white as death, and slapped Aislynn again. "Everyone knows what you are—*stray*."

Aislynn shoved Maris away. The other girl stumbled, her bare feet slapping against the stone. Eyes round and wild, she took a step back, and then another, before turning and fleeing down the stairs and into the garden.

Frozen on the terrace, Aislynn watched Maris run toward the hedge that encircled the garden. Suddenly a tall figure emerged from the shadows, face obscured by a hooded cloak. At first, Aislynn thought Maris's fairy godmother had come to fetch her, but then the figure stepped into the moonlight, and Aislynn saw that the cloak was not purple but black. No one wore black. Especially not at a ball.

A strange and awful feeling prickled at the back of Aislynn's neck as she watched the figure grasp Maris by the hand and pull her through the hedge. They disappeared from sight.

"Looking for someone?" Aislynn jumped. It was Violaine, her lips pursed in scorn, her hand resting on a gentleman's arm. Behind them, guests were streaming out of the ballroom, the ladies fanning themselves delicately. Servants followed, carrying silver platters of fruit and glass goblets of champagne.

"Has Maris deserted you yet again?" Violaine asked with an unpleasant smile. But Aislynn ignored her, turning instead to her companion. The gentleman on Violaine's arm was no stranger.

"Everett!"

"Hello, Aislynn." It had been years since they last met, but the smile that bloomed across his face was exactly as she had remembered. His wide nose had grown perfectly into the squareness of his face, and his brown eyes were now lined with thick lashes. Unlike Violaine, his green suit perfectly complemented his skin, which was several shades darker than Aislynn's.

"I almost didn't recognize you!" Aislynn exclaimed, stepping forward to hug her childhood friend but quickly realizing that such a greeting would be exceptionally inappropriate. They were no longer children, but young ladies and gentlemen. So she curtsied instead. Everett gave a slight bow and then took her hand. A thrill coursed through her. He was the kind of suitor she was barely brave enough to hope for. She prayed that his name was on her dance card.

"You look exactly as I remember," he said, smiling so broadly that the dimple in his left cheek showed.

A throat cleared, and Everett glanced at Violaine, who looked none too pleased. He coughed and dropped Aislynn's hand. "I'm so sorry. Where are my manners? Lady Violaine, this is Princess Aislynn."

"We've met," said Violaine tartly. "Sir Everett . . ." She purred as she sidled up against him. "I'm getting chilly."

"I thought you were warm," he countered, clearly confused.

"I was." Violaine pouted prettily. "But not anymore." Just then a servant dipped a tray gracefully between them. Everett handed each girl a goblet of champagne before taking one for himself.

"Why don't we make a toast?" He raised his glass. "To old friends!"

Violaine sniffed.

"To a wonderful party?"

There was no objection, and all three glasses were raised and clanked together—Violaine's toast so fierce that it was surprising the crystal didn't shatter.

The champagne burned Aislynn's throat. She was used to wine, sour and heavy, not these light, sharp bursts against her tongue. One sip, and she was already looking for a place to discard her goblet. Violaine lapped at it like a cat, but Everett drained the entire glass in one gulp.

"It's a lovely evening," he said, signaling to a nearby servant, who replaced his empty glass with a full one. He drank this one more slowly.

"It's a bit brisk," Violaine replied.

"I'm quite enjoying the decorations," Everett said. He directed his statement toward Aislynn, but she didn't have a chance to respond before Violaine spoke up.

"They're a shambles compared to the last spring ball."

Aislynn realized that the other girl was flirting. It was the method of Practiced Disinterest, one of the many styles of flirtation they had been taught at the academy. The first step was to act unimpressed with anything one's partner suggested, thus providing him with the challenge of pleasing you. Though there were at least a dozen types of flirtation, Aislynn had only attempted Practiced Ignorance, but her teachers had told her she was too genuinely curious to be any real success at it.

Violaine seemed to be doing only slightly better. She batted her eyes at Everett, who had now started on his third glass of champagne. "I simply love to dance," she said.

"I'm enjoying the breeze, actually," he responded. The smile he gave Aislynn was a little looser than the one before. "I think I'll stay out here for a while."

"You'd let me enter the ballroom alone, sir?" There was a bite to Violaine's words. Everett finished his drink and gave the glass to a passing servant, then gently detached Violaine's hand from his arm.

"I can't very well leave Aislynn out here by herself, now can I?" he asked.

Violaine's eyes narrowed. "You'd rather stay out here with *her*?" she sneered. "You do realize what she is, don't you?"

Aislynn sucked in a breath, her spine as straight as a

spindle. She could only imagine the stories her classmate would be more than happy to share.

"A childhood friend?" Everett asked, smiling. He wrapped his fingers around Aislynn's wrist, and she felt her breath release. His touch was soft and reassuring.

Violaine turned as red as a poisoned apple. "I would have expected that someone in your . . . situation would be more discerning when selecting a partner." This time it was Everett who flushed. "You two deserve each other," she hissed, throwing her goblet to the ground.

Everett and Aislynn barely had time to jump away before the glass shattered. With a flounce of her skirt, Violaine stalked into the ballroom without a backward glance.

"She's lovely," Everett said drily, taking Aislynn's goblet and draining it before she could say anything. Shards of glass glittered up at her, caught in the folds of her dress. She gently shook them free.

For a moment, neither of them spoke. Everett placed their empty glasses carefully on one of the terrace benches and strained to see down into the darkness. "What's down there?"

"The gardens—" The words were barely out of Aislynn's mouth before Everett grabbed her hand and steered her toward the steps.

"I don't think we're allowed . . . ," Aislynn said faintly,

knowing that her parents were probably looking for her but not really wanting to return to the ballroom, not really wanting him to let go.

Everett gave her a mischievous smile and led her down the steps. They followed the stone path until they reached a small gate nestled in a boxwood hedge. The sounds of the party grew fainter as they entered the hidden space, the lights of the ballroom just barely visible. Everett swung himself onto the edge of a sleeping fountain and lifted his face to the moonlight. It didn't seem possible, but the quiet of the evening and the secrecy of the rose garden made him seem even more handsome than before.

Suddenly he flung his arms wide, and Aislynn was afraid for a moment that he'd topple into the fountain. Instead he pitched forward, his knees hitting the ground hard, then his hands. Aislynn rushed to his side.

"Are you all right?" She knelt next to him, her lovely blue dress sliding over the dusty gravel. He blinked at her, once, twice, and finally when he opened his eyes a third time, he seemed to recognize her again.

"Aislynn," he said, his playful smile gone.

Grasping his elbow, she helped him to his feet. "Are you all right?" she asked again.

"I guess I've discovered my limit on champagne." He

frowned, and Aislynn longed to smooth away the line that appeared between his eyes. "Though it was likely I would have continued to indulge if you hadn't saved me."

"Saved you?"

"From your friend." Everett wrinkled his nose. "The *Lady* Violaine."

"She's not my friend," Aislynn said. The distaste must have been evident on her face, because Everett laughed.

"No, of course not." His teeth were white and perfect as he smiled at her. "Competitors should never be friends."

"I hardly think she imagines me as competition," Aislynn muttered, more to herself.

"Well, she should." Everett took her hand, his fingers brushing against the inside of her wrist. "I can't imagine who would marry someone like her, lacking in both modesty and connections. Not like you." His dimples deepened. "Violaine is a piece of green glass, while you . . . you are a sapphire."

Aislynn wished she had a fan to calm the heat that spread across her chest and throat. But Everett quickly dropped her hands, and she did her best to conceal her disappointment, pressing her damp palms against the skirt of her dress.

"What do you think she meant by it?" he asked. "When she said we deserved each other."

"I don't know," Aislynn said, but it was a lie. She knew

exactly what Violaine had meant. While Aislynn's chances of a good marriage were threatened by her inability to control her magic, Everett's opportunities were limited not only by his status, but by his birthplace as well.

Like Maris, his family was originally from the West. Every day seemed to bring news of another family leaving the embattled kingdom. No doubt Everett's family had fled with others, in hopes of a better marriage for him and a better life for them all. Unfortunately, rumors of Josetta's growing influence in the West had made some royals uneasy about forming alliances with her former subjects, even if they had been unwilling ones.

Both Aislynn and Everett were in need of good marriages to counteract things they could neither change nor control. No wonder Violaine had said they deserved each other.

"Can't imagine you're worse off than me." Everett looked up at the sky, where millions of stars glittered like crystals. "No land, no home, no house to take a bride to. Our true monarch is unable to protect us, and the new, unwelcomed *ruler*"—his voice was full of disdain—"is not a benevolent one." He faced Aislynn. "Her husband was a commoner, you know."

She nodded. Although the Midlands were not recognized as a kingdom, the self-appointed monarch queen had extended her wicked rule as far as it could reach, forcing many

Westerners out of their homes when they refused to swear allegiance to her. But Josetta was more than just cruel. She was dangerous, having rejected the Path completely, proudly flaunting her wicked magic.

"When did you leave home?" Aislynn asked.

"Last season." Everett returned to the edge of the fountain.

"Will you settle here, in the North?"

"If the monarch king grants us land." He didn't sound very optimistic. "She's building an army, you know, the Wicked Queen," he continued. "Of royal maidens. Of strays."

Aislynn recoiled, still feeling Maris's slap on her cheek, still able to hear her bitter slur.

"It's said that they're drawn to her. That she speaks to them in their dreams," he said.

The Wicked Queen's army must be growing, thought Aislynn. There had always been whispers of girls who had strayed, but lately it seemed as though there was a new girl and a new story with each season.

Swallowing painfully, Aislynn thought of her nightmare, of wolves and their sharp white teeth. The wolves that lived in Josetta's woods.

"Stupid witch," Everett muttered.

"Do you miss the West?" Aislynn asked, eager to change the subject.

He nodded. "But it doesn't matter," he sighed, dragging his feet through the pebbles. "I'd still be this way, no matter which kingdom I came from."

The dust was making Aislynn's eyes water. She coughed as delicately as she could manage. The kicking stopped.

"Sorry." Everett pushed himself off the fountain edge where he had been leaning. He seemed to be walking an invisible line, with his arms straight out on either side. "I spend most of my time in the stables with the horses and Emil anyway."

"Who's Emil?" Aislynn watched him walk his imaginary tightrope back and forth, back and forth.

"He's our new stable hand." The smile that had been hinting at the corners of his mouth dropped away abruptly. "But my parents hate horses. They canceled all my riding lessons. It's for the best, they say." The exaggerated manner made it clear he was mocking his parents, who, Aislynn knew, always used very proper diction.

"Perhaps it *is* for the best?" Aislynn offered.

"Yes, I suppose you're right," he said, still frowning.

Suddenly Aislynn heard the squeak of the gate and turned toward the sound. A man was standing in the garden.

"Adviser Hull." The greeting got lost in her throat, the words nothing more than a wheeze. His white suit gleamed in the moonlight. Aislynn knew she should have not have followed Everett into the garden. A proper young lady was never without a chaperone.

After a long silence, Adviser Hull spoke. "Who is this young man?"

"Everett, formerly of Willowisps, sir." Everett bowed, but his face showed the same nervousness that Aislynn felt.

"Luring this young man out here so you two could be alone." The adviser sighed. "Aislynn, I'm disappointed in you."

"I'm afraid I'm the one at fault—" said Everett, but he was quickly interrupted.

"If Princess Aislynn had listened to her Path, she would never have left the party," said Adviser Hull, his fingers linked together, as if he was addressing two very young children. "I think it's best that you go back inside, Everett, formerly of Willowisps. Let us hope no one else noticed your . . . disappearance." He held up a hand before Everett could argue. "I'll escort the princess in myself."

"Yes, sir." With embarrassment plastered all over his face, Everett bowed again and quickly retreated from the garden.

Adviser Hull sat down on the edge of the fountain. A quick jolt of dread filled Aislynn as he patted the space next to him. She wanted to be back at the ball, with Everett, with her parents, but she dutifully sat beside him on the cold, unyielding stone.

"You don't have to worry," he said, his voice calm and smooth. "I am here to guide you."

It was said that the husband was the ruler of that which could be touched: food, clothing, a home, a bed. One could not hold what advisers offered, yet their domain filled each person like air. They ruled no land or servant and had no wives. They answered only to themselves and the Path. The sacred text said of them, in Advisers 6:34: "An adviser might serve you, worthy king, but have you served him?"

To betray or reject their counsel was unheard of.

Aislynn twisted her fingers together as Adviser Hull continued to speak. "I promise not to tell your parents about this." He reached for Aislynn's hand, untangling it and running his thumb over her knuckles.

Aislynn knew that she should listen carefully, that she should follow his advice, but she couldn't help the wish that sat on the back of her tongue. The one that wanted him to stop touching her.

She swallowed it down.

"I know that you are dedicated to following your Path, and that is the reason I will keep this interlude a secret from your parents," Adviser Hull was saying.

His perfectly combed hair was just beginning to gray at the temples, exactly like her father's. But he wasn't anything like her father.

"Naturally this rebellious behavior, on a night so important, concerns me." He stroked the back of her wrist. "Perhaps you would benefit, as some do, from private meetings, where I can teach you how to better . . . curb your impulses." His hand moved to her leg.

Aislynn bit her lip and pressed her palm against the cold stone fountain. Magic churned in her heart, and Aislynn stifled a groan as it boiled inside of her, struggling to get out.

"I am very dedicated to your future, Princess. It would do you well to remember that most girls would consider themselves lucky to have not only my support, but my attention." His finger marked the tip of her nose.

"Please . . ." She tried to speak, tried to warn him as magic shot through her.

For a moment there was nothing. Nothing but the adviser running his finger along the line of her jaw. Then the ground began to shake.

Adviser Hull snatched his hand away and leaped to his feet.

"Stop that immediately," he commanded, but Aislynn realized with horror that even if she wanted to make it stop, she could not. The magic seemed unending, flowing through her like a river, spreading from the palm of her hand. The fountain gave a loud crack, and ice-cold water drenched her. Where it spilled, the ground heaved and buckled, expelling forth a tangle of thick briars that reached toward Adviser Hull.

The brambles wound their way up the adviser's legs, around his waist, and finally across his struggling arms, their thorny vines pinning his wrists together. As they curled toward his neck, the vines shivered, and roses burst into bloom.

With a tremendous roar, Adviser Hull pulled free, tearing his suit and scratching his hands on the sharp thorns. The sound was so loud and terrible that Aislynn fell backward, and the magic retreated inside of her like a frightened dog. Immediately the shaking ceased and the vines stilled. The only sound was the heavy heave of her breath.

This, like everything, was her fault.

From his pocket, Adviser Hull retrieved a small knife and began to hack away at the brambles around his legs. He glared at Aislynn in the moonlight.

"You stupid girl," he sneered before stalking away in his shredded and stained suit. Aislynn heard the garden gate slam behind him. She lifted her hands. They were bleeding.

Chapter 4

The spindle had been cleaned and polished since its last use. Aislynn did her best not to cower as the headmistress removed the long, thick needle from its case and presented it, first to her parents on either side of her, and then to Adviser Hull, who was standing in the corner.

"Is this absolutely necessary?" the queen asked as the spindle's sharp tip caught the light.

"Oh, yes," said the headmistress. "It is vital for Aislynn to understand the consequences of her actions."

"Your Majesties," Adviser Hull interjected coolly. "Madame Odette deals with such . . . transgressions on a regular basis. I assure you that her methods are in accordance with the Path."

There was no sign that less than an hour ago he had been
wrestling with an enchanted rosebush. His white suit was
pristine. Even his hair was impeccable. Aislynn could not
say the same for her own dress, which was just as stained and
soggy as it had been when he left her.

Adviser Hull examined his perfectly shaped nails.
"Perhaps a firmer hand with Aislynn would have allowed
us all to avoid this unpleasant situation." With a sigh, he
pressed his fingers together. "I believe I warned of such
disobedience when you bowed to her tantrums regarding her
fairy godmother—against my recommendations."

It had been those tantrums that had caused most of the
damage still visible in Aislynn's bedroom and on her skin.
When she had arrived at Nerine, she had longed for comfort
and care from her new fairy godmother. Instead she was treated
with disinterest and impatience. After months of unintentional
destruction, Aislynn had awakened one morning to find Tahlia
sitting patiently next to her bed, a cup of tea in hand. How she
wished her fairy godmother was here with her now.

With a firm, icy grip, the headmistress snatched Aislynn's
left wrist, not seeming to care that it was already riddled with
scratches. She pressed the sharp point of the needle against the
fleshy pad of one of Aislynn's fingers until the skin gave and a
single vibrant drop of blood appeared. Aislynn bit her lip.

"It's hurting her," said the king.

"If you'd rather leave . . . ," the headmistress offered coldly as she pricked the next finger.

Aislynn's father shook his head and was quiet.

"I'm afraid I blame myself," Adviser Hull said, once each of Aislynn's fingers had been pierced and Madame Odette had wiped the blood from the spindle. "I allowed my affection for your family to cloud my judgment."

"I don't understand." The queen took Aislynn's hand gingerly.

"Obviously, the occasional occurrence is to be expected—though never encouraged—while a young girl adjusts to the curse. We all have our moments of weakness." Adviser Hull's smile quickly faded. "But we can no longer overlook Aislynn's . . . stumbling. I know I first mentioned my concern when her initial occurrence happened at such a young age."

Aislynn watched her father. He looked at the floor. As the only witness to her first occurrence, he knew firsthand the extent of her abilities. When she had reduced a pile of his books to ash, the flames had been so hot that they had singed her hair and burned a hole in his desk. Before, she had been precious and loved, but in that moment she had become someone unfamiliar and strange. Someone to be feared and kept at a distance. Someone unsafe.

Most girls experienced the curse when they were around fourteen or fifteen. Aislynn had been twelve.

Adviser Hull continued. "It is now clear that Aislynn's Path requires Redirection."

There was silence. "A fairy godmother," said her father after a few moments.

A roar filled Aislynn's ears, and for a moment it felt as if she was still submerged in the bath, everything around her echoing and distant.

"But she only just turned sixteen," her mother said frantically. "She hasn't even been Introduced."

"Waiting until she turns seventeen is callous and unnecessary and would only invite more chaos. Understand that this is for her own protection." Adviser Hull's voice was firm. "She is in grave danger of straying. According to the headmistress, Aislynn's only friend is a young girl who spent her childhood in the Western Kingdom. While her family escaped from Josetta's grasp, I'm afraid it is likely too late for their daughter."

"One's kingdom of origin does not determine the surety of one's steps." The king's voice was steady. Aislynn knew her father was proud to come from the Western Kingdom and refused to allow its current reputation to tarnish his own. She felt sick knowing that her Redirection would only bring him humiliation and shame.

"No, of course not." The Adviser bowed his head in deference. "I only mention this because the young lady in question has disappeared."

"We believe Maris has strayed," the headmistress added.

Aislynn gasped. She remembered what Maris had said— that she would not allow herself to be Redirected. But to become a stray? To abandon the Path and be forever shunned by her family? To be forgotten, completely stricken from memory? She would rather all that than accept life as a fairy godmother?

"I have no doubt that if Aislynn is not Redirected, she will follow Maris to a devastating end." Adviser Hull took Aislynn's hands from her mother. She tried not to flinch as he leaned closer. "I hope you understand that this is for your own good. It is safer for everyone to prune you of your dangerous desires."

It took all of Aislynn's strength to stay in her seat when she wanted to run from the room, from the castle, from the academy. But she would not be like Maris. She would not. She would not abandon the Path, even as her journey along it had changed.

"It is best for all of us if Aislynn leaves for a new academy in the morning," Adviser Hull said, straightening and returning to the desk.

"In the morning?" the queen cried. She and the king exchanged a frantic glance.

Adviser Hull pressed his lips together, annoyed. "Her outrageous actions this evening should be enough to illustrate how quickly we must act."

Aislynn's cheeks burned with shame.

"I assume you trust me." Adviser Hull frowned.

"Of course, Adviser," Aislynn's father said quickly.

"May we say good-bye to our daughter?" asked the queen. Her eyes were brimming with tears.

The adviser seemed to consider the request. "I'll permit it," he finally said, and stepped to the headmistress's side. They stood there as if they were observing a staged play.

"Alone, if you don't mind," said the king.

The adviser gave him a cold smile. "Of course," he said, taking the headmistress's elbow. "Come along, madame." The heavy door closed behind them.

A thousand apologies filled Aislynn, but she kept her lips pressed together, knowing that if she spoke, she would begin to cry.

"Oh, my darling." The queen gently pulled Aislynn into her arms.

Aislynn rested her cheek on her mother's shoulder, breathing in the scent of her perfume. Orange and spices. Just as she remembered from when she was a little girl.

"I will accept the Path I am taking. I will not stray. I will not yearn for what I cannot have. I will heed the words of my adviser and guard my loving heart against cursed magic. Ever after." Her mother's words were like a lullaby in her ear.

Aislynn's locket pressed into her breastbone, hard and unyielding. Her hands ached and her leg burned, but she welcomed the pain. None of it compared to the injury she had done to her parents by failing to control her wicked magic.

She knew this might be the last time she would see her mother or father. Fairy godmothers did not have parents. They belonged to the family they served until their death.

"We have to go." Her father's voice was quiet as he embraced her, and then he too pulled away. Aislynn filled with panic—it hadn't been enough time. There were still so many things about her parents' faces that she had not yet memorized, so many things she had not yet said. But they were already leaving, her mother's head bowed, her father's hand resting on her shoulder. Before he left the room, the king glanced back.

"I'm sorry," he said and shut the door.

Chapter 5

Aislynn left a smear of blood on the doorknob. She could not remember leaving the headmistress's study or walking up the stairs to her room. A single candle burned on her bedside table, and a nightgown was spread across the bed. Tahlia had already been there. Did her fairy godmother know what had happened? Aislynn collapsed into a chair, her stiff gown crunching beneath her.

She looked in the mirror, and it took everything she had to keep from screaming at the reflection. The girl staring back at her was a disgrace. She was not a princess at all. If only she had tried harder, if only she had been better, if only . . .

With a trembling hand Aislynn began to uncoil her hair.

Section by heavy section it fell. When it was all undone and curling across her shoulders, she took her handkerchief and smeared away the powder on her face. Then she reached for the many slippery buttons running down her spine. Unable to undo them, she gripped her dress in frustration and pulled. It took a few tugs, each more vicious than the last, but finally the buttons burst from their threads and scattered across the room.

"Who could ever love you?" Aislynn snarled at her reflection. The girl there was familiar again, cheeks ruddy and hair wild. Everything else had been pretend. She was a girl who wasn't meant for ever after. But even though her head knew this, her heart refused to accept it. Her foolish, loving heart. A heart that would soon be gone.

Suddenly unable to breath, Aislynn scrambled to undo the slippery laces of her corset, but the knots were too tight. She yanked open the drawers of her vanity, ignoring the pain in her fingers and the lines of blood she left behind. Underneath a pile of ribbons she found it—a small pair of scissors that Tahlia used to snip unruly threads. The scissors were barely longer than her pinkie.

Gritting her teeth, Aislynn began to drag the tiny blade across the silk laces, sawing at them viciously until they finally snapped. She pulled the stiff corset away from her body and threw it across the room. Kicking off the rest of her undergarments, she pulled on her nightgown, her ruined legs bare beneath it.

She slipped out of her room. The castle was silent. The ball had ended, and all the other girls were now tucked into their beds asleep, their heads no doubt filled with dreams of dancing and romance. Aislynn knotted her robe tightly and quietly made her way downstairs.

At the bottom of the staircase was a series of portraits depicting the tale of the four sisters. Aislynn kept her eyes down as she passed them, though she knew their story by heart. According to *The Path*, they had mistakenly believed their magic to be a gift, not the punishment it truly was. Each portrait represented one of the four brambles that could grow within a maiden and overpower her loving heart: selfishness, pride, arrogance, and vanity.

The sister who cared only for her own needs wore a ring and sat despondently in an empty room. Once proud of her masculine strength and power, another could barely hold a jeweled dagger in her crippled hand. Arrogant in her cleverness, one sister's lips stretched in a mad smile beneath a sparkling crown, while the fourth was painted facing away. Her vanity had transformed her into a wolflike creature, and her stove-black eyes were reflected in the mirror she held in her hands.

Aislynn knew this part of the story best. Using magic to make herself beautiful, the vain sister could have had any man she wanted. Instead, she used her power to steal suitors away from their true loves. But as soon as her beauty began to decay, revealing the monster underneath, her admirers abandoned her, and she was forced to flee to the woods with her ruined sisters.

Aislynn hurried through the dark hallway toward the kitchen. Somehow she knew her fairy godmother would be waiting for her. The lamp on the table was lit, and Tahlia was pulling ingredients from shelves, humming to herself. She didn't look up as Aislynn entered, but there was a sad little smile on her lips as she finished collecting the necessary items: bowls of varying sizes, a whisk, measuring cups, and a wooden spoon. A jar of cinnamon. A pinch of yeast.

There was a wonderful predictability to baking. Adding warm water and yeast to flour would make it rise. Dough was sticky and porous. Cinnamon always mixed well with the sugar, and no matter how careful she was, Aislynn would always get flour in her hair.

Before tonight's disaster, before Nerine Academy and before magic, Aislynn had learned how to bake.

STRAY

And it was because of her fairy godmother. Tahlia was unusual, as fairy godmothers were assigned when a maiden entered school, not passed down from generation to generation. But Aislynn's magic had been too much for anyone else to manage.

Tahlia, as clever as she was unusual, always found ways to sneak Aislynn into the kitchen, even though it was against the rules. Each recipe Aislynn learned, she copied into a small, hand-bound book. Her favorite was the first recipe Tahlia had taught her: cinnamon bookbinder's bread.

Slowly the oven's heat began to warm the kitchen, and the bitterness that had filled Aislynn began to fade away. She lost herself in the careful measuring of ingredients, the smell of cinnamon, and the glorious blooming of yeast in warm water. She didn't even realize that her fingers had started bleeding again until a drop of red fell into the bowl, staining the white flour.

"Thorns," she swore under her breath.

"Let me see that," said Tahlia gently, pulling Aislynn's injured fingers toward her. She placed them between her palms and closed her eyes. Slowly Aislynn's fingertips grew hot, and there was a strange tickling sensation that fluttered over her. It was like magic, but it wasn't inside her. It was around her.

Tahlia released her hand. The cuts, the blood, and the

pain were all gone. Aislynn stared at her fairy godmother, who just smiled serenely and turned back to the bowl.

There were very strict rules regarding how fairy godmothers could use magic. No one was unguarded. Not students, not teachers, and especially not fairy godmothers. Magic, no matter how controlled, was never to be trusted. But Aislynn said nothing.

Instead, she watched her fairy godmother bake. A swatch of red hair, lined with gray, had escaped Tahlia's wimple and was curling toward her temple. Against the purple of her uniform, the color contrasted pleasantly, reminding Aislynn of carrots and lilac.

She swallowed hard. Tahlia had always taken care of her. Now Aislynn would become someone else's fairy godmother. But she would never be like Tahlia. No, Tahlia was warm and safe, not cold and distant like the others. Like fairy godmothers were expected to be.

Tahlia glanced up, and Aislynn realized that she had been staring.

Her fairy godmother smiled. "It's quite comfortable," she said. At Aislynn's puzzled look, Tahlia gestured to her uniform. "And it's long enough so you won't need to worry about hiding your legs," she added gently.

Aislynn flushed at her own foolishness. She had done her

best to hide her scars, but her fairy godmother was smart and observant. Of course Tahlia knew.

"Sometimes we need to keep secrets," said Tahlia, and Aislynn thought of the other secret she was keeping. The dreams that haunted her sleep, of the forest and the moon. And the wolf.

A tear dropped into the dough she was kneading. "And if those secrets are dangerous?"

Immediately her fairy godmother was at her side.

"In my dreams, I'm in the forest and it's dark." Aislynn's confession was a whisper. "And there's a wolf." She watched Tahlia carefully. If she hadn't, she might have missed how her fairy godmother's eyes widened, if just for a moment.

"A wolf?" Tahlia asked, turning back to the bowl.

"It follows me. It has yellow eyes." Aislynn twisted her hands together. "I know what it means. That my thoughts are wicked and impure. That I'm dangerous."

"You shouldn't believe everything they tell you," Tahlia said quietly, deftly shaping the dough into a smooth ball. She placed it in a bowl on the stove top and covered it. "Do you know why I leave the bread there?" Tahlia asked, and Aislynn shook her head, even though she did. "Because it needs heat to rise. Nothing matters more. You could have all the right ingredients, have measured them carefully and mixed them perfectly, but without warmth, you'll end up with a loaf of bread flatter than a plate. And while you might be able to eat it, it won't feed you."

Aislynn was not sure that she understood. Tahlia's face, which was usually as open and clear as the sky in the summer, had clouded over.

"Tahlia?" Aislynn asked hesitantly.

Without a word, her fairy godmother swept aside the bowl sitting on the stove. It hit the floor with a muffled smash, their evening's work destroyed in a gust of flour, cracked porcelain, and sticky dough.

Startled by Tahlia's actions, Aislynn bent down and began to carefully pick up the pieces. Tahlia knelt next to her, face now sunny.

"Let me take care of it," she said, and Aislynn understood this to mean that she was going to use magic once more. There was no doubt in Aislynn's mind that this was against the rules.

For a moment, the air was full of nothing but flour and silence. Then, like before, came the hum of magic. The bowl, now repaired and full of rising dough, was thrust into Aislynn's hands.

"Just remember," Tahlia said fiercely, her grip firm on Aislynn's wrists, her gaze unwavering. "Never let them take what you're not willing to give."

Chapter 6

The carriage waiting for Aislynn was so small it seemed like a toy version of itself. On the top was tied one modest trunk. Clearly she would not be needing her fancy dresses, perfumes, or powders anymore. From his post next to the carriage, an elderly coachman opened the door and helped Aislynn squeeze herself inside.

"Thank you," she said.

He closed the door, and Madame Odette's hand extended through the open window. "Your locket, please." She gestured impatiently. "Now." Her command was as sharp as a blade.

Aislynn had not removed her necklace since it had been given to her as a child. She handed it to the headmistress and watched with horror as Madame Odette opened the locket and snapped off the front half—the half that would have been inscribed with the name of Aislynn's husband.

"You won't be needing that anymore," Madame Odette said with satisfaction, returning what was left of the locket to Aislynn before heading back into the school.

"All right in there, my lady?" The footman peered inside the coach, his face kind and concerned. "I know it's a bit snug."

"I'll be fine." Trying to ignore her trembling hands, Aislynn put her necklace back on. "Where are we headed, please?" Madame Odette had not bothered to provide any information.

"Elderwood Academy, Princess. Near the eastern border."

"How long is the journey?" Aislynn asked, knowing that Redirected girls were sent to academies far away. It would be her first time outside the Northern Kingdom.

"It's not a quick one," he said apologetically. "We'll get there after nightfall. We'll likely eat dinner in the nearest township." Reaching up, he checked the tightness of the rope securing her trunk. Aislynn wondered which of her personal items the headmistress had allowed Tahlia to pack.

"Ready to go, Princess?"

"Yes, thank you," she said, and as a smile brightened the coachman's weathered face, she caught a glimpse of the handsome young man he had been in his youth. "What is your name?"

"Ford, Princess."

"You can call me Aislynn," she said.

With a tip of his hat, he disappeared from sight. The carriage shifted as he climbed up behind the horses.

When she had first arrived at Nerine Academy, Aislynn had imagined she would leave with a name on her locket and a celebration, not with a small trunk early in the morning before the rest of the school awakened. With a jolt, the coach rolled forward, and Nerine soon disappeared behind them.

Aislynn discovered quickly that she hated riding in carriages, at least those no bigger than some of her mother's hats. Every bump was like being jostled apart and then put back together incorrectly. At each stop, leaving the vehicle required learning to walk again. The poor horses seemed as tired as she was when they finally rested for lunch, still hours from the border.

Ford, on the other hand, appeared to relish their journey.

"It's the wind, Princess," he told her when she asked why. "Never was made for the life of an indoor servant, and I can't farm. But I love the wind." Ford didn't say much more, keeping his head bowed respectfully as they ate.

The journey was lonely. Aislynn had only her thoughts to keep her company, and sad and scared as she was, they weren't much comfort. To keep from crying, Aislynn recited the daily supplication:

"I will accept the Path I am taking. I will not stray. I will not yearn for what I cannot have. I will heed the words of my adviser and guard my loving heart against cursed magic. Ever after."

If she had been a clever girl, she would have prepared better for this moment. There was a part of her that had always known she would be Redirected. Like the four sisters, she was full of wicked, covetous thoughts. But she couldn't ignore the aching of her heart when she thought of Everett and the life she had so desperately wanted. Her mind knew that it was foolhardy, but her heart remained stupidly hopeful.

The carriage lurched to a halt. Aislynn leaned her head out the window to see why they had stopped. The horses pawed at the ground, wild-eyed. Ford was in front of them, his hand on their harness, speaking softly. A brisk wind blew through the carriage, and Aislynn shivered. Perhaps there was a blanket or cloak packed away in her bag. Ford came rushing over when he saw her struggling with the rope holding her trunk to the roof.

"Princess!"

"I was hoping to find something to keep me warm." She rubbed at her arms, which were covered in goose bumps. "Your wind is quite cold."

"I'll find you something. Just please stay in the carriage."
The fear on his face was so palpable that Aislynn nodded and
climbed back inside.

Outside her window was a forest, dense and dark, like the
one in her dreams. The tree trunks were old and gnarled, the
leaves almost black in the fading light. The branches were so
tangled together that it was impossible to tell which tree they
belonged to. From the stories she had heard, she would guess that
they were at the edge of the great forest, the one that surrounded
the Central Mountains and protected Queen Josetta's kingdom.
Aislynn could not help but imagine the Wicked Queen in those
woods, beckoning to her. One of the horses reared up with a
loud whinny, and Aislynn dropped back in her seat, glad that
she had been ordered to stay where she was.

When Ford reappeared at the window, he had a thick red
shawl in his hands. It was soft and large, with long tassels at
each end. It looked like it had been made by someone who
loved him very much, and Aislynn felt undeserving as she
wrapped it around her shoulders, covering her thin blue riding
gown with the warm knitted wool.

Aislynn could swear that Ford was pushing the horses to go
faster and faster. At some point they must have passed the
border between the Northern and Eastern Kingdoms and left

the threatening forest behind. Their pace eased up after that.

After hours of travel, they reached the Elderwood township. Ford helped her down from the carriage in front of the inn where they would be eating dinner. It was only a few more hours to the academy, she was told.

"It's a rough place and not what you're used to," Ford said apologetically as he handed the horses' reins to the inn's stableboy, but Aislynn shook her head.

"I'm not a princess anymore." It was the first time she had said it out loud, but it helped that she no longer felt like a princess, with her crumpled dress and dusty face.

Ford led her into the busy inn, making sure she was settled at a small table in the corner before excusing himself to tend to the horses. The dining room was full of people dressed in a wide array of colors. Aislynn had never seen anything like it. Among commoners, there was no need to display rank or status.

When she was a little girl, she had often grown tired of wearing only blue. Her mother would sigh and throw up her hands. "We can't just wear whatever we want," she would say. "We are not peasants." Aislynn remembered those words now as she watched a young woman, dressed in a dizzying blend of reds, purples, and yellows, serving food. Her clothing was quite different from the gray uniforms and head scarves academy servants were required to wear. Aislynn drew the red shawl tighter around her blue dress, hoping it would disguise her royal status and allow her to blend in.

Aislynn had never spent much time thinking about the servants at home or at school, beyond being grateful that after their first occurrence, all peasant women were required to report to the ruler of their county. A fairy godmother would then perform the custody spell, a charm that limited their magic and kept them safe. If these unfortunates would not protect themselves, it was a royal's duty to shelter them from harm.

The room was full of noise, of talking and laughter. Aislynn felt alone at her little corner table, and the thin broth she had ordered was a miserly comfort. There were rolls too, but one bite revealed that they were slightly stale, the crust sticky instead of crunchy. Aislynn remembered the warm, fragrant bread she had made with Tahlia, hardly able to believe that only a day had passed. So much had changed already.

She spotted a girl about her own age sitting close to a young man. Their heads were bent together, their hands clasped. Was this how peasants fell in love, their desires clearly displayed?

Aislynn thought about Queen Josetta. How she had forsaken the Path and her family and married a peasant. Had she been wooed like this young woman, her suitor's arms wrapped boldly around her while everyone watched?

As the girl tilted her face up to be kissed, Aislynn turned away. Despite the indecency of it all, she couldn't help the swell of jealousy that burned in her throat. She had been silly enough to hope that she would find love, but she quickly banished that longing. Such wishes were now traitorous to her Path.

Aislynn was looking toward the door, wondering when Ford would come back, when a young man sat down across from her.

"Is this seat taken?" His hair was dark and rumpled. Like the others in the inn, he was dressed in a variety of colors, and he was using his green vest to clean off the apple he held. As he leaned forward, Aislynn could feel heat radiating off him.

"I . . ." Aislynn glanced around for Ford but was still unable to find him in the crowded room.

"Headed to Elderwood, aren't you?" The stranger took a bite of the apple. His shirtsleeves were rolled up to his elbows. Aislynn had never seen a man's forearms before.

She realized she was staring.

"How did you know?" Aislynn dropped her eyes to the table, only to find herself looking at his strong, sun-browned hands.

"Oh, I know everything." He tapped his temple, his green eyes flashing. "Except your name. I'm Thackery," he said, holding out a hand. She stared at it for a moment before shaking it. It was warm and firm.

"Aislynn."

"Where will you be working at the academy?" he asked.

"The kitchen." The lie was out of her mouth before she could rethink it.

"Ah, so you're a cook."

"A baker." It somehow seemed better than the truth.

"I like baking," he said, leaning forward on his elbows. "Are you any good?"

"I'm the best." Aislynn sat up, pulling the shawl tight around her shoulders. Of course she had never baked without Tahlia's supervision, but there was no reason he needed to know that. She wanted to impress him, but she didn't know why.

Thackery raised an eyebrow. "Surely not!" He pointed at the half-eaten bun on her plate. "Those are the best rolls in all of the Eastern Kingdom."

"The *best*?" Aislynn sputtered. "I would hardly call them rolls. They are an insult to bread." She winced a little at her dramatic tone, but she couldn't help being horrified at the prospect of living in a kingdom that had no proper concept of what made a good roll.

"Well, I suppose they're not the *best* . . . ," Thackery said, grabbing the second, untouched bun and taking a bite. He chewed slowly, thoughtfully. "Maybe a little dry."

"A *little*? They're stale where they should be soft, chewy where they should be crisp, and completely and utterly—"

"Terrible," he concluded.

Realizing that he was teasing her, Aislynn flushed with embarrassment. "I never meant to say . . ."

He smiled, and Aislynn could see that his bottom teeth were crooked. "Why apologize for expecting something better?"

"Leave the young lady alone." It was Ford.

Thackery grinned sheepishly as the older man shook his head.

"Is he bothering you?" Ford asked Aislynn.

"Yes," she said, although she wasn't sure it was the truth.

"He's harmless," Ford said as he sat down. "Bothersome but harmless."

"I prefer charming but harmless," Thackery corrected with mock seriousness.

"I heard you were looking for a ride back to the academy," said Ford.

"I was. If you don't mind, of course." Thackery stood, smiling down at Aislynn. She looked away, wondering why he wanted to go to the academy.

"It's not my minding that would be the issue," Ford said.

Aislynn's cheeks, already warm, grew even hotter at the thought of spending the rest of her journey tightly pressed against Thackery in the tiny carriage. She turned to Ford. "Is there room?"

"There's a step on the back of the carriage. You won't even know I'm there." Thackery leaned forward, his eyes innocent. "Of course, I could always walk back. It's only fifteen miles or so, and I've done it before. I would get back awfully late, though. I only hope I can arrange the bouquets in time for the morning bell."

"Bouquets?" Aislynn asked before she could stop herself. Thackery laughed.

"I'm the academy gardener." He said it with pride.

Of course he worked there. He must have seen her arrive with Ford, which was how he had known where she was going. He might even have known that she was lying about being a baker, or if he didn't, he would find out soon enough.

She should tell him the truth, but couldn't. "I suppose that would be fine," she said instead. After all, what did it matter what a gardener thought of her?

"Thank you, Aislynn."

She didn't want to like the way he said her name. With the shawl tight around her shoulders, she rose from the table, grateful for the long skirt that hid her wobbly, traitorous knees.

"I didn't mean to be so sharp before," Ford said as they walked along the uneven cobblestones to the stable, Thackery several steps behind them. It took a moment for Aislynn to realize he was talking about his earlier insistence that she not leave the carriage.

"It's all right. You just wanted to settle the horses."

But Ford shook his head. "It's not just that." He slowed his steps. "There was a girl the other night. A girl who vanished."

"Maris?" Aislynn was surprised he had heard about Maris—did servants usually concern themselves with the goings-on at other academies? "She didn't vanish. She strayed."

Ford shook his head again.

"She was taken." There was genuine fear in his voice. Aislynn thought of the hooded figure she had seen in the garden with Maris. But both Adviser Hull and the headmistress had said that Maris had strayed. It was the only possible explanation for her disappearance.

"Oh, Ford," said Thackery, his breath visible in the cold night air. "Aislynn doesn't want to hear your ideas on some girl's disappearance. It's nothing but gossip. You of all people should understand that there are reasons why people disappear."

But Ford shook his head. "This is different. She didn't disappear and she didn't stray. She was taken."

Aislynn shivered.

Thackery wrapped his arm around her shoulders. "You're upsetting my new friend with your strange theories," he said.

Aislynn quickly unwound herself from Thackery's grasp.

He winked.

"I'm not upset," said Aislynn.

"Bet you anything she just did it for a little attention," said Thackery with mock sympathy. "Must be boring to be a spoiled little royal girl. All those balls and gowns and all that fancy food. How terribly dull to have everything you want."

Aislynn bit her tongue, glad that she hadn't told him who she really was. Ford swatted at him, but Thackery, laughing, easily avoided his hand.

The stables were behind the inn, away from the street lamps and the crowds. The carriage was waiting outside. One of the horses gave a snort as they approached. With a single fluid movement, Thackery swung himself up onto the tiny perch on the back of the coach.

"You just be careful of the woods, my boy," Ford called up to him. "They're dangerous."

"Not if you know what you're doing," came the reply.

With a shake of his head, Ford helped Aislynn back to her seat, and they were on their way again. As the carriage rumbled along, the sounds of the town fading behind them, Aislynn thought about Maris. Was she at Josetta's palace now? Had she been welcomed with open arms, a place in the Wicked Queen's army reserved just for her? Or had it been Josetta herself beneath that black hood, pulling Maris into the shadows?

Just thinking about it made Aislynn shudder. Proper young women did not entertain thoughts of those who had strayed. It was better to forget. After all, Maris had made it clear that she would do anything to keep from being Redirected. Aislynn wondered how quickly she would regret her decision.

Closing her eyes and leaning her head back against the carriage seat, Aislynn vowed that she would not make the same foolish mistakes. She would become a fairy godmother and follow her new Path diligently. She would be grateful. She would not be like Maris.

The sound of Thackery's feet hitting the ground woke Aislynn. She started as he thumped on the carriage door and poked his head through the small window. "I'm sure I'll be seeing you around," he said with a wide smile.

Before she could respond, the carriage pulled away. Ford drove on to what looked like a back entrance, where a single lantern was lit, swinging in the breeze. The building's solid stone walls and circular courtyard looked unnervingly similar to Nerine, and for a moment Aislynn was terrified that she had simply been returned to her old academy. But as Ford helped her out of the carriage, she noticed that the flags waving from beside the door were a different shape and color than the ones at Nerine, and she let out a sigh of relief.

"You can knock," Ford said as he reached for her trunk. "They'll be waiting for you."

Aislynn rapped her knuckles on the door. After a few moments, it swung open to reveal a girl, a little older than Aislynn, dressed in the traditional gray servants' uniform: an ankle-length skirt under a matching apron, her blouse buttoned to her chin. She was carrying her own lantern, and its flame flickered and danced in the wind. Her head was uncovered, tight dark curls pulled back from her tired face.

"We were beginning to worry," she said to Ford, who had placed the trunk at Aislynn's feet.

"No need to worry," he said.

The girl nodded, her shoulders relaxing. Her eyes were dark and beautiful, like two chestnuts, her skin almost the same shade as Aislynn's.

"I'll be tending to the horses unless you need me," said Ford.

"No, that should do." The girl hoisted Aislynn's trunk up against her hip and turned back into the dimly lit building.

"Thank you, Ford," said Aislynn. She unwrapped the shawl from her shoulders and gave it back to him.

"Good night," he said.

"Good night." Aislynn watched as he climbed onto the carriage and, with a *tsk* to the horses, slowly rattled away.

"You must be tired," the servant girl said, startling Aislynn. "I'm Brigid." It seemed as though she gave a slight curtsy, but it was hard to tell if she was just shifting the weight of the trunk against her hip.

"Aislynn."

"Come with me; I'll show you where you'll be staying." Brigid ushered her inside.

The room was dark, and it was hard to see beyond the small circle of light cast by the lamp's candle, but Aislynn could tell it was the kitchen. They passed a large iron stove and shelves overflowing with pots and pans and a doorway adorned with dangling onions and garlic. The embers in the fireplace were still glowing, and Aislynn could see a spit for roasting meat.

She followed the servant girl into a grand hallway. The walls were lined with sconces that cast a splash of light on the plush carpet covering the stone floor. Everything looked new. Even the paintings seemed to gleam with fresh paint. Despite its exterior, Elderwood Academy was very different from the formal, bare Nerine.

Aislynn followed Brigid up the center staircase and toward the dormitories. At the very end of the hallway, Brigid paused in front of a simple red door with a plain latch. Next to it, just a few feet away, was another door, also red. Unlike the one they stood in front of, it had dramatic curved handles with meticulously carved patterns in the wood.

"Would you mind?" Brigid asked, passing the lantern to Aislynn before opening the simple door. It squeaked in protest.

Aislynn followed Brigid into the room. The lantern revealed dingy walls and scratched wood floors. A bed, dresser, and chair seemed to be fighting one another for space in the tiny room. There was another door on the wall to the right, which presumably led to the room next door. The only window was high up and covered in soot.

Brigid set the trunk on the floor, while Aislynn did her best to suppress a growing sense of despair. Somehow the sad, pathetic bedroom made everything unbearably real. She sat on the bed, which was lumpy.

"Best get some sleep," Brigid said with what appeared to be sympathy. "You've got a long day ahead of you."

Chapter 7

In the dim light of the lantern, Aislynn pushed away her
sadness and began unpacking, pulling the three plain cotton
nightgowns and a supply of undergarments from her small
trunk. There would be no more blue dresses, not for tomorrow
and not ever again.

At the bottom of the trunk was the journal where
Aislynn kept the recipes she had learned from Tahlia. She
pulled it out and was surprised to find an oddly shaped
package beneath it, covered in brown paper and tied with
purple string. Aislynn turned it over to discover Tahlia's
familiar handwriting on the wrapping. Tracing her fingers
over the words, she read:

My dearest Aislynn,

Keep my gift close to you always, and remember that there are no truths, only stories.

Your forever fairy godmother,

Tahlia

Puzzled, Aislynn tore off the paper and found that it was the mirror Tahlia had given her for her sixteenth birthday.

Aislynn was as surprised now as she had been when the present was first given to her. Hand mirrors were a common Introduction present, but they were usually given by a girl's parents, or her adviser. And they never looked like this one. The gift of a hand mirror, typically with an oval face and unadorned wooden frame, reminded a maiden of the necessity of humility. But Tahlia's gift was ornate and small, silver edges dotted with tiny red gems. Set in the handle was a deep blue stone, almost as dark as the night sky.

Aislynn was filled with loneliness. She missed her old room and her old clothes, but mostly she missed her parents and Tahlia. Carefully she folded the wrapping paper inside her journal and placed it in the dresser. Then, pressing the small mirror to her chest, she crawled into her new, unfamiliar bed and waited for the sun to rise.

♡ ♡ ♡

The uniform itched. It was loose everywhere except around her throat, where it was pulled tight. The wimple covered her hair and wrapped down under her chin. At least there was no need for a corset, because Aislynn no longer had a waist—or a figure of any sort. Her entire form was hidden in the billowing purple fabric.

She had been sitting in the headmistress's study for what seemed like an eternity, staring at the oak desk that dominated the room. Behind it, set in the wall, were dozens of small doors. Each was the size and shape of a small book, and each was fitted with a dainty gold lock. Aislynn did not know what was behind those doors, but she welcomed the mystery, as it distracted her from the itchy headdress.

The room was warm, and Tahlia's hand mirror, which fit perfectly in her pocket, was pressed against her thigh. Aislynn didn't know if Tahlia's request to keep the gift close to her always was meant to be interpreted literally, but she knew she felt better having the mirror with her. She fought off a yawn.

With a startling *whoosh*, the door swung open, revealing a thin woman in a headmistress's uniform carrying a pile of scrolls. She looked familiar.

Following her, dressed in a white suit, was an adviser Aislynn had never seen before. The woman deposited the scrolls on the desk. They rolled across the wood, followed by a shiny red apple, like the one Thackery had been eating the night before. Aislynn thought of his crooked teeth and bare arms and felt a hot flush across her chest.

"You may call me Madame Moira," said the woman, peering over the top of her desk with a flat expression in her dark eyes. Despite the plush carpeting and the bright paintings, it was now clear to Aislynn that this academy was just like Nerine, and that Madame Moira was just another Madame Odette.

And she now realized why this woman looked familiar. Aislynn had seen Madame Moira with her former headmistress at the ball, which meant she had likely been privy to the specific details of Aislynn's Redirection. Anxiety inched up Aislynn's spine like a long-limbed spider.

While fairy godmothers were unmarried maidens, the women who taught at the academies had once been Contained, had once been loved. But because of an inability to bear children, a betrayal of their marriage vows, or any other act of impropriety, they had been Redirected. Now, instead of serving one family, one daughter, they served many. As teachers they were expected to lead their students away from wickedness and guide them safely down the Path.

"What I see before me is a spoiled little girl who caused her headmistress nothing but trouble." Madame Moira fixed her eyes on Aislynn. "Such willfulness will not be tolerated here. You will follow your new Path with grace and obedience. Do you understand me?"

"Yes, Madame Moira," Aislynn whispered.

"Good." The headmistress gestured to her left. "This is Adviser Lennard."

He dipped his head in greeting and Aislynn did the same, wondering suddenly if she should have risen when they both entered. It was quite possible that all of this was a test that she was failing horribly.

"You are being assigned to Monarch Princess Linnea," Madame Moira continued.

Aislynn almost gasped. She knew that name. Everyone knew that name. Linnea was the daughter of Monarch King Dominick and his wife, Morganne, from the Eastern Kingdom. Both had died when Linnea was only an infant.

During her four years at Nerine, Aislynn had heard many versions of the story, and all of them came to the same conclusion—that the death of the beloved rulers was in some way caused by Monarch Queen Morganne's sister.

"No doubt you've heard of Linnea's aunt," Adviser Lennard said, his tone as smooth as fresh butter. "Josetta, formerly of Eriostemon."

"The Wicked Queen," Aislynn breathed.

The adviser shook his head disapprovingly. "We do not encourage the use of that title," he said. "It gives her a power she does not deserve."

Chastised, Aislynn lowered her eyes.

"I have done my best to keep the monarch princess away from the damaging influences of her family," he continued. "Both in distance and knowledge. She arrived at the academy only a few weeks ago. Almost sixteen, and her first curse came only last season." He looked proud.

Indeed, it was unusual for a maiden to reach the bloom with so few incidents, and Aislynn felt a familiar rush of embarrassment for her own failures.

"As is traditional," said Madame Moira, "once a young maiden enters the academy, she is given a new fairy godmother. You will be the monarch princess's. I'm sure you understand the importance of that position." She gave Aislynn a withering glance. "She was insistent on claiming the next available fairy godmother. If it were up to me, I would have recommended she wait."

"If you fail her, then you have failed me," Adviser Lennard added, quiet and calm. He did not blink. "And if you fail me, then you have failed the Path. Do you understand?"

Aislynn swallowed. "Yes, Adviser."

"Very good." He gestured for her to kneel. "Now it is time for your covenant."

The stone was hard against her knees. Crossing her wrists over her chest, Aislynn bowed her head and tried not to flinch when Adviser Lennard placed his hand on the back of it.

"Repeat after me," he said. "I pledge my loyalty to the Path and all who tend it."

"I pledge my loyalty to the Path and all who tend it."

"I vow to protect the purity of Monarch Princess Linnea until she is Contained in marriage."

"I vow to protect the purity of Monarch Princess Linnea until she is Contained in marriage."

"I shall guide her steps, never allowing them to falter as mine did. Ever after."

"I shall guide her steps, never allowing them to falter as mine did," Aislynn whispered, shame drying her tongue. "Ever after."

It struck her how similar they were, fairy godmother and adviser. Servants to the greater good, they both lived a life that required devotion and sacrifice. Like fairy godmothers, advisers never married, spending their lives in counsel to others.

Yet they were not equal. *The Path* said that an adviser carried his knowledge like a lantern, one that illuminated the way to ever after. While he led the way, the fairy godmother remained a step behind. If a young maiden stumbled or doubted her journey, she need only look back to see what she would become if she did not follow the Path. Adviser Lennard was a guide for the monarch princess; Aislynn was a warning.

With a flourish, Adviser Lennard gestured for her to sit again. "Well then," he said, smoothing down the front of his suit and adjusting the handkerchief in his front pocket. "I shall now take my leave. Good day."

With a graceful bow to the headmistress, he left, and the room settled into silence, interrupted only by the soft scratch of ink on parchment. Aislynn waited awkwardly as the room grew stuffier and her uniform grew itchier.

Finally Madame Moira put down her quill and opened one of her desk drawers. She withdrew an empty glass jar with a white label covered in thick black writing. "Now," she said. "We'll need to remove your loving heart."

Aislynn's entire body stiffened. With an impatient gesture, the headmistress indicated for Aislynn to stand, but her legs seemed to have grown roots, and she was now part of the chair, part of the floor.

"It's a necessary sacrifice." The headmistress crossed the room with measured steps, her long robes brushing the ground. "We are servants of purity. Our loving hearts are a luxury and easily corrupted. Only by ridding ourselves of such vulnerability can we properly assist and protect our wards."

Aislynn prayed that her legs would hold her as she stood.

She wanted to be strong and brave. She wanted to be devoted. But her pulse quickened. Should she say good-bye? Could she? Was her loving heart something to be mourned, something to be missed? Or was it, as the headmistress said, a luxury and a danger, and therefore something that would be forgotten once it was gone?

Madame Moira raised her hand in front of Aislynn's chest. "I dedicate your sacrifice to the protection of our sisters. May you turn away from the love of men and keep your Path clear."

Aislynn squeezed her eyes shut but felt the spell as it hit her. A chill spread through her, frost dancing across her ribs. Her body became as thin as air, and she felt something like a hand pass through her, its fingers curling around her heart. It tugged. Then tugged again. And then, as if it had plucked the bloom from a flower, it withdrew. Aislynn's body was solid once more. The cold slid down from her chest and settled into her hands, crystallizing her fingerprints. She looked up.

Madame Moira held the glass jar aloft. Inside was a glowing orb, pulsing and blinking like a firefly. Its bright blue light filled the room. The headmistress quickly sealed the jar and, with a ring of keys, unlocked one of the doors in the wall. She placed the jar inside, the glowing thing that had once been a part of Aislynn swiftly locked away.

Aislynn waited for pain. She waited for a sense of loss,

of unfathomable sadness, but nothing came. She felt the same. Had it worked? She glanced over at the apple on the headmistress's desk. The heat that had been there earlier when she had thought about Thackery was gone. She thought about Everett too, and there was no twinge, no ache. Her heart beat steadily on, no longer stopping at the thought of him.

It felt wonderful.

Chapter 8

"Your schedule revolves around the monarch princess," said Madame Moira as she led Aislynn out of the study.

Aislynn placed her palm against her chest and felt a gentle, normal pulse. She could feel the chill from her fingers through the fabric of her uniform. Her heart was there, but it was different. It was a misleading description, she decided as she followed the headmistress. Having one's loving heart removed didn't feel as though anything had been taken from her. Instead, it was as if her heart had been frozen, that the part of her prone to foolish fantasies and swooning daydreams had been stilled, mid-beat.

That wasn't the only thing that felt different. Even the

jagged longing she felt when she thought of her parents and Tahlia was now muted. The scent of her mother's perfume, the sound of her father's laugh. Her memories of them felt faraway, blurry and half recalled. As if they were a poem whose words she had memorized but no longer understood. Her heart felt cold, like a block of ice in her chest, the chill inching gently through her body.

A proper fairy godmother had no need to remain connected to her past life. She would be grateful being freed of such unnecessary distractions. But Aislynn remembered what Tahlia had said to her that last night in the kitchen; that she should not let them take what she was not willing to give. Recalling those memories was like chasing a fading dream, but she couldn't help herself. Not completely. Not yet.

Madame Moira took her through the academy's quiet main hallway until they reached the bustling kitchen. The air smelled of butter and tart apples. A servant was whisking a bowl of cream into soft peaks of sweetness, while another sliced strawberries into glistening red triangles. Oven doors swung open and slammed shut as other servants removed freshly baked scones and replaced them with sheets of uncooked dough. All of it was a dance more intoxicating than any ball Aislynn had ever attended.

The appearance of the headmistress caused everything to

stop. Madame Moira's eyes swept the room. She beckoned to the servant who had let Aislynn in the night before.

"This is . . ." The headmistress's hand gestured vaguely at the servant. It took a second for Aislynn to realize that Madame Moira was trying to recall the girl's name.

"Brigid," said Aislynn. Both heads pivoted toward her. "I th-think," she stammered.

The servant girl gave a barely perceptible nod.

"Brigid." Madame Moira pursed her lips briefly before continuing, "Brigid has been helping the monarch princess since her arrival. For a servant she is quite . . ." She paused, seeming to search for the right word. "Satisfactory."

If Brigid was insulted, her expression didn't reflect it.

"We thought it best for the monarch princess that Brigid assist you during this time," Madame Moira said as they left the building through the door where Aislynn had first entered. The pale light from the early morning sun made Aislynn aware of how long the day ahead of her would be and how little sleep she'd gotten. Hiding a yawn behind her hand, she caught a glimpse of Brigid, who was doing the same. The ground was dewy and sparkling, and tiny droplets of water clung to the hem of Aislynn's robe.

"You will be in charge of the monarch princess's wardrobe; of helping her dress in the mornings and evenings, attending to any necessary cleaning or mending. Of course, your role is of extreme importance when it comes to balls; you will be in charge of the gown that she will wear, from measurements to execution. All of this will be discussed in greater detail in your fairy godmother courses, which you will attend while the monarch princess is focusing on her own studies."

Needlework, flower arrangement, calligraphy, dancing, singing, riding, and flirtation. Aislynn remembered her former classes well. She could only hope that she'd prove to be more successful at her fairy godmother lessons.

Having now passed through the well-manicured grounds below the grand ballroom, Aislynn and Brigid followed the headmistress through a small gate tucked into a tall hedge. On the other side were several buildings, including the stables. To their right was a large garden, overflowing with roses and surrounded by trellises bursting with morning glories, their bright purple faces open and turned toward the sun. Next to the garden was a tiny cottage—and standing in front of it, his arms full of roses, was Thackery.

He dipped his head respectfully as they approached. But his polite smile faded as his gaze climbed from her uniform to her face, his eyes flashing with recognition. He said nothing, turning instead to place the roses on a long table in front of the cottage. Unlike last night, when he had been dressed like the other peasants at the township, he now wore the ash gray of a servant. Along the side of his neck, from ear to throat, was a raised and puckered scar that she had not noticed in the dark of the inn.

Aislynn felt nothing except a detached curiosity. No wobbly knees, no damp palms, and no heavy thud in her chest. She felt light and clear, no longer muddled by Thackery's green eyes and tousled hair. And she felt no need to search for *these* missing feelings, no need to draw them back to her.

"This is our gardener . . ." Madame Moira paused again, clearly unable to recall the names of any of her servants.

"Thackery," said Brigid quietly.

"Ah yes. This is our gardener, Thackery."

It seemed strange to just stand there, so Aislynn dipped in a small curtsy. Instead of bowing in return, though, he thrust a bundle of red and orange roses at her. She took them in confusion.

"Every morning you will deliver fresh flowers to the monarch princess. There is a vase in her room specifically for these." The headmistress continued to talk as Aislynn examined the roses, which were tied with a red ribbon around their thornless stems. Each flower was perfect.

"Thank you," she said, raising her eyes to Thackery. His dark eyebrows were slanted downward in a frown. He was angry, Aislynn observed with her new sense of detachment, but that couldn't be right. If anything, he should be embarrassed. After all, she remembered his rant about spoiled royal girls.

Why was he angry? Aislynn realized she was curious, but there wasn't much time to dwell on it because the headmistress was already turning back toward the castle.

"Hurry now," Madame Moira said with an impatient jerk of her hand. "We must not keep the monarch princess waiting."

Aislynn looked back at Thackery, but he had already turned away.

Upon entering Linnea's room, the first thing Aislynn noticed was how different it was from her own. Brigid pulled back the curtains, and the morning light revealed the luxurious suite. Aislynn's room seemed even smaller and darker, more like a box than a place to live. Even her old quarters at Nerine Academy paled in comparison to the beautifully decorated space. The walls were a buttery yellow, the furniture a rich mahogany, and the girl herself was luminous as she sat up in bed, her copper hair bundled up in ribbons. The monarch princess yawned delicately as Brigid helped her into a red dressing gown.

"Your Majesty." Madame Moira curtsied deeply, and

Aislynn imitated her. "I'm sorry to disturb you so early."

"Not at all." The monarch princess smiled, looking as if her night had been filled with nothing but sweet dreams. Her blue eyes were bright and her skin like fresh milk. Gliding across the room as if she was walking on silk, Linnea stopped in front of Aislynn. "I assume you're my new fairy godmother." Her voice was as light and high as a little bird's.

"I am, Your Majesty." Aislynn bowed again, thinking how odd those words felt in her mouth.

"You're very tall," Linnea said, coming closer. The young princess barely reached Aislynn's shoulder, her diminutive height only adding to her doll-like appearance.

"Thank you," Aislynn stammered, unsure what the proper response should be. The monarch princess merely lifted an eyebrow and moved to sit at her vanity, where Brigid joined her and began unwinding the ties from her brilliant red locks. Aislynn stood awkwardly next to the tall dresser against the wall.

Madame Moira cleared her throat. "I'll take my leave," she said.

When the door closed behind the headmistress, Linnea's chin popped up like the lid of a pocket watch, and she swung around to face Aislynn, her eyes narrow.

Aislynn shouldn't have been surprised by the monarch

princess's suspicious gaze. Most young ladies kept their fairy godmothers at arm's length, and with good reason. Their loyalty was not to their ward, but to the leader of the household, whether that be a girl's father, an academy's headmistress, or a spouse.

Once a girl was married, it was the responsibility of the fairy godmother to report any occurrences, and while some instances of magic before matrimony were tolerated, any indication that a married woman was stumbling along her Path was taken very seriously. Under the guidance of his adviser, a husband could revoke his vows and have his wife Redirected.

"What have you heard about me?" Linnea demanded.

"I . . . uh . . . ," Aislynn stammered.

"I'm sure you've heard something," the monarch princess said. "Everyone has."

Aislynn's mind seemed to spin away from her, a top without a string. The story of Queen Morganne and King Dominick was one so tragic and beautiful that people couldn't help but bring it up when conversations turned to such topics. Aislynn's mother had a particular fondness for it, as she did for all tragic and beautiful tales.

According to the story, they had been a handsome couple, deeply in love, deeply happy. Queen Morganne had been the youngest of several girls, all of whom had once been very close. But as they grew older, it was clear that while Linnea's mother was finding her ever after, her eldest sister was straying further and further from the Path, pulled by dark jealousy for her youngest sibling. When Morganne married, Josetta began to show her true side—her cursed side—and King Dominick refused to welcome her into his home, even when his daughter was born.

Furious at being excluded, Josetta used magic to get past the guards, with the intent of stealing the infant and raising Linnea away from the Path. When Morganne refused to give her up, the queen was brutally murdered. Before Josetta and her huntsmen could abduct the child, however, the king intercepted them. It was only through magic that Josetta had managed to escape, fleeing to her wicked kingdom.

The poor king died soon after, his heart broken.

"I've heard that your mother was beautiful and your father very devoted to her," Aislynn offered.

"Is that all?" It was clear now that Linnea was testing her new fairy godmother, and it seemed as if Aislynn had failed. "I think you're lying. They've told you everything, haven't they?" Linnea sniffed and began to turn away.

"No," Aislynn said, surprising herself. "Truth and honesty, they didn't tell me you were so short." She quickly clapped her hand over her mouth.

The room was quiet, and then, to Aislynn's surprise, the monarch princess let out a snort, which grew into a full laugh. Aislynn felt a flicker of warmth at the sound, but it quickly faded, swallowed by the chill that had spread through her. She curled her cold hands into fists.

When the giggles subsided, Linnea, with a genuine smile on her face, waved a hand toward the dresser. "Well then, hand me my hair ribbons, won't you?"

"Yes, Your Majesty." Caught in the reflection of Linnea's mirror, Aislynn saw herself for the first time that day. She was barely recognizable, swathed entirely in purple, with only a tiny triangle of her face showing. And in that triangle was a pair of huge brown eyes. Aislynn expected them to look different, dulled somehow, but they didn't. They looked as they always did. Lost and a little sad.

"You should be an excellent source of advice when it comes to these parties I'm going to be attending." Linnea's voice startled Aislynn out of her thoughts. "You've been to a few, haven't you?"

Aislynn looked away from the mirror. "Yes, Your Majesty."

Brigid had begun to tie Linnea's curls into ribboned pigtails, making her look even younger. "I'll need you to tell me all about them." Eagerness lit the monarch princess's eyes. "Every single detail you can remember. I want to be as prepared as possible. Let's begin with the decorations."

Aislynn smiled, remembering that she had demanded the same of her parents after each party they attended. But she also knew that there were no proper words to describe how it had felt to walk into a ballroom for the first time, how her heart had felt like a candle flame, shimmering and bright. How she could never remember anything about that first party except the way the punch had tasted—fresh and sweet—and how no punch had ever tasted that good again. She was still unsure of what she would say when she was interrupted by the sound of the first bell.

"Well, I suppose we'll have to discuss it another time," the monarch princess said sadly. Turning back to examine her hair in the mirror, she gave a sigh too great for someone of her beauty and wealth, but just right for a girl waiting for her first ball.

Chapter 9

Aislynn concentrated on the cup of tea in front of her. It had been twenty minutes since the teacher had instructed the class to bring their water to a boil, and Aislynn's was still ice cold. But a glance around the room revealed that each of her fellow fairy godmothers was squinting at her own teacup with the same determination—and a similar poor result. Aislynn raised her hand tentatively, leaving it up until she caught her teacher's attention.

"Do you have a question?" Madame Posey was a robust woman, and she moved like someone who was not quite aware of the space she took up, knocking against desks and students' shoulders as she made her way to the back of the room.

"I'm just not sure how to make it boil," said Aislynn in a low voice. Though none of the other girls had found any success, she still felt as if she was missing some important information or direction. As if she was doing something wrong.

"You must concentrate." The teacher repeated the only instruction she had given when the class first began.

"Concentrate?" Aislynn asked confused. "Should I be thinking about magic?"

"No! Don't think about magic." Madame Posey gave a nervous laugh, glancing around as if she hoped no one had heard Aislynn's question. "We are trying to protect you, you foolish girl." She now sounded annoyed. "Think of the tea. Think of what you want it to do." As Aislynn looked blankly up at her, the teacher's eyebrows slanted downward, her frustration evident. "Think of the tea, Aislynn," Madame Posey repeated. "Concentrate on it, but think of the Path too. It will help guide you."

Aislynn was baffled. How was she supposed to think of using magic without actually thinking about magic? She had spent so much time trying to keep herself from having occurrences, she never imagined she'd someday be trying to encourage one.

Her entire day had been like this. She had been told

that until she performed the requisite task in the presence of a teacher, she was not allowed to use magic outside of the classroom. Therefore she was required to learn how to do many of her chores by hand and had spent the morning being taught how to make beds and darn socks and dust furniture. Her head felt so full of new information that she was afraid it would crack open like a pumpkin, thoughts spilling everywhere like pale oval seeds.

Focusing her gaze on the tea, she pictured tiny flames bubbling underneath it. Nothing.

Next to her cup was the pocket-sized manual she had been given that morning. Though there were spells listed, there were no instructions there either. The book mostly outlined, in detail, exactly which of Aislynn's daily fairy godmother tasks permitted magic and which did not. Heating tea or bathwater with magic was allowed. Arranging hair or fastening buttons was not—as magic in front of a royal maiden was strictly off limits. Which meant that when Tahlia had healed Aislynn's hands in the kitchen, she had broken the rules.

Aislynn couldn't help thinking of her fairy godmother now, reminded of the first time Tahlia had taught her how to bake in the kitchen back home. But the memory had been stripped bare. Aislynn could see the familiar walls and uneven floorboards, but she couldn't feel anything. Not the heat of the oven, not the warmth of the dough in her hands, and not even the excitement she had experienced when Tahlia had removed the finished loaf from the pan.

Suddenly she was furious. Furious at Adviser Hull for Redirecting her. Furious at her parents for letting her go. And furious at herself for being completely and utterly useless. All these years of powerful occurrences, and now, when she needed to, when she was expected to, she couldn't conjure enough magic to heat one simple cup of water.

Then Aislynn's nose filled with the scent of bread, the memory of Tahlia baking entering her mind like a burst of color, and she could smell the cinnamon and sugar as if she was pulling the bread from the oven at that very moment. And deep within her chest, her kettle heart began to warm.

Wrapping her fingers around the teacup, Aislynn focused on the still water. She did what Madame Posey had instructed and thought about the tea, concentrated on the tea. A tiny bubble rose from the bottom of the cup, popping as it reached the surface. It was followed by another and another until the water in the teacup was bubbling steadily, a soft halo of steam floating above it.

Aislynn glanced around to see if anyone had noticed, but all of her classmates remained focused on their own cups, their heads down.

The water bubbled more frantically, the hot cup burning her fingers, and it began to rattle against the table. Aislynn tried to calm her thoughts and stop the boiling, but it just got worse. Some of the fairy godmothers glanced over and shrieked as they were sprayed with drops of scalding water. The commotion alerted Madame Posey, who rushed to the back of the room, displacing chairs and students as she ran.

"What have you done?" she demanded.

Aislynn had no answer as a final burst of magic surged through her, causing the teacup to explode in her hands. Shards of porcelain flew across the room, striking several other fairy godmothers, who started wailing. Madame Posey wiped water from her cheek and glared down at Aislynn.

"You'll be washing dishes tonight and for the next month," she said. The room was full of angry faces. "And I'll be reporting this to the headmistress."

"Yes, ma'am." Aislynn carefully gathered what she could of the shattered teacup, her hands nearly blistered and soaking wet.

The kitchen was lit with a large lantern, but the light was not bright enough to fill the room. Uneasy shadows crawled along the walls. It appeared that everyone in the castle was asleep but Aislynn.

Crowding the counter was a seemingly endless pile of dishes. Aislynn picked up a plate encrusted with gravy and potatoes and realized that she had no idea how to properly wash a dish. Before today, she would have assumed there was nothing to it, but after spending a morning failing to make a bed correctly, Aislynn no longer had confidence in any of her assumptions.

Turning on the faucet, she plugged the sink and poured some soap into the cold water. She scrubbed the plate a couple of times with a rag, but the food didn't budge. Instead her sleeves got wet and soapy.

"It's easier if you roll them up," said Brigid, entering the kitchen.

Startled, Aislynn dropped the rag and plate; both disappeared into the mountain of bubbles in the sink. She attempted to roll up her sleeves past her elbows, but they were too big and kept sliding back down to her wrists. Shaking her head, Brigid seemed to take pity on her as she grabbed the material and, with a graceful twist, tied each sleeve back into a neat little bow. It was such a small kindness, but it warmed Aislynn like a blanket, the chill inside her dropping away, if only for a brief moment.

"There," said Brigid, and rolled up her own sleeves. Around each of her wrists was a thin red line, almost like a bracelet that had been drawn across her skin with a quill. Aislynn had never seen anything like it, but quickly looked away as Brigid dipped her arm into the sink and pulled the plug. Once it had drained, Brigid turned on the hot water. As the sink filled, steam rose above it, drawing wispy designs in the air.

Soon the kitchen was warm and fragrant from the soap. Aislynn watched carefully as Brigid pulled a plate from the enormous pile of dishes. Dunking it into the water, she removed the crumbs and stains with a graceful swoop of her rag before handing it to Aislynn.

"Why don't you dry?" she said, gesturing to some dry cloths.

They worked in silence, Brigid speeding through her pile and Aislynn struggling to keep up. Every once in a while, she sneaked a look at the thin red marks around the servant girl's wrists, wondering what they were for. It didn't take long for Brigid to notice her staring.

"Have they taught you this charm yet?" she asked, lifting her hands.

Embarrassed at being caught, Aislynn could only shake her head.

"They will," Brigid continued. "How else can a master keep his peasants in line?"

The servants at Nerine Academy and back home in Nepeta must have always worn their sleeves rolled down. Or perhaps Aislynn had never noticed. It made sense though, that the custody spell left a physical mark. One quick look, and you could see which peasants were safe and which were wild. She wondered if it hurt. It looked as though it did.

Aislynn picked up a dish and began drying it. The bitterness in Brigid's voice made her nervous. After all, the custody spell was performed for a peasant woman's own good. Without it, she would be prey to her own uncontrollable urges.

Maybe Brigid just didn't know any better. The advisers always said that servants were unable to welcome the help they so desperately needed, since they didn't have the same capacity for self-preservation that royals did. As *The Path* stated, "A wolf raised in a barn may have food and warmth, but if the gate is left unlatched, it will return to the forest it came from." It was up to royals to latch that gate.

"I can finish the rest of them," Brigid said quietly. "It won't take me long at all." Suddenly the air in the kitchen felt hot. Aislynn backed away from the sink.

"I'm allowed," added Brigid mildly, and though it seemed logical that a kitchen servant would be allowed to use magic in the kitchen, Aislynn wanted no part of it.

"I'll head to bed, then," said Aislynn. Brigid nodded.

Moving quickly, Aislynn left the kitchen, not stopping until she had climbed the stairs, crossed the hallway, and locked her bedroom door behind her.

Chapter 10

Aislynn ran. She could not see the wolf, but she could hear it, racing through the twigs and leaves that covered the forest floor as it pursued her. With her arms lifted in front of her like a shield, Aislynn felt the slap of branches whipping against her skin. She ran faster.

The only light came from the brilliant moon, giant and round, casting a bluish glow through the thick branches. But it was not enough light to illuminate the thick tree trunk until it was too late. Aislynn fell. There was no containing the cry of pain as she slammed into the earth.

Whipping her head up, Aislynn searched the night for the wolf, catching only glimpses of its silvery coat as *it darted in and out of the shadows, circling her. Then the moon shifted and the wolf stepped out of the darkness, its yellow eyes glowing.*

With a gasp, Aislynn woke. Legs aching and heart racing, she lay still, trying to understand what was happening to her. How was this possible? Her loving heart was gone. That dangerous, corruptible part of her had been removed. Why had the nightmares returned?

Rescuing herself from the damp snarl of her blanket and nightgown, Aislynn pressed a cold fist to her chest. The teacup, and now this? Removing her loving heart was supposed to protect her, but she felt just as dangerous as before.

The early bell had yet to ring, but Aislynn dressed anyway, eager to leave the nightmare behind.

Getting into the fairy godmother uniform yesterday had been a struggle, and this morning was no different. But Tahlia had been right, Aislynn thought as she tugged the purple fabric into place, the hem spread out on the floor around her. No one would ever see her legs.

With her hair twisted into a tight braid, she arranged her wimple as best she could and slipped Tahlia's mirror into her pocket. Its small weight was a comfort against her hip.

The academy was quiet. Aislynn hurried toward the

kitchen, where the servants' day had already begun and the sounds and smells of breakfast greeted her.

Her stomach grumbled, but she didn't stop. As she headed out the back door, the early bell sounded, no doubt waking the rest of the fairy godmothers. The grass was wet with morning dew, and though Aislynn did her best to hold up her robes, the hem of her uniform was quickly soaked. She reached the bouquet table just as Thackery was exiting his cottage, his arms full of roses.

Fixing a smile on her face, Aislynn decided that she would forgive him for his comments the night she had arrived and for his rude behavior the next morning. There was no reason for either of them to hold a grudge. She lifted her hand in greeting, hoping to start anew, but before she could say anything, Thackery threw Linnea's bouquet into her arms and went back into the cottage, slamming the door behind him.

Clearly he was still out of sorts.

Aislynn gave a small huff of frustration, turned on her heel, and stomped back to the castle. As she passed the rest of the fairy godmothers just exiting the kitchen, she told herself that it didn't matter what the castle gardener thought of her.

♡ ♡ ♡

Linnea's room was still dark when Aislynn entered. She placed the flowers on the dresser and went to open the curtains, just as Tahlia had always done. As morning spread across the carpet, Aislynn carefully arranged the roses in their vase. She was examining her handiwork when she remembered that her fairy godmother had also greeted her each morning with a tray of tea.

"Thorns," she swore under her breath. It wasn't even eight o'clock, and she had already made a mistake.

"Hmmm?" came a sleepy voice. Linnea was sitting up in bed, rubbing her eyes.

"Good morning, Your Majesty," said Aislynn, inching toward the door. There was still time. Chances were that the tray was waiting for her downstairs. It wouldn't take long to get it. But before she could, she noticed that Linnea was holding out her arms with a look of confusion.

The robe. Aislynn snatched up the dressing gown that lay across the plush chair next to the bed. The delicate fabric seemed to tangle and wrinkle as she struggled to wrap Linnea in it. Finally the monarch princess kindly batted her away and put on the robe by herself.

Rising from her bed, Linnea made her way to the vanity and, once she was seated, looked at Aislynn expectantly. There was a quiet knock on the door and Brigid entered, carrying a tray of tea.

"Good morning, Your Majesty." The servant girl gave a bow and was gifted with a dazzling smile from the monarch princess. "Aislynn thought we should divide responsibilities so as to best ease you through this transition."

"Oh, Aislynn." Linnea beamed up at her fairy godmother. "You are so thoughtful."

"Shall I help you with your hair?" Brigid asked. She set the tray down on the dresser next to the flowers.

"Yes, thank you, Brigid." Linnea's posture was in line with the back of her chair.

Over Linnea's head, Brigid nodded toward the tea set, and eager to do something useful, Aislynn busied herself with pouring a cup. Enough to drink, but not too full. She even blew on it a little.

Placing the delicate porcelain teacup on an equally delicate saucer, Aislynn brought the tea to Linnea. Brigid had begun to unwind the monarch princess's hair, and Aislynn stepped back to observe.

With gentle fingers, Brigid untied each of the ribbons that secured Linnea's curls. She unfurled each glossy lock until it rested against Linnea's pale neck and shoulders.

The monarch princess seemed to appreciate Brigid's assistance. Her eyes were closed, a small smile appearing in the corner of her lips . . . a smile that quickly faded when she took a sip of her tea.

"Your Majesty?" Brigid's hands stilled as the princess placed the tea on her vanity and with a delicate finger pushed it toward Aislynn.

"Perhaps I could have some sugar in this?"

Aislynn cursed her pumpkin-headedness. She took a deep breath. She could do better. Quickly spooning sugar into the cup, she handed the doctored tea back to the monarch princess.

It wasn't long before each curl was untied and draped across Linnea's shoulders like an ocean of red waves. "Thank you, Brigid," Linnea said as the servant girl gathered the cloth ribbons into a basket.

"Your Majesty." Brigid curtsied and departed.

Linnea's tea had been abandoned. Perhaps it had been too sweet this time around. The air in the room seemed heavy with Aislynn's mistakes.

"I am so sorry, Your Majesty," she offered.

"It's quite all right," said Linnea. "I suspect it will take some time to get used to each other. And you'll need some time to get used to—" She gestured to the fairy godmother's uniform. "This, I imagine. It must be difficult for you."

"It's my Path." But instead of pride, Aislynn felt only shame and embarrassment. She cleared her throat and lifted her chin. "I will not yearn for what I cannot have." She said it more for herself than anything.

"Yes, of course." Linnea seemed strangely flustered, and her eyes dropped to her teacup. "I never meant to imply . . . that is, I was getting quite used to Brigid, and it will most likely take some time for us to become accustomed to each other."

"I'm sorry, Your Majesty." Aislynn rushed to apologize again. The last thing she wanted was to cause her princess discomfort. "Perhaps if you told me the things your last fairy godmother did that you'd like me to do, then I could be of better assistance."

"I never really liked my last fairy godmother." Instantly Linnea's hand flew to her mouth and her eyes grew round with shock, as if she couldn't believe what she had just said. Then a tiny sputter burst from her lips, followed quickly by an eruption of giggles. "I'm sorry, that's a sooty thing to say."

"Not if it was true," said Aislynn, causing Linnea to laugh harder.

"It was true! Oh, goodness." Linnea wiped her eyes. "Poor woman. It wasn't her fault, really. She was more like Adviser Lennard's fairy godmother than mine. He's been my guardian since . . ." Her tone grew more somber. "Since my parents died. And I think sometimes he forgets that I'm older now." She turned her head, watching her locks bounce and sway. "He still thinks I'm a little girl with little-girl curls."

Frowning at her reflection, Linnea wrapped her finger around a chunk of copper hair and pulled. Hard. Aislynn winced. The monarch princess did not.

Across from the kitchen was a small room with no windows and one long table jammed up against the wall. To the left of the door was a trolley bowing under the weight of a tureen of steaming porridge, flanked by bowls of apple slices and dishes of brown sugar.

The other fairy godmothers had already collected their breakfasts and were crammed together on one side of the table, eating silently, their eyes directed downward. They all glanced up when Aislynn entered. Some of them glared, clearly still angry about yesterday's incident with the exploding teacup, but quickly returned their attention to their meals. Their movements were unnervingly uniform. They even appeared to be chewing in unison.

Her stomach gurgling with hunger, Aislynn filled her bowl halfway with the hot porridge, trying to keep her sleeves out of the gooey, bland breakfast. That morning she had tried to tie them up as Brigid had done the night before, but it had been impossible, and she had the sense that the headmistress would not look too kindly on such adjustments.

Still, despite the sleeves and the constant itching around her neck, Aislynn was surprised to discover that she actually enjoyed her uniform. She appreciated how invisible it made her and how the draping fabric completely obscured her figure. A figure that no one would ever look upon again.

The realization should have made her sad, but Aislynn only felt a dangerous trickle of excitement. She added another heaping scoop of porridge to her bowl. And then another, adding a pile of brown sugar to the top. Then, gathering up a handful of apple slices, Aislynn took her heavenly smelling breakfast and settled at the far end of the table.

With a wall of blank eyes watching her, Aislynn took a thick section of apple and dipped it into her porridge. The chewy oats and sweet sugar softened each crunchy bite, infusing the warm concoction with a cool, tart finish. Without a corset tight around her ribs, she could swallow comfortably. She wasn't afraid of taking one bite too many and pulling her perfectly tailored gown unpleasantly against her skin.

It didn't take long for her to clean her bowl. The others stared at her the entire time. For a moment, Aislynn thought of suggesting that they might enjoy doing the same with their breakfasts, but she quickly rejected the idea. After all, their time together was only temporary, and it was better to focus on pleasing the monarch princess than on trying to form friendships. Searching for companionship among fairy godmothers was as pointless as befriending a winter's frost, or so *The Path* said.

Aislynn rose and fixed herself another serving. As she was stirring the sugar and oatmeal together, one of the teachers appeared in the doorway.

"Thea," she said, summoning a fairy godmother with a curled finger.

Everyone else stayed at the table, playing with what remained of her porridge and watching Aislynn as she ate. It wasn't long before Thea returned and the teacher gestured to another fairy godmother at the far end of the table. "Cecily," she said, but the girl shook her head. "Nothing to report?"

"Nothing," said Cecily.

"Very well. Juliana?"

This time, she was rewarded with a nod as a petite fairy godmother rose and followed her out of the room.

Thea leaned over to Cecily. "Maybe you're not watching her closely enough," she said.

Cecily's eyes narrowed. "I watch her as closely as is necessary."

"I don't have anything either," one of the other girls interjected, and Thea shook her head condescendingly.

"You know the headmistress won't like that."

"What do you want me to do?" Cecily responded. "Make something up? Is that what you do?"

"I don't need to." Thea shook out her sleeves. "I have plenty to tell Madame Moira."

"I'm sure Princess Reata's book is as thick as she is," Cecily said, lifting her lip in a sneer.

"At least Princess Reata comes from a good family," Thea said, her eyes sliding over to Aislynn. "Unfortunately that's not the case with all the students here."

Taking her bowl, Aislynn left the table. Her fingers were cold, her heart like a lump of snow, and she wasn't hungry anymore.

The bell rang, and the hallway, which had been silent and still only hours before, became a bustling mass of girls and giggling. Just like Nerine, the academy echoed with the footsteps and gossip of its students. Aislynn waded through the crowd looking for the monarch princess, who was standing calmly outside the dining hall. There was barely enough room to curtsy, but Aislynn managed, and the two girls set off for Linnea's first class.

Everyone moved less like a group of young women and more like colorful schools of fish, darting in and out of classrooms, until only a sea of purple remained. Each time

Linnea was delivered to one of her classes, Aislynn silently joined the rest of the fairy godmothers for her own lessons at the other end of the academy.

There were breaks for meals, as well as the usual hour for reflection and personal study, and it wasn't until she found Brigid waiting for her in the kitchen after dinner that Aislynn realized she had hardly spoken more than a few sentences all day. The servant girl smiled, and Aislynn felt some of the cold within her recede, if only for a moment.

"I thought," Brigid said, filling the sink with water, "I thought we could talk about Linnea."

Aislynn had never heard a house servant use a royal's proper name. Even Tahlia had referred to Aislynn as "my lady."

"I mean, her royal highness." Brigid paused. "I thought we could discuss her preferences and schedule."

"Such as how much milk she likes in her tea," said Aislynn moodily. She popped a bubble rising out of the hot water.

"She doesn't like milk. Only sugar. Two cubes. She has a bit of a sweet tooth. If she's upset, a dish of sugared fruit will cheer her up. The cook keeps them in the pantry. Ask for cherries or cranberries." The plate she was scrubbing was clean, but Brigid didn't seem to notice. "If she's sad, fix her a cup of elderberry tea with a plate of shortbread biscuits. She likes her gowns laid out the night before, and any letters should be placed on the small table next to her yellow chair. She prefers her bathwater warm, not hot, and if she decides that she doesn't want to eat in the dining room—which is often—the headmistress should be informed immediately."

"Does Linnea have 'a book'?" asked Aislynn as soon as the other girl took a breath. "The other fairy godmothers were talking about them this morning—"

"Perhaps you should ask them."

"I don't think that will get me any answers," Aislynn said wryly. "Do you know what they were talking about?" From the way Brigid looked away, it was clear that she knew exactly what Aislynn was referring to.

"The book is where a maiden's magical occurrences are recorded." Brigid dried her hands and turned to Aislynn. "The headmistress maintains it, and it is passed on to the girl's husband once she marries. He keeps track of any continuing events after the wedding."

Aislynn knew, of course, that fairy godmothers were expected to report any instances of magic, but she had never imagined that it was done in such a meticulous way. Words in a book were so permanent, so damning. . . .

Had Tahlia contributed to the volumes that must have

been created about her? Aislynn quickly dismissed such a thought. Of course she hadn't.

"The headmistress asks for reports once a week," Brigid said, returning to the dishes.

"Has there been anything to report about the monarch princess?" asked Aislynn hesitantly, noticing how the other girl's jaw tightened.

"Nothing." But it sounded like a lie. Brigid thrust a wet bowl into Aislynn's hands. "We should hurry."

"Of course." Drying the dish dutifully, Aislynn wondered what else she didn't know about the responsibilities of a fairy godmother. She desperately hoped there would be no more surprises like this one. "Brigid?"

"Mm-hmm?"

It was clear that Brigid did not want to continue the current conversation. So instead Aislynn asked, "Why are you being so kind to me?"

Brigid gave her a small smile and passed her another dish. "Because you remembered my name."

Chapter 11

By the time she had completed her month of dishwashing, Aislynn knew more about Linnea than she did about her own parents. Brigid finally conceded all responsibility for the monarch princess to Aislynn, though she made it perfectly clear that she was available if there were any questions.

There was a part of Aislynn that was disappointed to leave her sessions with Brigid behind. Most of the time, the servant girl was the only person that Aislynn spoke to, except for the increasingly brief exchanges she had with Linnea.

The monarch princess was warm and open with Brigid, but once Brigid returned to her regular post in the kitchen, Linnea's temperament shifted, and she began to behave toward Aislynn as a royal maiden was expected to act toward her fairy godmother: largely indifferent.

She asked for details about the balls once or twice but for the most part was undemanding, which allowed Aislynn to focus on her own studies. While Linnea was curled up in her yellow chair with her needlepoint, Aislynn was free to read and reread her fairy godmother manual. Though she never attempted any of the spells, she soon had them all memorized.

One evening Aislynn was trailing behind the rest of the fairy godmothers as they headed to the dining hall to retrieve their wards.

"There's a reading tonight," she heard Cecily say to Juliana. "Three pages. Princess Sibyl has a very articulate suitor."

"We'll be up all night," said Thea. "Doesn't he know that any maiden would prefer a proposal over poetry?" Cecily, who was Princess Sibyl's fairy godmother, only shrugged.

It was common practice for the princesses to share the letters they received from their suitors, often staying up past midnight to judge the quality of poetry and prose. The library would be filled with sugar cookies and tittering. Linnea never attended.

Which was why Aislynn was surprised when the monarch

princess left the dining hall and began following the other girls to the library. She seemed more ready for battle than an evening of listening to the meandering rhymes of Sibyl's suitor.

"Can you imagine?" Princess Rochelle said, glancing over her shoulder. "Such an embarrassment."

"After what her aunt's done—" Lady Ellyn replied.

"I can't believe she'd show her face."

Linnea inhaled sharply and stopped in her tracks. Then, pivoting on her heel, she took off toward the staircase. Aislynn had to rush to keep up. They wove silently through the corridors to their rooms. Linnea slid through her door and quickly blocked Aislynn's path.

"I'm feeling rather tired," she said.

"Why don't I help you get ready for bed?" Aislynn offered, but Linnea shook her head.

Aislynn tried again. "Would you like some sugared cherries? Or a cup of elderberry tea?"

But there was no response. Linnea had already shut the door.

The walk to and from the rose garden was a small piece of freedom for Aislynn, nothing but the grass beneath her feet and the sun against her face to keep her company. There were even moments, if she closed her eyes, when she was able to forget who and where she was.

On those days, even Thackery's childish behavior couldn't irritate her. His new tactic was to ignore her completely, but Aislynn had stopped trying to understand why and instead kept reminding herself that she shouldn't even care.

But today she had overslept. Rushing down the stairs, she practically collided with a gaggle of fairy godmothers just outside the kitchen. Annoyed at herself for being late, Aislynn had no choice but to follow the others, imagining how they probably appeared to Thackery, an enormous, gossiping purple wave sliding over the landscape.

"The headmistress should make him wear gloves," Thea said as they drew closer to the small cottage. Thackery's back was toward them, his head bowed over the flowers. "It's unseemly."

"They're so rough," said Juliana, causing several heads to swivel in her direction. "His hands," she clarified.

"You've touched them?"

"He touched me," Juliana was quick to correct, her chin jutting out defensively. "I think he did it on purpose, too." There was a sharp intake of breath from the other girls.

"He's such a beast," Cecily hissed. "His kind shouldn't be allowed near the academies. You know they can't control themselves."

Though most of *The Path*'s chapters on commoners were dedicated to the dangerous and wild nature of the women, there were the occasional passages devoted to the unsavory tendencies of peasant men. It was considered best to keep them at a safe distance.

"He's much better suited for the fields," said Thea. "And that scar." She shuddered. "It's so hideous."

Aislynn hoped he couldn't hear them. Though he had been rude and childish to her, she didn't think he had earned such treatment.

But as they approached, the faint blush that stained his cheeks made it clear that he had heard. When he looked up, his eyes found hers. The disgusted look on his face made her stomach twist.

The summer air, which moments ago had been clear and fresh, now felt thick and stifling. Thackery handed out the bouquets in silence, and it seemed that even the birds were too ill at ease to sing. Aislynn waited for the other girls to depart, watching them hurry across the lawn, uniforms fluttering. For some reason it was very important to her that Thackery know she did not agree with the other fairy godmothers.

Too embarrassed to look at him, Aislynn reached out for her bundle of roses. Thackery's fingers brushed hers as he gave them to her, and then, in a whisper so quiet she almost missed it, he asked, "Too rough?"

Surprised, she looked up. "No," she said, wrapping her hands tightly around the stems.

He gave a small shake of his head, almost as if he was laughing at her. Then he bowed deeply, and she was sure he was laughing at her. But she liked it better than being ignored, so she didn't say anything as she curtsied low and turned away. Crossing the lawn, she forced herself not to look back.

As the cool air of the castle embraced her, she was reminded of her responsibilities and of the unhappy princess who waited for her upstairs. She headed for the pantry. Linnea hadn't wanted any comforting treats last night, but perhaps she would appreciate them this morning.

Brigid, tying up her apron, entered the kitchen as Aislynn was steeping the elderberry flowers.

"What happened?" Brigid asked, looking at the tea.

Aislynn recounted last evening's encounter outside the library. When she had finished, Brigid scooped a handful of sugar cookies from a jar and placed them on a plate.

"Why don't you bring her the tea and cookies, and I'll bring up breakfast? I doubt she'll be dining with the others this morning," Brigid said, and Aislynn nodded, grateful the other girl knew Linnea so well.

The roses tucked securely under her arm, Aislynn took the tray and squeezed out of the now-bustling kitchen. She entered Linnea's room quietly, and as usual, it took her eyes a few moments to adjust to the darkness. When they did, she was surprised to see Linnea kneeling on the carpet next to her bed, wrists crossed over her chest.

"Good morning, Your Majesty." Aislynn placed the tea and cookies on the vanity and moved to the windows to open the curtains.

"Wait!" Linnea cried, but it was too late. Light sprang into the bedroom, spilling onto the sheets and blankets that Linnea was frantically trying to shove into the corner. When Aislynn had made the bed the day before, the linens had been pure white – now they were completely red, as if they had been dyed during the night.

The scene was so familiar that it made Aislynn breathless. On her first morning at Nerine Academy, she had awoken to find her ivory nightgown had been transformed to a sapphire blue. The punishment had been severe, but had done nothing to keep her from ruining her carpet in a similar fashion the following evening. It had been years since those occurences, but Aislynn could still feel Linnea's shame and fear as if they were her own.

"I'll take care of it," Aislynn said immediately, even

though she had no idea how. Gathering the sheets in her arms, she pushed open the door adjoining their rooms and dumped them onto her own bed. When she returned, she found that Linnea had curled up in her large daffodil chair, looking even smaller and paler than usual.

"Drink this," Aislynn said, giving Linnea a cup of warm, sweetened tea. Then she handed her a cookie, hovering over her until she ate it. When the color was restored to Linnea's cheeks, Aislynn went back to the task of arranging the bouquet of roses. She didn't know what else to do.

"Brigid will be bringing your breakfast shortly," she said, keeping her voice calm and quiet as she gathered yesterday's wayward petals from the top of the dresser. She knew a proper fairy godmother would report Linnea, but one look at the monarch princess's despondent face and Aislynn knew she could not.

"She is?" Linnea's voice rose hopefully. "Perhaps you could tell the headmistress I'm not feeling well," she added. "That it's best that I stay in bed today."

"Of course, Your Majesty," said Aislynn. She knew that if Tahlia were here, she would have gone into the other room and reemerged with pure white sheets. But even if Aislynn had those skills—which she did not—the thought of doing something so against the rules terrified her. She couldn't tell the headmistress and she couldn't fix it. So Aislynn curtsied and left, nearly crashing into Brigid, who had a heavily laden tray in her hands.

"How is she?" Brigid whispered.

Lowering her voice, Aislynn quickly explained the situation. Maybe the other girl would know what to do.

"I'll take care of it," said Brigid, her face unreadable.

Aislynn thanked her and swallowed her guilt, hoping that she had done the right thing.

It was the first time since her arrival that Aislynn had found cause to visit Madame Moira. She rapped on the heavy wood door.

"Come in." The headmistress was sitting behind her desk as if on a throne.

"I just wanted to inform you that the monarch princess is not feeling well and has decided to stay in bed for the day." Aislynn's words tumbled out of her.

Nodding, the headmistress opened a drawer and retrieved a leather-bound book with Linnea's name written across the cover in neat gold letters. "Is there anything else you would like to report, Aislynn?" she asked, her quill posed expectantly over a blank page.

"No, Headmistress," said Aislynn, eager to leave the dimly lit office.

"I'm afraid I don't believe you," said Madame Moira after a moment of silence. "The other fairy godmothers reported that the monarch princess was very upset last night." She sighed. "Perhaps I have not made clear what is it expected of you in these situations."

Aislynn understood exactly what was expected of her, and she also knew that a proper fairy godmother would tell the headmistress everything. Yet as Aislynn stood there in Madame Moira's gloomy study, she knew that she would never be able to tell the headmistress what she wanted to hear.

"I'm sure you think that your loyalty will be appreciated by the monarch princess—rewarded, even." Madame Moira leaned forward until her sleeves spread out across the desk like spilled ink. "However, you are only doing her, and yourself, a grave disservice. Indeed, shielding her from the consequences of her occurrences is not only dangerous but selfish."

Madame Moira stood and turned to the collection of tiny doors that lined the wall behind her. "I once knew of a fairy godmother who kept the secret of her mistress's wicked occurrences from those who could have helped her, mistaking her own greedy need for the princess's affection for true devotion." She paused, running her fingers along the hinges and locks, seemingly lost in the story.

"When she turned sixteen, the princess married, for

she was beautiful and beguiling. Her husband, equally handsome and charming, loved her very much. And the princess loved him. More than she had ever loved her fairy godmother."

Aislynn noticed that Madame Moira's features had softened and her eyes, previously so flat and cold, had become dewy. Was this story about her? Was she the princess?

"But she was naive and foolish." Quick as a mousetrap, Madame Moira's face snapped back to its former hardness. "Eventually the prince discovered the fairy godmother's lies and realized the wickedness that lurked inside his bride. When he told the young princess he could not remain married to her, she flew into a rage. Since she had never been chastised or punished, she was unable to control the magic that overpowered her and, in an instant, ruined her life and that of her husband."

Aislynn could only stare as the headmistress slowly relaxed her fist.

"Let me be clear. If you are not careful, your childish infatuation with the monarch princess will be your downfall. And hers. Make sure you think about that the next time you come to my study. I don't need to be saddled with another failed fairy godmother." She slammed Linnea's book shut. "You are dismissed."

Aislynn scurried from the room, thinking of only one thing. It was clear what had happened to the princess in Madame Moira's story. But what had happened to the fairy godmother?

Chapter 12

Madame Moira's story haunted Aislynn throughout the day. Several times she even found herself heading in the direction of the headmistress's study, the truth burning in her throat. But every time she reached the end of the hall, where she should turn left, she would always turn right, taking herself on several tours of the western wing of the castle.

Part of her knew that the headmistress was right, that keeping Linnea's secret was more of a betrayal than an act of kindness. But even knowing that—even knowing that she was putting her ward in great danger—was not enough to loosen her tongue.

How had Tahlia done it? How had she kept Aislynn's secrets and her own guilt at bay? Did she regret not reporting Aislynn's occurrences? Did she feel some blame for the Redirection?

Aislynn passed the library for the seventh time that day, pivoted, and began marching in the direction of the kitchen. She knew that contact with anyone from her former life was strictly forbidden. But surely the Path looked kindly on those who aimed to move forward, even if their steps were not always straight.

Aislynn found Brigid in the pantry, peeling potatoes. "Can I help?" Aislynn asked, watching Brigid remove the skin from a large potato in one long curl.

Eyebrow lifted, Brigid handed over a small knife. "Have you ever peeled potatoes before?" Aislynn shook her head. "Well, try to cut the potato, not your fingers."

Holding both knife and vegetable delicately, Aislynn managed to detach several thick patches of potato skin. They worked in silence for a few minutes before Aislynn, trying to keep her voice casual, asked, "Linnea doesn't send many letters, does she?"

"No, not many." A few curls had escaped from Brigid's head scarf and trailed across her forehead. "She occasionally writes to her cousin Gregor and to Prince Westerly, though those letters are sent through Adviser Lennard, of course."

"Prince Westerly?" It was a name Aislynn had not heard before.

A shadow seemed to flit across Brigid's face, but it passed so quickly that Aislynn wasn't sure she had seen it at all. "If all goes well, he'll find himself sitting on the throne next to the monarch princess. You'll meet him soon enough." Brigid paused in her peeling and looked up, her eyes clever and bright. "Is there someone you were hoping to send a letter to?"

"You know that wouldn't be allowed," Aislynn said automatically.

Brigid reached for another potato with a smile. "You should talk to Thackery." The small hope that had begun to bloom in Aislynn wilted immediately. Thackery would never help her. He wouldn't even speak to her. "He can send your letter in town, and you can have any responses delivered to him there. He goes every week to sell the extra flowers and vegetables."

"Isn't there anyone else who could help?" asked Aislynn.

"Ford travels when they need the carriage, but you can't depend on that. And none of the rest of us can leave the academy. Madame Moira doesn't want her servants disappearing like they've been doing at other schools. It would be quite the inconvenience for her."

"Disappearing?" Aislynn thought about Maris for the first time in weeks, and a chill went up her spine.

"There have been some servants . . . unaccounted for."

But Brigid didn't seem very concerned. In fact, she seemed slightly amused.

"Do you think they were taken?"

Brigid chuckled. "You've spoken to Ford, haven't you?"

Aislynn ducked her head sheepishly. "A girl at my academy strayed," she explained, lowering her voice, "but if people are disappearing . . ."

"Not people, servants." Brigid stood, scooped the peeled potatoes into her apron, and walked over to the large butcher's block in the corner. "And they aren't being taken, they just don't want to be found." She began to chop the potatoes, dropping the even slices into a nearby pot. She looked at Aislynn, who was still sitting on the stool. "Is there a reason you don't want to ask Thackery about the letter you don't want to send? He's very trustworthy, and he'd be happy to help."

"I don't think he would." Aislynn continued to peel her potato. "He doesn't care much for me. In fact, I think he hates me."

Brigid's burst of laughter was a surprise. "He doesn't hate you," she said, wiping her hands on her apron. "It's just, well—"

Aislynn waited expectantly for Brigid to continue, confused by her obvious mirth.

"It's this he hates." Brigid waved her hand at Aislynn's

uniform. "He's not particularly fond of fairy godmothers. He wants to like you. He just gets a bit prickly, that's all." Brigid paused. "Why don't I talk to him? I bet he'll appreciate that you're willing to break the rules."

"I don't want to break the rules," Aislynn insisted, but Brigid had already returned to her chopping and didn't seem to hear the lie.

The next morning there was a note addressed to Aislynn on Linnea's tea tray. Catching Brigid's eye, Aislynn was gifted with a quick smile. She shoved the note into her pocket, wishing she could read it right away.

She delivered the tea to Linnea, who seemed eager to forget the events of the previous morning now that her bed linens were back to a pristine white. She even chatted eagerly about the book she was reading while Aislynn untied her hair.

Finally the monarch princess was herded down the stairs and off to breakfast. Bypassing the fairy godmothers' dining room, Aislynn went back upstairs, her curiosity overwhelming her hunger.

Thackery will take your letter. There is ink and parchment in your top drawer.

Brigid

♡ ♡ ♡

Aislynn pulled her dresser open. The top drawer resisted as usual, but she found a roll of parchment, a quill pen, and a small bottle of ink sliding around inside.

Placing everything on her bedside table, Aislynn carefully dipped her quill in the ink and wrote, *Dear Tahlia . . .*

She quickly filled the parchment and found herself wishing she had more. There were so many questions she wanted to ask, mostly about how to be a good fairy godmother to Linnea. She folded the letter carefully, addressed it, and sealed it with her candle. The bell rang. Breakfast was over.

Ignoring her angry stomach, Aislynn made her way downstairs to start the day. She was horribly distracted throughout her first two classes, her leg keeping a frantic rhythm beneath her desk. The bell signaling the beginning of lunch seemed to come at the end of seven seasons, and when Linnea was finally seated in the dining hall, Aislynn wove through the bustling kitchen and out into the brilliant yellow light of the afternoon. Compared to the cold stone of the castle, the summer sun felt wonderful on her face.

She spotted Thackery working in the vegetable garden. His pants were rolled to his knees and his shirt shucked off to the side, the muscles in his back flexing as he thrust his shovel into the soil.

Aislynn stepped closer. On his shoulder—the left one—she could see a plum-sized mark. There was an image inside the circle that she couldn't make out, but she could tell clearly that his skin was raised and puckered, like the brands she had seen on horses.

"Oi!" Thackery snatched his shirt off the fence and quickly threw it on. "Can I help you with something?"

"I . . . I have something for you." Picking up the hem of her robe, Aislynn made her way to him. The interested look on Thackery's face dimmed when she pulled the parchment from her pocket.

"Brigid said that you could send this letter for me."

"Did she now?" said Thackery. Aislynn was close enough to see the sweat on his brow as he frowned, and for a moment she thought that she had made a mistake. Had she misread Brigid's note? But he snatched the letter out of her hands and smiled, holding it up to the sky as if he was trying to read it. "I'm going into town tomorrow. I'll make sure it gets to where it's going," he said. "Who's Tahlia?"

Aislynn hesitated. "My fairy godmother." She corrected herself. "My former fairy godmother." Thackery tilted his head, clearly curious. Aislynn rushed to explain herself. "I know I'm not supposed to question my Path, and I'm not, I just . . . I just had a few things that I needed to ask her. It won't happen again . . . it won't happen often, I swear. I know it's very unusual behavior."

He shrugged. "I'm no authority on what's usual behavior for fairy godmothers." His expression was a strange combination of pity and amusement. "You're the first one I've known to ever ask for anything."

"I am?" But Aislynn wasn't really surprised.

"Your lot tend to stick to your own kind," he said, tucking the letter into his back pocket.

"Not an admirer, are you?" She tried to make her words light, but Thackery's face grew serious.

"Of fairy godmothers? No. But you're hardly as bad as the others." He shrugged again. "Nothing personal, you understand."

"It sounds rather personal."

"Yes, I suppose it would." He ran his fingers through his thick hair. "Cheer up," he said, giving her a gentle jab on her arm. "I'll still send your letter. And deliver any that arrive." He lifted his shovel and began to head back toward his cottage.

"How did you get that mark on your shoulder?" Aislynn called without thinking. He stopped, and she could see him tense before he glanced back.

"Noticed that, did you?" Wiggling his eyebrows, Thackery gave Aislynn a playful leer. "Notice anything else?"

"Nothing of interest," she shot back, surprising herself.

His laugh was genuine, but it faded quickly. "Let's just say the answer to your question has a lot to do with why I'm not especially keen on your kind," he said. His gaze swept the length of her, as if he was searching for something.

It wasn't an unusual experience; advisers, headmistresses, teachers, and peers had been doing the same to Aislynn her entire life. Only this time, she didn't feel as if she had been found lacking.

"However," Thackery continued, shifting the shovel to his shoulder, "I'm starting to think you're not really like them at all."

Chapter 13

Even though she knew not to expect a quick response, or one at all, Aislynn couldn't help but be disappointed as weeks went by without any news from Tahlia.

As summer neared its peak, the days began to blur into one another. Her new Path became routine, and Aislynn found that her mistakes grew less and less frequent. There were even times when she was able to anticipate the monarch princess's needs and fulfill them accordingly. She was surprised by how satisfying it was to make the princess smile.

After the incident with the sheets, Linnea had not made any further attempt to interact with her classmates. She spent most of her time alone in her room reading or writing to her childhood friend, Westerly, who now sent her a letter almost every day. Aislynn was grateful for his constant, if mysterious, presence in Linnea's rather lonely life.

Each week brought the promise of a visit from Adviser Lennard, but on the day he was scheduled to call, Linnea would inevitably be greeted not by her adviser, but with an apologetic note. The monarch princess never complained but returned to her room each time visibly disappointed.

So Aislynn was surprised when they entered the private drawing room one morning and found the adviser waiting with a smile. He bowed, and Linnea beamed. Taking her hands, Adviser Lennard greeted her with a kiss on her cheek. It had been mentioned, on numerous occasions, that after the death of the monarch king and queen, Adviser Lennard had taken special care of the young princess, but his informal salutation and Linnea's delighted response confirmed that he was more of a surrogate father to her than a family adviser.

But if he cared so much for Linnea, why had it been so long since his last visit? Didn't he know how lonely and sad she was? Didn't he realize how much it hurt her when he broke his promises to come see her? Aislynn felt a twinge of annoyance, one she was quick to push away. It was not her place to question an adviser's actions.

"You are the very image of purity," Adviser Lennard said with pride.

The monarch princess blushed and settled onto the chair he offered. He took the seat opposite, staring at her with a strange smile on his face.

It was an admiring look, but it reminded Aislynn of the way one might study a butterfly on a pin. After a few moments of silence, it became unnerving, and even the monarch princess had begun to fidget.

"Would you like some tea?" Aislynn asked, hoping to distract the adviser. It didn't work, but when Linnea nodded eagerly, he seemed to come out of his trance. Aislynn curtsied and quickly slipped from the room, heading toward the kitchen. It was spotless and deserted. Through the window, Aislynn could see several servants plucking chickens for dinner.

"He's here?" Brigid asked, entering the kitchen with two of the naked chickens, which she put next to the fire. Tiny white feathers were caught in her hair and eyelashes.

Aislynn nodded as she assembled the tea tray.

"I'm glad." Brigid brushed off her apron. "I'm sure it was nice to see her happy."

"It was," Aislynn said, and the two of them shared a smile. The kettle on the stove whistled.

As Aislynn filled the teapot, she watched Brigid inspect

the tray. Then, without a word, the servant girl walked over to the window, where rows of small jam tarts were cooling. Aislynn studied Brigid out of the corner of her eye as she first arranged four of the treats carefully on a plate and then quickly shoved two more into her own pocket.

"He likes sweet things," Brigid said, adding the plate to the tea tray.

Aislynn nodded, choosing not to mention the stolen treats. It wasn't her business anyway.

Adviser Lennard and Linnea were deep in conversation when Aislynn entered the drawing room. The monarch princess paused long enough to smile up at her. Adviser Lennard continued to ignore her, even when she placed the plate of tarts and a cup of tea in front of him.

"I nearly forgot," Adviser Lennard said after finishing his second jam tart and dabbing up the crumbs with his napkin. He patted his coat, withdrawing an elegant box in the shape of a thin book, which he handed to the monarch princess. "You'll be sixteen soon and ready to be Introduced. Or did you forget?" he teased as she quickly opened her gift.

It was a hand mirror, its oval face surrounded by a simple and traditional wooden frame. Aislynn touched her pocket, where she always kept the mirror Tahlia had given her.

"It's wonderful," Linnea breathed. "Thank you."

Smiling, Adviser Lennard leaned back in his chair and took a sip of tea. His grin disappeared. "This is cold," he said, lowering the cup to its saucer. He reached for Linnea's teacup and took a drink, a muscle in his jaw tensing.

His eyes swung round to Aislynn, standing in the corner. The intense anger in his eyes made her shrink back against the wall. She wished she could explain that she was still learning, that she had not yet been given permission to use such spells on her own, but she knew better than to offer an excuse.

"Why has the tea gone cold?" he asked in a low voice, rising from his chair. "Isn't it your responsibility to make sure that the tea remains hot? Isn't that your very purpose? Does *The Path* not say 'Give me a fairy godmother, so I may not wish. Give me a fairy godmother, so I may not want'?"

"I—"

"Do not speak to me," he hissed, eyes flashing with anger. "If you are unable to provide the simplest of necessities, then what is your use? What is your purpose?"

Aislynn hung her head, filled with shame. She wished Linnea were not here to see this.

Adviser Lennard let out an unpleasant laugh. "Pathetic, even for a fairy godmother," he said, pointing in the direction of the door. "Get. Out."

Chapter 14

Aislynn fled, fighting the tears of humiliation that burned her eyes. With her head down, she rushed through the kitchen and headed straight out the back door into the blinding sun. She hurried past the manicured hedges, through the gate and to the stables.

The horses didn't even look up as she entered the dim, cool building and settled on a bale of hay in a dark corner. She pulled her knees to her chest, trying to make herself as small as possible. As small as she felt. She told herself not to cry but was unable to stop the tears that rolled down her cheeks.

No matter how hard she tried, she always seemed to stumble.

She couldn't fail at this. Failure would mean another Redirection, but this time to the life of a teacher. And the thought of being stuck at Elderwood with Madame Moira for her entire life made her ill.

Aislynn had been trying to protect Linnea, trying to keep her own dangerous and uncontrollable magic as far away from the monarch princess as possible. Surely Adviser Lennard could understand that, could forgive that.

It wasn't fair, she thought, slamming her fist into the bale of hay. All these years she had been punished for using magic, and now she was being punished for not using it. If only Adviser Lennard had seen what she had done in class, what she was capable of. Perhaps then he wouldn't be so eager to ask her to heat his tea.

Magic rattled against her ribs like a fox clawing at a cage. She was ashamed of herself for thinking such things. But she was a wicked girl, and she was full of wicked thoughts.

Aislynn pushed back her sleeve. She had always imagined that she could have claimed modesty or shyness and kept her legs hidden under stockings and nightgowns forever. Arms were harder to hide. But there was no longer the chance of a husband's gaze on her bare skin—it didn't matter what she did to herself. Pressing her palm into the fleshy part of her forearm, Aislynn released the curse, the pain both awful and necessary. Familiar and terrible.

When the magic faded, the wretched sensation in her ribs was gone, replaced by a steady throbbing in her arm. Peeling back her fingers, she found a mark almost as large as her fist.

The size of it shocked her. She couldn't stop staring at it until the sound of wheels on gravel forced her to look away.

A carriage came to a stop outside the stable door, and Aislynn heard the muffled sounds of conversation. Pulling her sleeve gently over the wound, she scrubbed the remaining tears from her cheeks.

Ford and Thackery were unloading empty baskets from a wagon, but they stopped when she approached. Ford touched his hand to the brim of his hat before returning to the task at hand, while Thackery jumped down from the wagon and followed her.

"Afternoon," he said conversationally.

Aislynn nodded and sped up her pace. He matched it.

"Spending some time with the horses?"

"Am I not allowed?" asked Aislynn sharply.

Thackery put up his hands in mock surrender. "I didn't say that. We just don't get many fairy godmothers over here."

"So I'm not like the other fairy godmothers," she snapped,

turning on him. "Trust me, I'm well aware of my failings—I don't need to be reminded of them."

The shock on his face was enough to make Aislynn feel immediately guilty.

"I'm sorry," she muttered, setting off toward the castle again.

"Bad day?" His voice was low as he caught up, his hands tucked into his pockets. "Looks like you've been crying."

Aislynn turned her face away, embarrassed that he had noticed.

"The stables are a good place for that," he said quietly. "The gardens, too, if you ever feel the need."

Aislynn managed a nod as they crossed the lawns toward the kitchen. Suddenly Thackery reached for her, unknowingly grabbing the newly scarred skin. Aislynn caught the inside of her cheek between her teeth to keep from gasping.

"I'm sorry." Thackery pulled his hand back immediately. "I never meant to . . . I didn't mean . . ." Kicking at the gravel on the walkway, he continued. "Being unlike the others doesn't make you a failure. At least"—he smiled tentatively—"not to me."

He pulled a thin envelope from his back pocket. "Maybe this will make your day a little more bearable," he said, holding out the envelope as if it was a precious gift. And to Aislynn, it was. The familiar handwriting filled her with a wonderful, warm glow, almost strong enough to chase the pain away.

"Thank you," she said. He nodded and turned back to the stables, leaving her alone. She was just about to open the letter when she heard Brigid calling her name.

"Where have you been?" Brigid huffed as she raced toward her.

"I—"

The other girl shook her head, still breathing heavily. "It doesn't matter. Let's get you inside before the headmistress notices you didn't take the monarch princess back to her room."

The letter in her pocket taunted Aislynn for the rest of the day, a day that seemed cursed with busywork. It wasn't until hours later, when she was finally back in her room that Aislynn found a moment to herself. Settling onto her bed, she pulled out Tahlia's letter and broke the seal.

Dearest Aislynn,

My wonderful, clever girl. You should not have contacted me. Though I have never regretted the decisions I made as your fairy godmother, I cannot protect or guide you any longer. Keep the mirror close, and you will never truly be lonely. You already know what is right, what is good. You already know what must be done—trust yourself.

Please know I will remain loyal and dedicated to you and your parents, no matter what. Your family was the brightness of my life.

Remember that it is warmth that makes bread rise.

Tahlia

Chapter 15

Something was wrong.

Aislynn stared at Tahlia's letter and tried to make sense of it. She read it a dozen times, but still didn't understand it. Protect her? Protect her from what?

Knowing she would be unable to sleep, Aislynn quietly padded downstairs. The kitchen was empty and dark, lit only by her candle and the glowing embers of the fire. It took her some time to find the necessary ingredients, but eventually she had everything she needed.

It was awkward at first. She cracked an egg too hard and had to fish out the shells, and she had forgotten how to hold a whisk properly, but it soon came back to her. While the butter and milk were warming together, she folded the eggs into the flour and yeast. Slowly, wonderfully, perfectly, everything came together to form a sticky mound of dough. She set it aside to rise.

The cinnamon tickled her nose as she grated it. With a spoon, she swirled the golden-brown spice into a bowl of sugar, stirring until they were blended together.

She knew the dough was ready when she pressed against its smooth top and it gently, softly pushed back. The room filled with the wonderful scent of flour and yeast when Aislynn sank her hands into the mixture, the dough clinging to her fingers like spiderwebs.

Each slide of the rolling pin swept a cloud of flour into the air, the white powder settling on her uniform and face like snow. Her mind was cleared of anything but this moment, this simple act. After the dough had been smoothed and shaped, Aislynn brushed the surface with melted butter, her mouth watering at the smell of it. The cinnamon and sugar came next, sprinkled evenly across the top.

With a sharp knife, she sliced the sweetened dough into small rectangles and gently piled them on top of each other, like pages in a book. Carefully, she turned the towering pile on its side and transferred it to a waiting pan. As it rose, she set to work restoring the kitchen to its previous state of cleanliness.

Once all the dishes were washed and put away and the pages of dough had doubled in size, she placed the bread in the oven to bake.

She sat down to reread Tahlia's letter, and she discovered something else strange. Her fairy godmother had written: *Your family was the brightness of my life.* Was. As if they no longer met this description. What had changed? Had something happened to her family? Aislynn took a deep breath and tried to calm herself.

Tahlia was just trying to help her. She knew that it was against the rules for them to write each other and that Aislynn would get in trouble if she was caught. That was all. If something truly was wrong, Tahlia would have told her. But still Aislynn could not shake the lingering weight of suspicion that lay across her shoulders.

The scent of cinnamon and sugar filled the kitchen, a reminder of the task at hand. Checking the oven, Aislynn was surprised to find the bread was already browned, her thoughts seemingly speeding the passage of time. Carefully, she took the loaf out of the oven and upended it into a clean towel. Suddenly she knew exactly what to do with it. She had never really given Thackery a proper thank-you for delivering the letter, and she imagined he would appreciate waking up to a gift such as this.

♡ ♡ ♡

The crickets kept Aislynn company as she crossed the grounds, heading for the cottage. A flicker of light caught her eye. It was coming from the stable windows.

She should just keep going. But her curiosity steered her toward the barn. She could hear bits of a muffled conversation floating through the partially open door.

". . . out of here?"

"There must be . . . figure it out."

"It's too dangerous . . . ?"

Thackery. Ford. Brigid.

Aislynn crept across the drive, accidentally kicking gravel against the building. The conversation stopped abruptly, and the door swung open. She had been caught.

"What are you doing here?" demanded Thackery.

Startled, Aislynn stepped back and caught her heel on her uniform. Stumbling awkwardly, she fell and hit the ground hard.

"For thorns' sake, Thackery." Brigid pushed past him to help Aislynn to her feet. "What's this?" she asked, looking at the bundle in Aislynn's arms.

"Bread." She held it out awkwardly. "Cinnamon bookbinder bread."

"We don't have time for this," said Thackery, looking

over his shoulder. In the shadows of the stable, Aislynn caught sight of a young girl with dirty-blond hair peering out from the heavy wool blanket that was wrapped around her shoulders. She was staring at the bread with hungry eyes.

She looked thirteen, fourteen maybe, and the dirt on her face was streaked with old tears. She was small and thin and almost disappeared into the moth-bitten blanket.

Aislynn held out the warm bread. "You can have it, if you'd like." The girl hesitated.

"It's all right." Brigid nodded encouragingly. "She's a friend."

"She's a nuisance," muttered Thackery.

Darting forward, the girl snatched the loaf from Aislynn and quickly retreated to the shadows. The blanket slipped from her shoulders, revealing a tattered rag of a dress. On her back was a circular brand, like Thackery's, but the skin around it was red and raw.

"We appreciate the food," Brigid whispered, "but you really should go."

Aislynn planted her feet. "I want to know what's going on."

"We don't have time to explain it to you," Ford interjected. "We need to send this girl away from here tonight."

"Elanor said that there would be a carriage waiting for her

in town," Brigid added, as if Aislynn knew who Elanor was. "But we have to get her there before sunrise."

"Elanor also said that she would have an appropriate disguise." Thackery's voice dropped to a frustrated growl. "We can't put her on the carriage dressed like that."

"I have something she could wear," Aislynn offered hesitantly. All three heads swiveled toward her. "I still have my traveling gown. My royal one." There was no response. "It's blue," she added, unnerved by their silent stares.

"This isn't a loan," Thackery said, his gaze boring into her. "You won't be getting your pretty dress back."

"I don't have much use for pretty dresses now, do I?" she snapped at him.

Thackery glanced at her purple robes, his face unreadable. "No, I suppose not." He didn't sound angry anymore.

Aislynn turned back to the others. "It's in my room. I can go fetch it."

"I'll go with you," Brigid said, glaring at Thackery as she took Aislynn's arm. "We'll be back shortly. You'd better prepare the horses."

Aislynn and Brigid rushed back to the castle and up to Aislynn's room in silence. Yanking open her dresser, Aislynn found the gown neatly folded, exactly as she had left it the night she had arrived. She ran a hand over the stiff blue fabric and waited for a sense of loss, a sense of longing for her former life.

It was strange, for although she still missed Tahlia and her parents, she had stopped missing the blue dress and all the trappings and attention that came with it.

"What are those?" asked Brigid, pointing to the bodice.

There were three small white dots on the fabric. "I'm not sure," Aislynn said, rubbing at them with her finger. "It looks like wax."

"I would have just given her one of my uniforms," said Brigid. "But I only have two, and if I ask for another one, they'll get suspicious."

Aislynn waved her off. "I don't mind. Truly. But I want to know what's going on."

Brigid frowned. "Not here. Let's get back to the barn, and I promise I'll tell you everything."

The young girl was sleeping when they returned, curled up on a bale of hay. Who was she? Aislynn wondered. What was she doing here in such a state? And why did she have the same mark as Thackery?

Brigid went to get the girl dressed, and Ford gestured for Aislynn to join him by the horses. He was gently stroking the nose of a beautiful white mare when she approached.

"It's a nice thing you've done," he said quietly. "I'm sure there won't be a day that goes by where she won't remember your kindness. We'll make sure to pay back that debt for her."

Brigid and the girl stepped out of the shadows.

Aislynn's heart sank. The dress was far too large for her. "It's too big. I should have known it wasn't going to fit," she said with regret.

But Brigid gestured dismissively. "That's easily fixed." She ran her hands lightly over the girl's shoulders and waist, over the skirt and down to the hem.

Magic perked up inside Aislynn like a friendly dog, as if to acknowledge the spell that now pulsed in the air, surrounding the young stowaway like an invisible, warm wall. The blue dress began to shrink. The shoulders tightened, the waist narrowed, and the hem crept off the floor.

It was astonishing to watch, and Aislynn was terrified.

Brigid rubbed her hands. "Thankfully, it was a little too large. I'm much better at shrinking fabric than I am at making it bigger." Aislynn could only nod as she waited for the magic inside of her to subside.

"I hope you're planning on doing something with her hair." Thackery appeared behind them. "Because I'm sure Her Former Majesty would agree that it's currently a dead giveaway."

"I think it's clear to anyone who doesn't have beans for a brain that I haven't finished yet," Brigid retorted.

"Well, you'd better hurry." He gestured to the carriage.

Brigid rolled her eyes and set about putting the finishing touches on the young girl's appearance.

Thackery stood next to Aislynn, hands shoved in his pockets. "Why are you doing this?" he asked. "Why didn't you just go straight to Madame Moira?"

"I don't know," she said. It was an honest answer.

Thackery kicked the gravel, his eyebrows furrowed. Aislynn couldn't tell if he was angry or concerned. She wished she had something to say. Something that would bring back the Thackery who had been so kind to her that afternoon. Before she could think of anything, though, Brigid returned. The girl's face was clean and her hair was perfect—she could easily pass for a princess.

"When you get to town, you'll be looking for someone wearing a dark green cloak and a brown hat," Brigid instructed her. "The hat will have a feather in it. Do you understand?" She handed the girl a canvas sack. "There's some food in there." Brigid glanced back at Aislynn with a slight smile. "A jam tart or two. Your sister will be waiting for you."

"Thank you." It was the first time Aislynn had heard her speak. Her voice was thin but clear. She spoke to all of them, her eyes lingering on each face. Brigid patted her hand as Ford helped her into the carriage and closed the door.

"Best be on your way," said Thackery.

"Wait!" Aislynn exclaimed, startling everyone, including herself. "I'm sorry, I just . . ." She reached through the coach window. "I'm Aislynn."

"Gilly" was the shy response.

"Nice to meet you, Gilly." She could practically feel Thackery rolling his eyes, but she ignored him and shook the girl's hand, which was dry and cold, her fingers as skinny as twigs. "Safe journey."

Ford climbed up onto the carriage and clicked his tongue at the horses. A small arm emerged from the coach window, waving a solemn good-bye as the horses started to move.

Brigid let out an enormous sigh, running a hand through her wild hair, but Thackery just kicked up some more gravel and stalked off. Aislynn felt a strange ache in her chest. Disappointment, frustration . . . and something else she couldn't name.

"I'm glad that's over." Placing an arm around Aislynn, Brigid gave her a gentle squeeze. "It will be dawn in a few hours. I can never sleep on nights like this. Want to watch the morning glories open?"

The night was quiet and the breeze ruffled the leaves and flowers, making them bob and dip almost as if they were bowing to those who passed. The scent of roses surrounded them. Aislynn and Brigid settled on one of the few stone benches scattered around the garden, the moonlight illuminating the purple buds of the morning glories that climbed each trellis.

But the moon wasn't the only light. Across the garden, Aislynn could see a faint yellow glow in the cottage window. A shadow paced back and forth. Thackery. Suddenly the cottage went dark, and Aislynn imagined him crawling into bed, settling into sleep. The idea of Thackery sleeping so close by made Aislynn feel uncomfortable, as if even imagining it was inappropriate. She ignored the strange twist in her stomach and turned back to Brigid, who had also been staring in the same direction.

"You can't let him bother you," Brigid said. "He just . . . well, we all deal with it in our own ways, I suppose."

"Deal with what? What was that? Who was that girl? What did I just help you do?" The questions fell from Aislynn's mouth like a broken strand of pearls.

"I didn't even think to ask her name. . . ." Brigid shook her head with a small humorless laugh.

"Why does she have the same mark on her shoulder that Thackery does?"

"How do you know about that?" Brigid asked with surprise.

"I saw it when he was gardening. What is it?" pressed Aislynn. "Do all commoners have them?" Instantly she regretted the question, but Brigid just shook her head.

"No, not everyone."

"Then what is it? Does it have something to do with why she was here?"

"It's why we're all here." Brigid undid the top clasp on her dress and pulled the fabric off her shoulder, revealing a circular brand just like Thackery and Gilly's. Close enough to see it clearly, Aislynn realized there were four dots inside the circle. It looked a little like a button.

Brigid restored her dress. "I didn't show you this so you would feel sorry for me," she said. "I showed it to you so you would understand how important your silence is. No one can know about this. Not just the headmistress and the monarch princess, but the other servants and other fairy godmothers. Not even the person you send letters to."

"I don't understand."

Brigid sighed heavily. She looked very tired. "Josetta gave us these marks, and she did it for many reasons. One was to remind us and anyone else that we were in her . . . care."

"You belonged to Queen Josetta?"

"As much as you belong to Linnea," Brigid responded drily.

"I'm sorry, I didn't mean . . ." Aislynn tried to apologize, but Brigid just shook her head.

"Of course you didn't." Her mouth was twisted in a humorless smile. "We only know what we are taught. I can't blame you for your ignorance."

"I'm sorry?" Aislynn's words were indignant and colored with embarrassment.

"Not just about commoners." Brigid tilted her head. "I saw the look on your face when I was fixing Gilly's gown. You were terrified."

"Magic is dangerous and should be treated with caution and restraint," said Aislynn primly.

Brigid let out a hoarse laugh. "You royals. I'll never understand why you started believing that. Magic is not dangerous."

Shocked, Aislynn stood and moved away. It was one thing for servant women to disregard the damage magic would do to them, but to deny its danger completely was insulting and misguided. "It absolutely is."

"If magic is so dangerous, then why are fairy godmothers allowed to use it?" asked Brigid calmly.

"We provide guidance! An example of why we should all follow the Path!" Aislynn struggled to explain something that needed no explaining. "Without fairy godmothers, royal women would be unable to resist the temptation to do magic, and they'd meet the same monstrous end as the four sisters."

"Monstrous end?" Brigid scoffed. "I think you and I have heard very different versions of this story."

"Yes, I daresay the one you learned from Queen Josetta is filled with all manner of interesting details." As soon as the words left her mouth, Aislynn wanted to take them back. But it was too late.

Brigid clenched her jaw. "You royals like to believe you're so different, so much better than the Wicked Queen, but when it comes to magic, you all think the same. And you all act the same, too." And before Aislynn could answer, Brigid was on her feet and stalking out of the garden.

Regret and confusion swirled through Aislynn. She was alone under the stars, and no longer sure of the things she thought she knew.

Chapter 16

Aislynn woke with a start. She had overslept. It was too late to get the bouquet, too late to get the tea. Hastily pulling on her robes, she rushed into the monarch princess's room and froze at the sight in front of her. Linnea was sitting in her chair, her dressing gown wrapped around her, and Madame Moira was standing in the center of the room.

"No flowers this morning?" asked the headmistress with a hard glare. Then, she turned back to Linnea. "I thought you said—"

"As I was trying to tell you before Aislynn arrived, I said she was going to speak to the gardener about my flower arrangements." The princess spoke in a haughty, unfamiliar voice. "If you had let me continue, I would have said that she was speaking to him about my desire to receive them every other day instead of every day." Rising from her chair, Linnea swept across the room to the dresser, where yesterday's flowers stood in full bloom. "It's a shame to waste them, don't you think?" She stroked the bloodred petals gently, and a few fluttered to the carpet near Aislynn's feet. The look on Linnea's face made it very clear that Aislynn should remain silent.

But Madame Moira was not to be deterred. "That still doesn't answer my question, Your Majesty."

"You asked if I knew where my fairy godmother was," Linnea retorted. "I think I've answered you already. Don't you think so, Aislynn?"

"Perhaps I should have clarified." Madame Moira clasped her hands together. "Do you know where your fairy godmother was last night?"

Aislynn's stomach dropped. Had the headmistress checked her room? There was a loud silence as a hundred laughable excuses raced through her head. She had gone downstairs for a drink of water and fallen asleep in the kitchen. She had been cleaning a classroom as punishment. She had gone for a walk and gotten lost.

"Of course I know where she was," Linnea snapped, her back as straight as a spindle. "She was here with me."

The headmistress's triumphant expression fell away, and Aislynn struggled to keep the surprise from her own face.

"On occasion I ask my fairy godmother to sleep here, in my chair," said Linnea. "Last night was one of those nights."

"If I may, Your Majesty . . ." Madame Moira was barely able to hide her annoyance. "Why do you require your fairy godmother to remain in your room while you sleep?"

"It really isn't any of your business." Linnea lifted her chin defiantly, though her lower lip wobbled. "But I've found that with my fairy godmother nearby, I have a tendency to sleep better."

"Everything that occurs within the academy walls is my business, Your Majesty," Madame Moira responded, directing a purposeful look at Linnea's unmade bed. "I'm sure I don't have to remind you of that."

"Yes, headmistress," said Linnea, lowering her eyes. Her cheeks were red.

"Good. Now I expect to see you at breakfast, Your Majesty," the headmistress said before sweeping from the room.

As soon as the door clicked shut, Linnea let out a shaky puff of air, followed by a whoop of laughter.

Struggling to catch her own breath, Aislynn felt her legs give. She stumbled and knocked into the edge of the dresser, causing the roses to wobble and fall. The vase hit an open drawer on the way down and scattered broken glass across the carpet. Dropping to the floor, Aislynn pulled the flowers from the broken vase, cutting her palm on a large shard of crystal.

"Aislynn!" Kneeling beside her, Linnea took her fairy godmother's hand in her own. She unwound one of her hair ribbons and gently used it as a bandage. The cut wasn't deep.

"I'm so sorry, Your Majesty."

"It's just a bunch of flowers." Linnea gathered the roses from the floor and placed them back on the dresser.

"Not just about that." Aislynn couldn't look at Linnea and focused her attention on mopping up the mess. "About you having to lie for me."

"Well, I'm afraid to admit there was some selfishness in my decision to do so." Aislynn glanced up to see an enthusiastic gleam in the monarch princess's eye. "I want to know everything about your secret tryst last night!"

"My what?"

"Your secret tryst. The reason you weren't in bed." Linnea's voice was full of excitement. "I want to know everything!"

Aislynn was speechless a moment. "I'm sorry to disappoint," she said. "But there was no tryst."

"Then where were you?" Linnea demanded.

For a moment Aislynn thought of using one of the many

terrible excuses she had thought up, but she owed Linnea more than a poorly formed lie. So she told the truth. Part of it. "I was baking."

"Baking?" Linnea crossed her arms over her chest, her disbelief obvious. "What were you baking?"

"Cinnamon bookbinder bread."

"Where is it?"

"Uh . . . I burned it?"

"You burned it."

"It didn't rise." Aislynn thought of Tahlia's letter. "It didn't rise, and that's why it burned. So I threw it away."

"Why were you baking?" It was clear Linnea didn't believe her.

"I was lonely." It wasn't quite the truth, but it wasn't exactly a lie either. Aislynn had promised Brigid she wouldn't say anything, and despite their argument, she had no intention of breaking that promise.

"Lonely," Linnea repeated.

Aislynn sighed. "I've been writing to my old fairy godmother," she confessed. At least that secret was hers to share. "I know I'm not supposed to, and I don't plan to do it again, but I just needed to ask her some questions."

"About baking?"

"I'm usually better at it, but I was . . . upset." Aislynn

swallowed, hoping Linnea would stop asking questions soon. "I went down to the kitchen and tried to make something, but I got distracted and it burned. Then I guess I fell asleep."

After a long pause, Linnea sighed. "I'm not sure I want to believe you. I was so hoping it was a romantic tryst."

"Unfortunately, Your Majesty . . ." Aislynn tapped her heart. "I'm not built for such things any longer."

Linnea's eyes widened. "Of course! How foolish of me to forget." The monarch princess lowered her voice to a conspiratorial whisper. "What was it like?" she asked, lifting a hand to her own chest. "Did it hurt?"

Aislynn shook her head. "It was like—like I was made of smoke and someone was reaching through me," she said slowly, trying to find the words. "And afterward, it's as if everything became clearer. Less distracting."

"And those feelings are gone? Completely gone? Do you still notice . . ." Linnea looked down, her cheeks pink. "When people are attractive?"

"It's different," Aislynn said. "It feels removed from me. I don't . . ." The word she was looking for was on the tip of her tongue and the back of her mind.

"Swoon?" Linnea offered.

That was the word. Aislynn nodded.

"Incredible." The monarch princess released a deep

breath. "Sometimes I think it would be good for all of us to be without such messy emotions clouding our judgment." Asking if there was anyone in particular clouding Linnea's judgment seemed rather impertinent, so Aislynn kept the question to herself.

"But before you were a fairy godmother," said Linnea pressing on, "did you ever . . . ?"

"Swoon?"

The monarch princess giggled. "Yes. Did you ever swoon?"

"There was someone," said Aislynn. "Once."

"What was his name?"

"Everett." She remembered the night of the ball, the quiet of the garden, his fingers on her wrist. Still, there was no longing.

Linnea leaned forward. "What happened?"

The breakfast bell rang.

"Oh, soot!" Linnea exclaimed. "Don't think this means you're out of the tower. I'll get the story from you yet!"

It took enormous willpower for Aislynn to stay awake during her classes that day. She also somehow managed to avoid Brigid, and she even found ways to distract Linnea so that she would stop asking about Aislynn's previous life.

That night, she didn't even bother to change out of her uniform, collapsing fully clothed onto her bed. She was asleep almost immediately.

Her feet slapped against the ground as she ran, but the trees kept pushing her back.

Suddenly she couldn't move. Her dress was caught, the tattered skirt wrapped around a snarl of branches. She tugged at the blue fabric until it ripped, freeing her and sending her stumbling forward.

When she regained her balance, she was no longer alone in the forest. Up ahead, she could see a pair of yellow eyes and a silvery coat gleaming in the moonlight. Waiting patiently for her. Gathering her dress in her arms, Aislynn took a deep breath and ran after the wolf.

She woke exhausted, as if she hadn't slept at all. Aislynn couldn't stop yawning as she stumbled down the stairs, through the kitchen, over the lawn, and toward Thackery's cottage.

"Morning," he said in a slow drawl when he saw her. At least he didn't seem angry or annoyed. "Your flowers, my lady." He handed them to her, a single eyebrow raised. "You look terrible."

"Much appreciated." Aislynn lifted the bouquet in a mock

salute, and her long sleeve fell back to her elbow. Immediately she grabbed at the sleeve, tugging it back over her most recent wound and down past her wrist. The flowers slipped from her hands.

"How did you get that?" Thackery's eyes were wide.

"How did you get yours?" Aislynn countered quickly, still holding her sleeve.

Thackery frowned. "I'll tell you if you tell me."

"You tell me first."

"Ah, ah, ah." He raised a finger. "That's not fair, is it? How do I know you'll still tell me?"

"You don't." Aislynn wondered what he would do if she bolted. The thought was incredibly tempting. "But you're the one who wants to know, so you have to follow my rules."

"Fine." Thackery shrugged, but Aislynn could see his jaw tighten. "Which one do you want to know about first? This one?" He touched the scar on his throat. "Or this one?" With a smooth tug, he pulled his shirt over his head.

The last time Aislynn had seen him without his shirt on, she had been too far away to get a good look. This time she was close enough to touch. She gestured for him to turn around and stepped closer.

Instead of the buttonlike design that had been branded on Brigid, Thackery's scar contained what appeared to be a crudely drawn shield. Without thinking, Aislynn touched the circle with her finger. With a start, Thackery jerked back, wrapping his large hand around her wrist and holding it away from his body.

"I didn't say you could touch," he said. "Your fingers are cold."

"It's a shield." Aislynn ignored his complaint. "Why is Brigid's different?"

"Because Brigid wasn't going to be one of the queen's huntsmen." Thackery let go of her hand. "She was going to be a seamstress. And Ford, master and lover of all animals, was going to be a butler."

"But Ford hates working indoors."

"And I'm terrible with a sword. Brigid is actually a fairly good seamstress, but don't tell her I said that." Thackery pulled his shirt back over his head. "We aren't consulted about our future. About the things we want to do." He looked at Aislynn. "I guess we're not so different in that regard," he said.

Aislynn was speechless.

But he wasn't finished. "At least I did something about it instead of just accepting what I was given." Thackery said it softly, but his meaning hit Aislynn like a slap in the face.

"I need to go." She turned to leave, but his arm shot out and he grabbed her wrist again.

"You said you'd tell me about yours." He pushed back her sleeve to expose the still-healing wound. It was a garish red, more ugly and shameful than she remembered. "Who did this to you?" Thackery asked.

She could feel his warm fingers encircling her wrists, gentle and dangerous at the same time. Carefully he touched her scar. And as if emerging from a long slumber, Aislynn's heart began to tremble in her chest. The heat from Thackery's hand spread through her body, and the invisible wall between them seemed to shift and buckle as a *whoosh* of agony and joy flooded her. Everything inside her seemed to simmer. Aislynn wished he would release her, but she felt as if she would die if he did.

"Who did this to you?" he asked again.

The spell was broken, and Aislynn jerked her arm away.

"No one did this to me," she said. "I did this to myself."

His eyes widened, maybe in shock, maybe in disgust, maybe in pity.

Aislynn turned and ran.

Chapter 17

It was impossible. What had just happened was completely and utterly impossible. But no matter how many times Aislynn said that to herself, it didn't refute the fact that her palms were sweating, her knees were shaking, and her heart was pounding against her ribs. Her loving heart was gone—she had seen it in that glass jar, locked away in the headmistress's cabinet. How was it possible for her to be feeling these things?

Stopping outside the kitchen courtyard, Aislynn took a moment to calm herself. She had just begun to feel normal again when the door burst open and Brigid stepped out into the early sunlight.

Guilt, as heavy as a golden ball, sank in Aislynn's stomach. She had managed to avoid Brigid all yesterday, but she knew that the responsibility of an apology lay completely on her shoulders. She stepped toward her friend.

"I'm sorry," she said.

"It was a long night." Brigid's smile was tired as she took Aislynn's hands and gave them a squeeze. "I said some unkind things when I should have thanked you for your help."

Aislynn squeezed back. When the other fairy godmothers started emerging from the kitchen, she lowered her voice. "Did Gilly find her sister?"

"Ford watched her get on the next carriage." Brigid waited until the fairy godmothers had left the courtyard before continuing. "Josetta likes to make examples of those who are reclaimed. It's usually a good sign when we haven't heard anything."

"Do you think that Linnea knows about her?" The monarch princess never mentioned anyone in her extended family, let alone her infamous aunt.

"She must know that she's a disgrace to the family and the Path, but I don't think she's aware of much more." Brigid suddenly seemed very far away. "Adviser Lennard keeps the monarch princess quite sheltered."

"Quite," Aislynn repeated, surprised by the venom in her voice. It was as if by saying it aloud, she realized how much she detested Linnea's adviser.

With Linnea's sixteenth birthday approaching, Adviser Lennard's visits became more and more frequent. Still too unsure of herself to use magic, Aislynn was forced to ask for Brigid's help each time he came for tea. But he never acknowledged her, and Aislynn was grateful to be ignored.

There was still no word from Gilly, but Brigid insisted that this was to be expected, and Gilly's safety became another thing Aislynn tried to stop thinking about. The incident with Thackery was harder to forget, so Aislynn did her best to avoid him. She began waiting for the other fairy godmothers in the morning so she didn't have to face him alone and was careful not to catch his eye or brush his fingers when he passed her Linnea's bouquet.

With the summer ball approaching, preparations for the monarch princess's Introduction began to dominate Aislynn's schedule. Nearly every week there was new information from Adviser Lennard, who now preferred to deliver his instructions in person.

"It's been decided that the summer ball will be held here, at Elderwood," he was saying as Aislynn entered the drawing room with a tray of tea sandwiches and scones.

"How wonderful!" Linnea gave a pleased little clap. Even Madame Moira looked somewhat gratified.

"Obviously, it is of the utmost importance that you present yourself properly. Your appearance, most especially, will need to be"—he shot a rare glance in Aislynn's direction—"impeccable. Dress, hair, slippers, jewelry, all of it will need to be executed precisely as designed." There was silence, and Aislynn realized with a start that he had been speaking to her.

"Do you understand?" The question was filled with impatience. She quickly nodded. "The details will be sent shortly. You are dismissed," he said with an annoyed wave of his hand. "Your presence is not necessary for the remainder of this conversation."

"Yes, sir." With a smooth curtsy, Aislynn retreated gratefully.

The adviser's voice floated out behind her. "And of course Prince Westerly will be your escort for the evening. Now, has there been any progress on securing a lady-in-waiting?"

The following day, Aislynn was summoned to the headmistress's study.

"You've disappointed me, my dear," said Madame Moira without preamble.

Aislynn was reminded of a snake she had encountered out riding once. The creature was in the middle of the road, its eyes open, revealing two endless pools of black. The snake was so still that Aislynn had mistaken it for dead. But the second she was close enough, it sprang forward and sank its fangs into her mare's leg.

Aislynn braced herself for an attack. The headmistress's gaze was sharp and unblinking. "I have been made aware of your . . . extracurricular activities," she said.

Aislynn held her breath. It had been weeks since Gilly's escape, but there had never been any word confirming her arrival. Had she been captured?

"I'm aware that you are often seen with one of the servant girls." The headmistress glanced down at the parchment in front of her. "One of the kitchen maids. Brigid." She glanced up at Aislynn, who gave a small nod.

"I assume you understand why this is distressing." Madame Moira linked her fingers together. Aislynn's panic grew, but she bit her tongue.

The headmistress slammed her hands down on the desk. "Your obtuseness annoys me. It is obvious that your ungrateful behavior is a misguided attempt at rebellion. Clearly you believe that you were placed in your current position unfairly, and instead of embracing the role of fairy godmother, you have decided to flaunt your dissatisfaction by fraternizing with a commoner."

Confusion replaced fear. Was the headmistress chastising her for spending too much time with Brigid?

"There is something you must understand about this life, my dear." Madame Moira's voice was low, eyes unwavering. "This life is not fair. One day you are a lady or a princess or a queen. And the next day you are not." For a moment she looked almost sad. "'No journey is taken alone. Parent, adviser, and godmother. No greater service than guiding the steps of another.'" The headmistress lifted her chin, looking down her nose at Aislynn. "You must realize that as a fairy godmother, your reputation is not your own. Your behavior is a reflection on the monarch princess, and currently you are not casting either of you in a particularly positive light. You still wear your locket, I presume?"

Aislynn managed a nod, trying to ignore the hot anger surging inside her. The locket felt like a tether around her neck.

Clasping her hands together, Madame Moira leaned forward. "Let it serve as a reminder to you of the importance of remaining with your own kind."

Her own kind? It was her own kind who had rejected Aislynn back at Nerine Academy, and the treatment here had been no different. How right Thackery had been to distrust the fairy godmothers! How justified Brigid's frustration toward royals was! And how ashamed Aislynn felt, knowing that she too had been guilty of such unfounded judgments.

"Is that all, Headmistress?" The words spilled out between Aislynn's clenched teeth. Anger had made her brave.

"Unfortunately not, my dear." Rising to her feet, Madame Moira came around to the front of the desk. "You may think that you can hide things from me, but let me assure you: I am aware of everything that occurs within these walls." She drew an icy finger down Aislynn's cheek. "Your teachers have informed me of your lack of progress with your required spells, and I suspect you've been using your servant girl to complete your tasks."

Aislynn said nothing, her heart pounding. She hoped Brigid would be spared punishment.

"Remember, a fairy godmother who cannot perform her duties might not remain a fairy godmother for long," said Madame Moira as she stepped back.

Aislynn did the same, praying that she was being dismissed. But instead the headmistress retrieved a long flat box from behind her desk, which she handed to Aislynn.

"Open it," she ordered.

Inside was a neatly folded bolt of satin. Monarch red.

"Your new lesson." Madame Moira gestured at the box. "You have a month before the monarch princess's

Introduction. Plenty of time to complete the gown Adviser Lennard has designed. Anything you can't do with magic in the presence of a teacher, you'll be sewing by hand. And I will know if you ask that commoner for help."

Madame Moira's words were a smooth drawl. "It would do well for you to think of this conversation any time you begin to . . . stray. I would hate for Linnea to have to train a new fairy godmother."

"I understand completely," Aislynn said. The threat was crystal clear.

"I'm so glad." The headmistress's eyes were sharp and cold. "It's time you learned how to use your magic properly, my dear."

Chapter 18

The instructions were twelve pages long. Adviser Lennard's handwriting was small and flat, his words like a line of orderly ants crossing the parchment. Even his final sketch of the monarch princess's gown was covered in notations. It made Aislynn dizzy just to look at it.

All around her, there was activity and chatter, the room full of beautiful dresses at various states of completion. Linnea's gown was still a pile of red fabric, neatly folded in its box. Aislynn was terrified to start, afraid of ruining the costly satin by putting scissors or needle to it.

Madame Posey was circling the room like a raven, occasionally stopping to dole out criticism. "The sleeves are uneven, Thea," she said, fanning herself. "And watch your lace, Juliana. It's beginning to bunch."

With summer at its peak, the heat permeated the normally cool stone and had inspired Madame Posey to carry a small fan with her at all times.

Behind the teacher's back, Juliana rolled her eyes before tugging on the misbehaving lace. It refused to smooth out. Aislynn watched her take a deep breath and close her eyes. Her eyebrows bunched together as she ran her hand over the delicate trim. Nothing seemed to happen, so she tried again. After the third time, the lace underneath Juliana's hand appeared smooth and perfect.

Next to her, Thea was doing the same thing with the sleeves of her princess's dress, but with less immediate success. It took her almost seven tries to get them even.

The air was thick with magic. When Madame Posey arrived at her desk, Aislynn realized that she had been holding her breath.

"I see there's been no progress," Madame Posey said, and the room went quiet.

Aislynn sank down in her chair. "No, Madame Posey," she said.

"Do you intend to send the monarch princess to her Introduction ball in her undergarments?"

There was muffled laughter.

Aislynn slid lower. "No, Madame Posey."

"Do you know what happens to fairy godmothers who are unable to fulfill their duties?" Madame Posey was so close that Aislynn could smell the porridge on her breath. She nodded. The last thing she wanted was to remain at Elderwood Academy forever.

"Then try harder," Madame Posey snarled.

"Yes, Madame Posey," Aislynn said, relieved when the teacher turned away.

"Get to work," Madame Posey snapped at the rest of the girls, and with her fan fluttering furiously, she strode to the front of the room.

Aislynn's palms were sweating, so she rubbed them quickly on her uniform before touching the satin. Carefully, carefully, she lifted the red fabric out of the box and unfolded it across the table.

First it needed to be cut. She pinned the fragile pattern to the satin, wincing with each stab. Holding the heavy silver scissors in one hand, she paused. Most of the other girls had done this step by hand, but Cecily, who was the most accomplished fairy godmother of the lot, had managed it with magic.

Glancing over, Aislynn was surprised to find the other girl watching her. Cecily quickly looked away, but the expression on her face was familiar and unmistakable—it was somewhere between pity and fear, and Aislynn had seen it every day on her classmates at Nerine.

But before that memory could fester and grow, Aislynn closed her eyes and focused her thoughts on the task at hand. She was running out of time.

The sketch was clear in her mind. Concentrate, she told herself. Think about the scissors. Think about what you want them to do. She could see them, slicing smoothly through the satin. There was a tiny twitch inside her chest. Magic.

Suddenly Adviser Lennard's angry face roared into her mind. "What is your purpose?" he thundered, and Aislynn's arm throbbed. She was back in the stables, and Thackery was there, with his face sad, so sad as he reached out to touch her. . . .

The scissors clattered to the floor.

Aislynn opened her eyes, relieved to find that no one had seemed to notice. Her throat burned as if she might be sick, and her chest felt as if it was filled with stone. Gently she placed her hand on her arm, tracing the scar through the material of her uniform. Even though she knew she should, she couldn't use magic. How could she trust something she couldn't control?

She picked up the scissors, took a deep breath, and made the first cut.

♡ ♡ ♡

Aislynn rubbed her eyes. Her spine was throbbing, her eyes blurry, and her fingers stiff. The ball was only a few days away, and Linnea's dress was about one hundred glittering beads from being almost very nearly done. Except there was also a problem with the fit, as well as an uneven hemline and a whole line of buttonholes that were too small. It was a disaster.

Since there was so much still to be done and there was so little time left, every free moment was spent rushing to finish the dress. After everyone had gone to bed, Aislynn would sneak downstairs and use a table in the fairy godmothers' dining room to work. Madame Posey had given her permission to work on it as long as she didn't attempt any magic outside of class. Laying the satin out on a sheet to keep it clean, she would sit on the bench, hunched over the increasingly hideous gown.

It was nearing midnight, and she was just about to gather up her supplies and depart for bed when she heard footsteps and whispers coming from the kitchen. Abruptly they stopped.

"Hello?" Brigid called out in a hoarse whisper:

"Hello." Aislynn's voice echoed in the quiet of the sleepy castle. She smiled when Brigid peered around the doorway. Then Thackery appeared next to her.

"Hello," he said, his own smile strained.

"What are you doing here?" Brigid asked, approaching the table. She held up the section of gown that Aislynn had been embroidering. It looked even worse in the light. "It looks . . . nice," she said kindly, even though the expression on her face said otherwise.

"It still needs work," said Aislynn faintly. She was growing more anxious at the thought of presenting the gown to Linnea. Such a monstrosity would ruin the monarch princess's Introduction, and Aislynn wasn't sure how she was going to fix it.

"I like the lacy things and the sparkly bits," said Thackery, dropping the burlap sack he was carrying and leaning his shoulder against the doorway.

"I never knew you to have such an extensive knowledge of women's attire," said Brigid, one eyebrow raised.

"I have unplumbed depths," he retorted.

Aislynn had never seen Thackery inside the castle. "What is going on?" she asked Brigid. "Is there someone hiding in the stable?"

Guilty looks crossed both their faces. "Not tonight. But . . ." said Brigid, glancing at Thackery. He shrugged and then gestured as if she should continue. "There will be. In three days."

"That's the night of the ball." Aislynn looked down at

the dress and back at Brigid, who nodded.

"We're hoping it will be a distraction, but we're not sure what to expect. They haven't hosted a ball here at Elderwood since we arrived," said Brigid, chewing on her nails.

Aislynn had been to so many parties that surely she knew something that could be of help. "Well, you can expect that most attendees will be in the ballroom for the majority of the evening, some of them spending time along the terrace or even in the gardens below," she said, thinking out loud. "The stables are visible from the far end of the terrace, so I wouldn't use any candles or torches that could draw attention. Carriages will be coming in around nightfall and leaving just before sunrise. If you want to get someone out undetected, I would leave when the guests leave. No one will be looking inside the coaches." Aislynn realized she was rambling. Brigid and Thackery were just staring at her, and she felt foolish. "I'm sorry."

"All that information is immensely helpful," Brigid said with a grateful smile. "The Orphans owe you a debt of gratitude. Again."

"The Orphans?" Aislynn noticed the nervous look Thackery gave Brigid.

"She's practically one of us already," Brigid said to him before turning back to Aislynn. "What you saw that night with Gilly, that's what we do. Taking back from Josetta what's ours. What's always been ours."

"It's not much right now," Thackery added. "But it won't always be that way."

"I want to help," Aislynn said, surprising herself, but it was impossible to ignore the rush of happiness she felt when Brigid had said she was one of them.

Brigid shook her head. "I don't want to get you in more trouble with the headmistress. I know she's been keeping a close eye on you."

"I'm not afraid of Madame Moira," said Aislynn. It wasn't exactly true, but Brigid and Thackery didn't need to know that.

Thackery shuddered. "I am. I value my toes far too much to make her angry."

Aislynn and Brigid both stared at Thackery, who was looking at his feet.

"What are you talking about?" Brigid asked.

"The thing with the fairy godmother and the toe and the—" He made a slicing gesture. When he saw their uncomprehending faces, he dropped his hands in exasperation. "She hacked off her fairy godmother's toe. Haven't you heard the story?"

"What?" gasped Aislynn, but Brigid just rolled her eyes.

"I swear on Jack's beanstalk, Thackery. You love gossip more than the princesses do."

"It's not gossip," he said seriously. "It's the truth."

"Madame Moira chopped off her fairy godmother's toe." Brigid sounded unconvinced.

"It happened before she was, whatever you royals call it—rerouted?"

"Redirected," said Aislynn.

"Apparently before Madame Moira was Redirected, she came from a well-connected family. And the man she married wanted very much to be well connected, too. Only he didn't want to remain connected to her for very long. So he reported her to the family adviser, claiming that her fairy godmother had told him that Madame Moira was willfully using magic."

Brigid scoffed, but Thackery continued. "So the charming husband was able to get his wife Redirected, keep the title she gave him, and marry the woman he wanted. But the headmistress, believing that her fairy godmother had betrayed her, flew into a rage and—chop, chop, chop." He made the slicing gesture again. "Terrible, isn't it?"

Aislynn felt sick.

"You know what's terrible?" Brigid asked. "That story. That story is terrible."

"It's the truth!" he insisted, and then added quietly, "I feel sorry for her."

"For who?" Brigid crossed her arms. "Not for the headmistress, I hope."

"I feel sorry for anyone who loves someone who can't love them back," he said.

He was looking at Aislynn. Those deep green eyes seemed so sad, so lonely. A spark of warmth flickered in her chest.

Thackery looked back at Brigid. "Anyone who loves someone they shouldn't love," he added.

"I'm sure Madame Moira would have no interest in your pity," said Brigid, but she seemed sad, too.

Thackery shook his head. "It's not pity if you understand how it feels."

There was silence then, a silence that seemed to go on forever. "It's late," said Brigid finally. "Too late to be talking about such things. Good night, Aislynn."

Aislynn watched them go, not exactly sure what had just happened, but the way Thackery glanced back at her made her feel as though she was somehow involved.

And then, suddenly, unbidden, she felt magic tickling her ribs. With nervous hands, she reached for the dress. Closing her eyes, she gripped the silk and pictured the gown as it should be. Perfect and elegant.

Like a loaf of bread, she felt herself expand and release, magic flowing from her palms. Then as quickly as it had come, it was gone. She opened her eyes.

The gown had been transformed. Each bead was neatly sewn, the uneven stitches corrected, the hemline straight. Even the buttonholes were the right size.

It was beautiful.

Chapter 19

"Did I tell you that my adviser is bringing Westerly tonight?" Linnea asked as Aislynn tucked another pin into her red hair. The monarch princess's elaborate braid started behind one ear and came around the back of her head in a twisted spiral. It looked almost like a rose.

"Yes, Your Majesty." Aislynn gently nudged the braid to make sure it was secure. As she slipped the rest of the pins into her pocket, Aislynn felt a strange stiffness in the material of her uniform. Pushing her sleeve back, she was surprised to find several dried circles of wax down the side of her robe.

"I haven't seen him since I've been at school," Linnea continued as Aislynn quickly scratched the wax off.

"He's very tall, very . . ." Linnea seemed to search for the word. "Very reasonable." The monarch princess had been talking about Westerly nonstop since his birthday gift to her—a thoroughbred pony—had arrived the day before. "Adviser Lennard thinks we would make a very agreeable match. And I'm inclined to, well, agree. He's practically a part of my family already."

While Aislynn laid out the undergarments, Linnea counted Westerly's admirable attributes on her fingers. "He's intelligent, brave, clever, and thoughtful. Wasn't that pony thoughtful?"

Aislynn got the impression that Linnea was looking for approval, not an opinion. So Aislynn did as she had been doing all day and nodded silently while she focused on lacing the monarch princess into her new corset.

"Take a deep breath," she said, tugging hard.

Linnea did so, holding on to the edge of the vanity as the boning cinched her already tiny waist. After that came the massive petticoat and then, finally, the dress.

It was truly spectacular, with a sweetheart neckline trimmed with lace, slim-fitting sleeves, and a matching red silk sash—but instead of being tied in a bow, the large ribbon fluttered down the back of the dress. Across the hem glittered a thousand crystal beads, as if Linnea had just emerged from the sea, droplets of water caught on the satin.

The monarch princess looked exquisite, but she wasn't looking at her reflection. Instead, her eyes were cast downward as she chewed on the corner of her lip.

"It's all right to be nervous," Aislynn said, remembering how scared she had been before her first ball.

"I'm not nervous," Linnea insisted.

"Of course not." Placing her hands on Linnea's shoulders, Aislynn turned her toward the mirror. "You look beautiful. Westerly will want to dance with you all night."

Linnea gnawed on her bottom lip. "That's what I'm afraid of." Her eyes were round as she looked up at Aislynn. "What if I forget the steps?"

"What do you mean?" Every noblewoman was trained in dancing. Daily. Aislynn knew the monarch princess had a tendency to skip classes, but it seemed impossible that she would be *that* inept at waltzing.

"I know them," Linnea amended, to Aislynn's relief. "I've just . . . I've never practiced with a partner. None of the other girls would dance with me. What if I step all over Westerly's toes? Everyone will be watching us!"

Aislynn hesitated. Though her own dancing skills were middling at best, her height had usually forced her to perform the man's role in class. It was often the only time the other girls would interact with her.

"I'll practice with you," she finally said, lifting her arms to the starting position.

Linnea gave her a skeptical look. But Aislynn grabbed her hands and put one on her shoulder and held firm to the other. Her own free hand went to the monarch princess's waist.

"Just pretend I'm Westerly," she suggested, which made Linnea giggle.

"You are almost as tall," she said.

"Ready?" And with Linnea's nod, they were off.

Aislynn kept the rhythm.

"One-two-three, one-two-three, one-two-three, keep your head up," she coached as they glided across the room.

"Sorry!" Linnea apologized each time her heel caught Aislynn's toes. But as they kept dancing, her steps became more confident and Aislynn's feet were less abused. By their tenth turn around the room, the monarch princess was barely making any mistakes and they were both laughing.

Aislynn stopped so they could catch their breath. "I don't think you'll have any problems tonight," she said with a smile.

"I'll just pretend Westerly is you," Linnea joked, her cheeks flushed. Smoothing her dress out carefully, she settled at her vanity and opened the top drawer. "He wrote me today," she said as she pulled out the letter. "He says he's looking forward to seeing me again and he hopes I am feeling the same." She chewed her lip again. "I suppose it isn't a romantic letter, but Westerly's not one for flowery language. Not that I mind, of course. I much prefer a straightforward approach." But that sounded like less of an opinion formed by the princess herself, and more like one she had been given. "Adviser Lennard has often said that romance is one of the many follies of women."

"My adviser used to say that as well." Aislynn remembered Adviser Hull's lectures on poetry, which he had deemed unnecessary frippery. Poetry was something to be shared between ladies-in-waiting, not expected from husbands, who had more serious thoughts to entertain. "But my father used to write the most wonderful letters to my mother."

"He did?" Linnea tried to turn around, but Aislynn stopped her so she could repair her hair, which had come a little loose during their dancing.

"He did." It had been a long time since she had thought about her parents, but in that moment Aislynn was flooded with a memory of her father waltzing her mother around the foyer after a party, their laughter floating up to her as she watched them from her perch at the top of the stairs. The memory was rich and full, and Aislynn was surprised to feel the twinge of loneliness that accompanied it. She shook it away. "He told her once that she was as lovely as freshly fallen snow. . . ."

Linnea stared at the toes of her shoes and sighed. "I think my father was terribly romantic as well." It was the first time the monarch princess had ever mentioned her parents.

"I think you should carry Westerly's letter with you tonight." Aislynn plucked the letter from the top of the vanity and tucked it into Linnea's silk bag. "Just to remind you that he's waiting for you." She placed a hand on the princess's shoulder. "There's nothing wrong with a little romance, once in a while. Even if it is one of our follies."

"You're right." Linnea smiled and turned around to examine herself in the full-length mirror. The princess in the reflection was a marvelous thing, regal and beautiful, but Aislynn saw that her eyes were filled with nervousness and doubt.

"How do I look?" Linnea asked.

Aislynn smiled, feeling nothing but pride and excitement for her young ward. "You look wonderful. Are you ready?"

A bell sounded. The ball was about to begin.

Aislynn discovered she enjoyed parties much more from a distance. From her designated spot, nearly hidden by the immense tapestries, she watched Linnea, who wore a blinding smile as she was Introduced. Just watching the monarch princess enjoy herself was more fun than Aislynn had ever had at any of the parties she had attended, except perhaps her first one.

The room was gorgeously decorated. Trellises stood in every corner, the morning glories somehow coaxed into blooming early. The tables were overflowing with sunflowers and roses as red as Linnea's gown. The vibrant color made her stand out in a crowd of blue, green, and yellow. Strewn on the gleaming ballroom floor were lush gardenia petals, so that every step the dancers took would perfume the air. It seemed Madame Moira and Elderwood Academy had spared no expense for the only living monarch of the Eastern Kingdom.

At Linnea's side at all times were two men. Aislynn already knew Adviser Lennard, who smiled graciously at everyone who passed, greeting the men with a shake and kissing the hands of the women. The younger gentleman had to be Westerly. Aislynn studied him as carefully as she could from her place against the fairy godmother's wall. He had obsidian hair, gray eyes, and was so sallow that he looked almost unwell. He was very tall and towered over Linnea. He seemed to stare rather sourly at everyone except her, and offered only the occasional awkward smile.

"The latest news about the stray . . ." Hushed muttering came from Aislynn's left, where several of the fairy godmothers were sharing forbidden gossip. Everyone knew it was improper to speak of a royal maiden once she had strayed. *The Path* stated that all knowledge of her should be erased, as her memory could prove just as dangerous as her presence, but Aislynn still strained to hear. Could they be talking about Maris? Or had yet another girl joined Josetta's army?

"Did you hear about her parents?" Juliana asked, and there was a slow rustle of shaking heads. "They believe she was taken."

"Ridiculous," Thea said quietly, sounding scandalized. "They're just trying to save her reputation and their own."

"*Shh, shh, shh,*" Cecily said urgently, and the group went silent as several couples walked by. But once they had passed, the fairy godmothers remained quiet, their conversation unfinished.

Aislynn directed her attention back to the dance floor, where Linnea was now waltzing with Westerly. They looked wonderful together, his blue suit a perfect complement to the red of her gown. His expression had softened slightly, but she was more radiant than ever, eyes shining brighter than every candle in the room. They glided across the floor with no indication that the monarch princess was anything but a perfect, practiced dancer. Aislynn was filled with pride and satisfaction. It didn't last.

"My goodness. Ashy-linn, is that you?"

Aislynn turned to find Violaine standing beside her. The other fairy godmothers quickly dispersed, scattering like startled mice that had just seen a cat.

"I can't believe it! What luck!" Violaine let out a piercing laugh. "I was so hoping for the chance to see you in your uniform one day."

"As always, it's been a pleasure to see you, Violaine." Aislynn gave a shallow curtsy and started to walk away, but the other girl's tiny, clawlike hand stopped her.

"I don't think I dismissed you."

Aislynn gritted her teeth. "I am not your fairy godmother."

"How dare you?" Violaine tightened her grip on Aislynn's arm, pulling her close. "Let's not forget the precariousness of our situation, *stray*."

"I beg your pardon." Linnea's sweetly polite voice interrupted them. "Haven't you been taught that it's rude to touch things that aren't yours?"

Violaine quickly let go of Aislynn and dropped into a deep curtsy.

"Your Majesty, if I had only known that this was *your* fairy godmother, I would have acted differently." Violaine rose, an innocent smile plastered across her face.

Linnea gave an unimpressed sniff and took Aislynn's

hand. They turned to leave, but Linnea took only one step before stopping abruptly. Glancing down, Aislynn realized that Violaine was standing on the hem of the monarch princess's dress.

"Is there something else you wish to say to me?" Linnea's eyes were hard as stone, but her voice quivered just a bit.

"I only wanted to compliment Your Majesty on your appearance this evening." Violaine batted her eyelashes. "It's been said that you inherited your looks from your mother. I was merely wondering if there's anything else you inherited from her side of the family."

It felt like the air had been sucked out of the room.

Suddenly Aislynn felt a surge of magic, but it wasn't coming from her. She glanced at the monarch princess, whose face was white.

"Come with me," said Aislynn, tugging her hand. But Linnea jerked forward. Violaine's foot was still on the hem of her dress, causing her to stumble. Grabbing a nearby table kept the monarch princess from falling, but it was too late. Before she could pull her away, Aislynn felt magic pour from Linnea. The table began to shake.

Glasses began to burst one by one, splattering wine all over the tablecloth, sending broken glass shooting through the air. Yowling like a cat, Violaine leaped away, her green dress splashed with red. A shard of glass flew across Aislynn's cheek, but she barely noticed. Quickly pushing up her sleeve, Aislynn grabbed Linnea's hand and placed it against her own arm.

It felt as though her bones were on fire, splintering from the heat. A red, twisting burn spread from beneath Linnea's hand across Aislynn's skin.

Then, as suddenly as it started, it was over. Quickly, the monarch princess pulled her hand away, her face filled with shame and horror. Violaine and her ruined dress had disappeared into the crowd.

"What happened here?" Madame Moira crunched shards of broken glass into the polished floor as she stalked up to the girls.

Even the music had fallen silent, and all eyes seemed to be focused on them.

"Who did this?" demanded Madame Moira.

Aislynn stepped forward, shielding Linnea from the rest of the ballroom. "I did, Headmistress." Aislynn's confession drew shocked murmurs from the crowd.

"I see," said the headmistress, clearly doubtful.

Then the dancers parted, and Adviser Lennard appeared with Westerly at his side. The young man stepped carefully over the broken glass and draped his jacket around Linnea's shoulders, practically swallowing her whole.

"Are you all right?" he asked quietly. Her tiny, pale face nodded uncertainly.

"I think it would be best if you come with me," Adviser Lennard said to Aislynn.

Head bowed, she followed him out of the ballroom. Just before the door swung shut behind them, she heard the music begin to play again.

Chapter 20

They were alone in Madame Moira's study. The candelabra on the top of the oak bookcase cast flickering shadows around the room. Adviser Lennard gestured for Aislynn to sit.

She declined. There was no reason for her to be comfortable.

Adviser Lennard slid a finger across the length of the desk and held it up to the light as if he was checking the cleanliness of the surface. "I know that you lied to Madame Moira," he said. "It wasn't you who used magic tonight. It was the monarch princess." He wiped his hand with a handkerchief, taking a moment to glance over the desk at Aislynn. "I assume she was being insulted."

Aislynn held herself still and said nothing, but Adviser Lennard nodded as if she had confirmed his theory. "Yes, that is usually what makes her more vulnerable to the curse. Your loyalty is admirable. . . ." He plucked at an imaginary thread on his sleeve. "But dangerous." Pressing his palms together, he let his fingers rest against his chin. He sighed. "The headmistress told me that you have not reported any occurrences since you became Linnea's fairy godmother."

"There haven't been any," said Aislynn quietly.

Adviser Lennard clicked his tongue against his teeth as he came around to the front of the desk. "Don't lie to me." He leaned toward her. "Madame Moira has warned me of your misguided devotion," he continued, "and how it may prove to be a liability. I am beginning to see her point.

"Your loyalty belongs not to the monarch princess, but to me, and eventually, Path willing, to Prince Westerly." A knock sounded at the door, but Adviser Lennard ignored it. "I shall leave your punishment to the headmistress, but if there is another incident like this one, I will not hesitate to have you Redirected once again. Do you understand?"

Her heartbeat echoing in her ears, Aislynn managed the smallest of nods.

"Good," he said. "Come in."

The headmistress entered and gave a perfunctory curtsy. "I'm here to take Aislynn to her room."

"Yes, of course."

Aislynn had turned to follow the headmistress out of the room when Adviser Lennard stopped them both. "Just one more thing. Madame Moira?"

"Yes, Adviser Lennard?"

"Please make sure Aislynn is disciplined appropriately."

"Naturally," Madame Moira said.

The sounds of the party could be heard faintly in the hallway. Aislynn's stomach dropped as the headmistress wrapped a cold hand around her shoulder.

"My dear, my poor dear." Each word was punctuated by a slow shake of her head. "I warned you, didn't I?" Aislynn forced herself to meet Madame Moira's eyes. It was like looking into two dark pits, but she did not falter.

"You may think you're being brave," said Madame Moira, taking a candle from the sconce at the bottom of the stairs. "But you're not." She brushed away the drop of hot wax that fell on her hand. "Now get out of my sight. I'll deal with you in the morning."

Aislynn looked straight ahead as she climbed stiffly up the stairs, her heart pounding. It was only when she was out of sight that she ran, her robes billowing around her.

♡ ♡ ♡

Safe in her room, Aislynn pulled Tahlia's mirror from her pocket and peered at her reflection. Though the cuts on her face were small, there were many of them. They didn't hurt. But her arm throbbed, and she rolled up her sleeve to discover a wound far worse than any she had given herself. It looked as if she had been burned, the twisted skin red and tender.

Aislynn undressed and crawled into bed, wrapping her fingers around her arm. She deserved this. It was agony, but she gritted her teeth and pushed harder, until there was nothing left to think about but the pain.

Chapter 21

Aislynn felt the midnight air against her bare legs as she raced through the trees, her dress gathered in her arms. Her breath was as loud as her footsteps, both echoing through the silent forest as she pushed forward.

There was no moon. Searching the darkness, Aislynn looked for the gleam of silvery fur, the glow of yellow eyes, but saw nothing.

She stumbled and dropped to her knees.

Something wet touched her hand. The wolf was beside her, its eyes round and curious. Aislynn took a deep breath and reached toward it.

♥ ♥ ♥

The pain in Aislynn's arm woke her. She dressed carefully, the burn throbbing like a heartbeat. It wasn't until she had closed the door to her bedroom and was heading down the hall that she realized that for the first time since her nightmares had begun, she hadn't woken with clammy skin and a racing pulse. Even thinking about the dream didn't cause the same fear and anxiety they usually did. That should have worried her, but she felt quiet and still, like an untouched lake.

Until she discovered she was late. Last night's frustration and disappointment came rushing back at her. She couldn't even wake up on time. What kind of fairy godmother was she?

As she stepped out of the kitchen, she saw the others coming back from Thackery's with roses for their princesses. They grew silent as she passed.

Holding her head high, Aislynn hurried to the cottage. Thackery was finishing the last bouquet—Linnea's—as she approached. He was whistling.

Aislynn cleared her throat, and the whistling stopped.

"Morning," she said, touching her injured cheek self-consciously.

"Morning." He raised an eyebrow. "I had no idea they were featuring knife fights at the evening's festivities."

"Only when the orchestra takes a break," Aislynn responded, and he grinned. She caught a glimpse of his crooked bottom teeth, and somehow that made her feel better.

"So, did you win?" he asked, handing her the flowers.

Aislynn thought about the way Violaine had screeched when she was pelted with red wine. "One might say that," she said, smiling.

They stood there in the morning sunlight, grinning at each other. Thackery took a step forward, and Aislynn's heart leaped into her throat. She backed up, and his smile fell.

"I just wanted . . . I wanted to say . . ." he started, but the morning bell rang. Aislynn was late.

"I have to go." She turned and hurried back to the castle, warmth spreading through her chest.

The kitchen servants were busier than usual, tending to the aftermath of the ball. In the middle of it all was Brigid, elbow deep in dirty wine goblets. Not wanting to disturb her, Aislynn grabbed the tea tray and rushed upstairs to Linnea's room.

The monarch princess was still in bed, her blankets bundled up around her neck. When she saw Aislynn, her face brightened, and with a great swoop, she pushed aside the blankets, scrambled from the bed, and wrapped her arms around her fairy godmother.

"Mind the tray," Aislynn said, but she quickly set it and the roses down and hugged the princess back.

"I thought they had sent you away," Linnea cried, leaving

large wet spots on Aislynn's shoulder. "I thought I was all alone. What did they say? Are you going to be punished?"

"Don't you worry," said Aislynn, but she was grateful for the concern. "The important thing is that I'm not going anywhere. I'm still yours." Her voice caught, but Linnea didn't seem to notice. Instead she just squeezed Aislynn tighter, rocking them both from side to side.

"I'm so sorry," she murmured into Aislynn's uniform.

"It's all right." Aislynn gently sat Linnea down at the vanity and began untangling her hair. "You just need to be more careful."

"I know. But that poisonous girl . . ."

"You can't let her and others like her affect you in such a way." It was hollow advice, as she had never been able to ignore Violaine herself, but Linnea nodded.

"I try, but sometimes it's just so hard."

"It's best to ignore whatever will make you lose control." Aislynn wished she had substantial wisdom to offer, but as *The Path* said, "A fairy godmother is only to caution, never to counsel." It was not her role to direct the monarch princess in such matters.

Linnea bent her head, and it took a moment for Aislynn to realize that she was quietly reciting the daily supplication.

"I will accept the Path I am taking. I will not stray. I will not yearn for what I cannot have. I will heed the words of my advisers and guard my loving heart against cursed magic. Ever after."

Linnea caught Aislynn's eye in the mirror. "Thank you for what you did last night. You saved me from . . ." The monarch princess didn't need to finish her sentence. They both knew exactly what Aislynn had done. She had saved Linnea from being Redirected, from becoming just like her.

"You're welcome." But Aislynn couldn't help feeling that it was a bit unfair. Adviser Lennard knew that she had lied, knew that it had been the monarch princess who had used magic, yet there had been no mention of the possibility of Redirecting Linnea. Aislynn quickly pushed that thought away—she had protected the princess—that was all that mattered.

A knock sounded at the door.

"Good morning." Madame Moira entered with a curtsy. "Your Majesty," she said. "Adviser Lennard and Prince Westerly are waiting for you in the sitting room." Linnea let out a happy sigh, sharing a smile with Aislynn, who began untangling the monarch princess's hair in earnest. They were already behind schedule.

"And Aislynn? Once you have delivered the monarch princess to her guests, come see me in my study."

Nervously Aislynn caught Madame Moira's gaze in the mirror.

She was smiling.

♡ ♡ ♡

Brigid swayed on her feet when she saw the blood. Aislynn would have gone straight to the sitting room to check on Linnea, but her fingers were bleeding so much that she needed them tended to.

"I didn't mean to scare you." Aislynn apologized as Brigid wrapped tiny strips of fabric around each fingertip. The blood instantly appeared in perfect red circles on the white cloth.

"I wish I could just heal them," Brigid muttered as she tied the last bandage. She lifted her wrists, looking at the red bands with irritation.

Aislynn shook her head. "It's a punishment, and it's supposed to be painful and evident. Even if you healed them, the headmistress would just do it again, and she'd take a certain type of pleasure from it."

Brigid looked disgusted as she emptied the bowl of water she had used to clean the punctures, the pinkish liquid swirling around the drain before disappearing. There were dark circles under her eyes and she tried, unsuccessfully, to stifle a yawn.

"Was last night a success?" Aislynn asked quietly, relieved when Brigid smiled.

"The information you gave us was incredibly helpful and—" Brigid went silent as another servant hurried past, then lowered her voice to a whisper. "We want to do something to thank you. Can you meet here after midnight tonight?"

With a nod and a quick good-bye, Aislynn was off—dashing down the hallway to the other end of the academy. She narrowly avoided a collision with Prince Westerly, who was standing outside the sitting room.

"Sir." Aislynn gave a curtsy, which the prince acknowledged with a slight, disinterested nod. Pushing open the heavy door, Aislynn found Linnea sitting on the couch with Adviser Lennard, while Madame Moira stood in the corner. The headmistress gave Aislynn and her bandaged fingers a cold look. Clearly her detour had been noted.

". . . evening, wasn't it?" Adviser Lennard was saying. "I think you presented yourself quite well. Considering."

"Thank you, Adviser." Linnea was sitting in a spot of sunlight from the window, making her features all the more porcelain and perfect. Even the blush that clung to her cheeks was becoming. "I had a wonderful time."

"Well, now." He stood and rubbed his hands together briskly. "I think we've kept Westerly waiting long enough. Shall we?" He offered the princess his arm. Before Aislynn could follow them, she was pulled aside by Madame Moira.

"They will be taking a walk around the gardens. Since I will be entertaining the adviser, you must act as their chaperone. Stay behind them. Do not let them out of your sight. Do not speak to them." Her eyes were fierce. "Do you understand?"

"Yes, Headmistress."

"Now stop wasting my time," Madame Moira hissed, "and fulfill your duties."

Aislynn raced out of the room to catch the monarch princess and her suitor.

The morning chill was already beginning to fade, indicating that the day would be warm. Aislynn remained several steps behind Linnea and Prince Westerly as they strolled through the gardens. Clearly Adviser Lennard was pushing for a speedy engagement. Aislynn knew that a chaperoned visit like this one was granted only to a suitor who had made his intentions clear.

Aislynn watched with displeasure as the prince wrenched a perfect red rose from one of Thackery's immaculately tended rosebushes. Its stem was mangled and twisted, but Linnea swooned over it as though it were a golden egg.

"I thought the candles last night were quite lovely," Linnea said, her hand tucked into Westerly's elbow.

"They were quite lovely," he repeated, his voice a deep baritone.

"It was so much better than I ever imagined it would be." Linnea's beaming face inspired only the slightest hint of a smile from her suitor. "I was disappointed that I didn't get a chance to see Princess Fallenne, though. The headmistress told me she was ill and unable to attend."

"Yes, I heard that as well." Westerly turned away from her and looked across the garden. His gaze caught Aislynn's and her throat tightened. His eyes were so cold.

"Her parents were very close to mine." Linnea's expression was thoughtful. "I should write again and see if we can meet another time."

"Darling." Westerly's term of endearment carried as much affection as the word "onion." "I thought we decided you were going to focus less on the past and direct your energies toward the future."

"Of course, dear." Linnea smiled up at him, demure and obliging. A perfect demonstration of Practiced Compliance. "You're right. It's much better to focus on the future."

"I just want what's best for you," said Westerly. He brushed a strand of hair from her cheek. "You understand that, don't you?"

"Yes, of course," Linnea whispered. "I will only think about the future."

Chapter 22

Someone far too tall to be Brigid was standing in the kitchen when Aislynn sneaked down after midnight. She wasn't surprised to see Thackery, but she was confused to find that he was alone. He was unpacking small cloth bags from a large wooden box, the final bag expelling a white powdery cloud when he set it on the table. Flour.

When she got closer, she saw that he had an array of baking supplies, from sugar to yeast to eggs. There was even a neat bundle of dried rosemary and lavender, tied up with a cheery yellow ribbon.

"Where's Brigid?" Aislynn asked, and Thackery jumped.

"Hi." He turned toward her, shoving his hands into his

pockets. "Uh, Brigid isn't coming. It's just me."

Aislynn's palms were suddenly damp. "Oh," she managed.

Thackery's smile was nervous as he swept up the rosemary-and-lavender bouquet and presented it to her. "I wanted to apologize," he said. "It isn't as fancy as flowers, but I thought you might be sick of roses."

"Thank you," said Aislynn, startled. "What are you apologizing for?"

"For a lot of things, I guess." Thackery shuffled his feet. "But mostly for how I treated you after I found out you were a fairy godmother. It was unkind."

"I understand," said Aislynn, because she did. She imagined that if she had been in his place, she would have reacted in much the same way. "Are you expecting me to bake for you?" she asked teasingly. "Is it really a proper apology if I'm doing all the work?"

Thackery blushed. "Not all the work," he said. "Think of me as your apprentice."

Aislynn knew she shouldn't think of him at all. She shouldn't be standing alone with him in the kitchen at midnight, and she shouldn't be smiling up at him. She lifted the bouquet of herbs to her nose and took a deep breath. The scents of lavender and rosemary made her dizzy, and she immediately knew what kind of bread she wanted to make.

"I need to get something from my room," she told Thackery. "I don't know the recipe by heart." He nodded, and she could tell that he wasn't convinced she was going to return. She pulled an apron off the hook on the wall and tossed it to him. "If you want to be helpful, you could try lighting the oven."

Aislynn raced to her room quietly and quickly. She grabbed her journal from the top drawer of her dresser and hurried back downstairs before she could talk herself out of it.

The kitchen was getting warm when she returned, and Thackery had the apron tied around his waist and a spring of lavender tucked behind each ear. Aislynn pulled another apron over her head, hiding her grin.

"What are we making?" he asked.

"Rosemary thumbprint bread," said Aislynn, opening her journal and flipping through the pages until she found the recipe.

"That doesn't look too hard." Thackery's breath caused her wimple to flutter against her ear. The back of her neck grew hot. Grabbing a large bowl, she pushed it into his chest, causing him to grunt and back up, still grinning.

"Why don't you do the first step, then?" she offered.

"It would be my pleasure." He bowed dramatically.

She watched as he carefully measured out the ingredients and poured them into a bowl. Then he slowly, slowly, slowly began stirring them together. It was like watching someone walking through a blizzard.

"Give me that," said Aislynn, taking the bowl from him. "You don't need to be so delicate with it." She mixed the ingredients quickly, the wooden spoon an extension of her wrist. When it was blended together, she added the next items and passed the bowl back to him. "Why don't you try again?"

He nodded seriously, his forehead creased as he took the bowl and gave its contents a nice powerful stir. The result was a huge puff of flour that exploded and settled over both of them. Without a word, Thackery pushed the bowl back at Aislynn, his expression sheepish.

She burst out laughing. "It takes practice."

He shook his head, dislodging flour from his hair and covering Aislynn anew. With a shriek, she jumped back. The sound echoed around the quiet kitchen. Quickly she clapped her hand over her mouth. Eyes wide, she listened while watching Thackery, who seemed to be doing the same thing. When the castle remained silent, she let out the breath she didn't know she was holding.

Thackery smiled and wagged his finger at her. "You're

going to get us in trouble," he said in a low voice.

"This was your idea," Aislynn whispered back. Carefully she began stirring again, the smell of flour all around her. "We should get the rosemary prepared," she said, reaching for the herb. But Thackery got to it first.

"It says fresh rosemary." He pointed to her journal. "This is dried rosemary." He waved the fragrant bundle under her nose.

"We can use dried rosemary." Aislynn tried to grab it, but he transferred it to his other hand, the one that stretched out nearly across the room.

"But it says fresh."

"Sometimes you can change the recipe." Aislynn glanced at the book. "For example, we didn't have any honey, so we used sugar."

"Then why doesn't it say sugar in the recipe?"

"Because that's the way my fairy godmother taught it to me." She reached for the rosemary, but he just raised it above his head. She huffed and crossed her arms. "It will taste the same."

"Exactly the same?" Thackery lifted a disbelieving eyebrow.

"Well, maybe not exactly the same. But it will still taste good." Aislynn finally grabbed the rosemary from him. She plucked the tiny leaves, and dropped them onto the dough.

Thackery leaned over to watch. He was very close, so close that if he lowered his head a bit, his chin would be resting on her shoulder.

"Sometimes you need to ignore the recipe," Aislynn added. She could smell the lavender in his hair.

"Interesting."

"What's interesting?" She began pressing her thumbs into the soft dough, kneading in the rosemary.

"It's interesting how easily you can ignore some rules . . ." He perched on the counter. ". . . and not others."

"I'm not ignoring the rules," she said indignantly as she covered the bread. "But there are times when you have to make . . . adjustments."

But Thackery's attention was now focused on her wimple. "Does that thing itch?" he asked abruptly. "It looks like it itches."

The change of conversation was surprising but welcome. "It used to. But now I barely notice it." Automatically she reached up to adjust it. "Though it does get hot sometimes."

"Like now?" Thackery gave her a knowing look, and she turned away instead of answering. She opened the oven door, checking the heat. "You could take it off, you know," he said.

"It's against the rules." She realized instantly that she had walked straight into a trap. Thackery smiled gleefully as she straightened.

"I wouldn't tell anyone." He leaned over and tugged at it, but she swatted his hand away. "You wouldn't be breaking a rule, you'd just be making an . . . adjustment."

She wanted to wipe that smug grin off his face, so she gave her wimple a yank and pulled her braid free.

"Happy now?" she said, folding the purple fabric neatly and placing it on the counter.

"Very," he responded, leaning back on his hands.

Aislynn lifted the braid off her neck. She untied the ribbon, uncoiled her hair, and ran her fingers through the waves the braid had created.

When she looked up, she realized that Thackery was staring at her. Aislynn felt her cheeks flush. She could only imagine how she looked.

Gently, as if approaching a wild animal, he reached out a finger and touched a curl. The heat from the stove behind her burned her skin.

"You have some flour in your hair," he said.

Aislynn's heart gave a lurch. She stepped away from him and turned toward the oven, shutting the door.

♡ ♡ ♡

By the time she made it back to her room, Aislynn's belly was full of warm bread and the sun was mere hours from rising. Wiggling out of her robes, she left them in a pool on the floor and put her journal down on top of the dresser. She was about to blow out her candle when she noticed that the journal was speckled with drops of wax similar to those that had dotted her robes and blue dress. Turning the book over, Aislynn found that the back and spine were untouched.

As she tilted her candle to get a better look, it dripped hot wax onto the cover, leaving an identical mark. Understanding clicked into place. The wax circles were from a candle.

The room was suddenly cold, and Aislynn's spine felt as if it was made of ice. Had someone been searching her drawers? Looking through her things?

No. She dismissed the thought quickly. Who would be interested in her belongings? And what could they possibly imagine they would find? An old dress, uniforms, and a journal full of recipes? A hairbrush and scraps of fabric to secure her braid? A couple of slippers and well-mended stockings? Needle, thread, and a pair of sewing scissors? The writing materials had been returned to Brigid ages ago, and none of her other meager possessions appeared to be missing.

The wax must have come from her own candle. Of course it had.

But when Aislynn crawled into bed, she was no longer tired. Suddenly every sound became a footstep outside her door, and she fell asleep with her hands clenched.

Chapter 23

Westerly's proposal came as summer departed. It arrived in the form of a letter, delivered by Adviser Lennard and twenty servants, each bearing an armful of roses. While the monarch princess buried her nose in the flowers, breathing in their extravagant scent, Aislynn thought of the bundle of herbs Thackery had given her. Not only had they inspired the creation of a particularly crispy and delicious loaf of rosemary bread, but they continued to make her smile every morning, hanging in her window.

After Adviser Lennard left, Aislynn escorted Linnea to her room. When they entered the suite, the monarch princess went immediately to her window and stared out across the grounds. She said nothing.

Aislynn busied herself with tidying up, occasionally glancing over at the monarch princess with concern. She had been expecting happy, excited chatter and was surprised at this sullen silence. After a long while, Linnea turned and quietly went to her vanity, where she unlocked a drawer and removed a small cedar ring box.

"Adviser Lennard thinks I should give this to Westerly as a wedding present," Linnea finally said, opening the box. Inside was a man's ring made of polished silver, set with a large white stone. Aislynn thought that she caught a glimmer of blue in the center of the stone, but Linnea snapped the box closed before she could be sure.

"It was my father's." The monarch princess looked miserable.

"It's beautiful," said Aislynn, and then, after a moment, added, "You don't talk about your parents much."

"I don't really need to, do I? Everyone has their own story, their own version of what happened." Linnea shrugged the smallest of shrugs. "I don't even remember him, you know. My father. My earliest memory is of Westerly. He brought me a stuffed horse when I was little, even named it for me. He would get so mad when I couldn't say 'Penelope' correctly." Linnea smiled when she saw the expression on Aislynn's face. "He's not as bad as you think."

"He seems . . . rational," Aislynn said cautiously, and Linnea laughed.

"Yes. He certainly is that. But he's always been a part of my life. Westerly may not be overflowing with romance or poetry, but he knows me better than anyone else. And he loves me." Linnea's jaw was set. "Despite everything that has happened, despite what my family is, I know that he loves me."

"And you love him," Aislynn offered, but Linnea had turned to the window again.

"Adviser Lennard is right," she said. "This would make a lovely gift." But by the way her fingers curved around the box, it was clear that she was not ready to let it go.

"Perhaps we can find something else to give Westerly," Aislynn suggested. "Maybe another ring, with a horse on it, like the pony he gave you."

"No, I don't think so." Linnea put the box back in the drawer and locked it. "I think it's best to do what Adviser Lennard recommends."

"Or commands," said Aislynn under her breath.

Linnea spun around. "What did you say?" she snapped. Her gaze was icy and sharp.

Aislynn was taken aback. "I . . . I only meant to say—"

"You only meant to say that I should disregard the advice

of my most trusted adviser? Tell me, fairy godmother, tell me what I should do about a gift for my future husband? You must be rich in knowledge about such things." Her eyes flashed, her words burning like a brand. "Please go now. I think I'd like to be alone."

Aislynn headed to the gardens, her hands linked together to keep herself from tearing at her uniform, which seemed to be growing tighter and tighter. She was filled with guilt and fury.

Linnea had everything she wanted. She was engaged. She was sixteen years old, soon to be a monarch queen, and she was going to be married, going to have a name on her ever-after locket. It was all that a girl could hope for.

The unfairness of it all clutched at Aislynn's throat.

She hated Westerly for proposing to Linnea. She hated Adviser Lennard for his unrelenting control of his ward. She hated Linnea for being so selfish. And mostly she hated herself.

Tears welled up in her eyes. In that moment, she wanted to be Linnea so badly it hurt. Wanted to be a princess again. Wanted her parents and Tahlia. Wanted to be safe and loved. Cared for.

"Aislynn?"

She spun around to find Thackery behind her, his arms

full of flowers. At the sight of her face, he dropped them and rushed toward her, scattering rose petals with every step. "Are you all right?" he asked, his hands finding her waist.

She fully intended to run away. But the concern on his face was enough to make the tears come in earnest. Throwing herself into his arms, Aislynn buried her face in his neck and sobbed. He smelled like earth and rosemary and bread. He stroked her head, and Aislynn suddenly hated her uniform, hated the distance it kept between them. She wanted his fingers tangled in her hair, his palm against her neck, his lips . . . she wanted . . .

She stepped back and wiped her eyes with her sleeve. Something was wrong with her. She had known it since the day Thackery had touched her arm, her scar. Her loving heart had returned. She was sure of it.

Somehow it had found its way to her again and beat inside her so fiercely that she feared it would burst from her chest. She ached with a desire to touch Thackery. It was a dangerous feeling. She knew that she should leave the garden immediately and lock away all of the wicked, treacherous thoughts that brewed inside her. But Aislynn did not move.

When Linnea married, and she would marry soon, she

would leave the academy. And when she left, she'd take with her all her belongings, her dresses, her jewelry, her perfumes, and her fairy godmother. For Aislynn belonged to Linnea, forever, like a necklace or a hair ribbon. And once they left, she would never see Thackery again. Her heart felt as if it was shattering into a million jagged pieces.

"Bad day?" Thackery asked. His hands were still around her waist.

Aislynn nodded, took a deep breath, and tried to smile. "I'll be fine," she said. "But your flowers . . ."

Thackery glanced at the ruined roses and shrugged. His hands lifted away from her. "I'll just pick some more." Aislynn nodded, and an uncomfortable silence settled around them.

"I should tell you," he said, rubbing the back of his neck. "That is . . . we're leaving. Brigid, Ford, and me. We're leaving Elderwood."

"What?" Her heart seemed to break anew.

"We don't usually stay in one place this long. We would have left a while ago, but . . ." He shook his head. "We have to move on. It's harder to get caught if you don't stay in one place."

"Do you think Josetta is still searching for you?" asked Aislynn, horrified.

"She'll always be looking for us."

"Where will you go?"

"Another academy." Thackery ran a hand through his hair. "Someplace that will feed and clothe us in exchange for work. Someplace where we can help others."

"Won't Madame Moira get suspicious if you all disappear?" A chill ran through Aislynn. "She could report you."

Thackery snorted. "She can't even remember our names. Leaving will be an inconvenience for her, nothing more. We'll be quickly replaced. Besides, I'll be leaving first, to scout ahead. Brigid and Ford will follow once I've secured new positions for us. It will make it less suspicious if we all depart separately."

"When are you leaving?" Aislynn held her breath.

"Soon," he said. "I'll be gone before the autumn ball."

"But that's in a few weeks!" Aislynn's voice cracked, and Thackery curled his hands into fists.

"I was thinking . . . that maybe . . ." He was so quiet and hesitant that she had to lean forward to hear him. "That maybe you could come with us."

Go with them? A life without a princess to serve, without teachers to impress, without advisers to obey? No more lessons, no more uniforms.

For a glorious moment, Aislynn wanted to say yes.

She wanted to go with Thackery.

And that's what stopped her. The realization that she was so willing to abandon the Path for him made her realize the true danger she was in. How close she was from becoming what everyone had always believed she was—a stray.

"I can't."

"I know." He didn't seem surprised, just sad.

The wind was picking at the rose petals on the ground and tossing them around like a kitten playing with string. Autumn was coming soon.

Suddenly Thackery took her hand. "Your fingers are warm," he murmured, pressing her hand to his chest. "Can you feel that?" And she could. She could feel his heart beating beneath her palm.

Aislynn raised her eyes to his. They were so very green. She saw herself in them, and it was like staring into the mirror she had always wished for, where the reflection was winsome and fine.

Then he kissed her, and it was better than dancing, better than summer, better than bread. All of her seemed to be turned inside out in one glorious swoop. But before she could kiss him back, his arms fell away.

"I'm sorry," he said, hanging his head. "I never should have . . ."

Before Aislynn could swallow the poisoned apple that was lodged in her throat, Thackery turned and walked out of the garden, never once looking back.

Chapter 24

Thackery was gone by morning. Aislynn tried to convince herself that it was better that way. For if he hadn't gone, if he had stayed just one more day, it was possible that she would have abandoned sense and reason, and gone with him.

Now she would never see him again, and Brigid and Ford would be following soon after. And the thought of their absence in addition to Thackery's was a new type of pain, not sharp and cutting, but dull and unending. It was a pain that turned the whole world gray.

Brigid promised that she'd stay at least until the wedding, which had been set for immediately after the autumn ball at Nyssa Academy and was approaching far too rapidly for

Aislynn's taste. As Thackery predicted, the headmistress found a new gardener, and he was a small, sour-faced man whose bouquets were scrawny and lackluster.

Each new day was as miserable as the last. But even Aislynn's mind-numbing unhappiness didn't stop her from noticing Linnea's new habit of disappearing for hours on end. On one particularly humid afternoon, Aislynn was told that Westerly was planning to visit that evening. The monarch princess had been missing since breakfast, and because it took several hours to dress for such an occasion, Aislynn was now desperate to find her. The dining hall was empty, her teachers unhelpful, and the other fairy godmothers uncaring. Aislynn left the castle and was heading to the gardens when she caught sight of Brigid.

"Are you looking for the monarch princess?" Brigid asked, pointing to the rose garden. Calling her thanks over her shoulder, Aislynn hurried on, realizing belatedly that Brigid had seemed upset. But there was no time to address it, as Aislynn soon came across the monarch princess sitting on a bench in the garden, reading a letter.

"Your Majesty?"

Linnea started and dropped the parchment. It fluttered to the ground, and Aislynn rushed to pick it up, but the monarch princess snatched it away and quickly folded it into her small bag. Her cheeks were flushed, and she gripped the clasp fiercely.

"What do you want?" Linnea asked, her tone sharp.

"I've been looking for you all afternoon," said Aislynn gently, trying to contain her frustration. "Prince Westerly is coming tonight."

"He is? Oh that's lovely." Rising from the bench, Linnea gave her fairy godmother an apologetic smile. It was the first sign of kindness the monarch princess had offered Aislynn since their argument. "It's the wedding," Linnea said. "So many decisions to make: the food, the flowers, the guest list. Sometimes I just want to get away from it all." She smoothed out her skirt. "I'm so glad Westerly is coming. He's always so certain when it comes to these things."

Aislynn followed the monarch princess out of the garden, neither girl saying another word.

The shiny red apple rolled unevenly across the table into Aislynn's hand. With a gentle push, she sent it back toward her other palm. Back and forth, back and forth the apple wobbled as Aislynn waited for the bell to tell them that dinner was over and she could head to the dining hall to collect the monarch princess.

Across the table, the other fairy godmothers were

gossiping, as they always did. Aislynn was barely listening when she heard Cecily lazily mention a Lady Maris. Aislynn stilled.

"Her parents never believed she strayed," Cecily was saying.

So, it was Maris they had been gossiping about at the most recent ball—had they heard something new? Aislynn strained to hear.

"They thought something terrible had happened to her, didn't they?" said Thea.

"And they were right?" asked Juliana.

"Well, not completely," Cecily corrected. "She strayed, but then something terrible happened to her. I heard her parents found a yellow shoe on their doorstep. Apparently it had a rose embroidered on the toe."

Aislynn remembered that shoe and how proud Maris had been of it. A dreadful feeling started to churn in her stomach.

Cecily continued. "Inside the shoe was a bramble, the very kind that is known to grow around Queen Josetta's palace. But that wasn't the only thing—" Cecily paused dramatically. "Inside the shoe was a severed toe."

The other girls gasped. Aislynn felt the small room grow hot, and the walls seemed to close in on her. She stood up quickly and rushed out through the kitchen, ignoring the stares of the servants. She slammed the back door and leaned against it, welcoming the cool evening breeze.

Josetta. That horrible, wicked woman. That monster. After what the Wicked Queen had done to Brigid, Ford, and Thackery, Aislynn supposed it was foolish to be surprised that she was so cruel.

What had Maris done to deserve such violence? Was this how Josetta repaid the service of her followers? Maris had been so proud of her tiny, delicate feet. Surely the Wicked Queen must have known that, if this was the message she chose to send Maris's parents.

But what kind of message was it? Head throbbing, Aislynn moved away from the kitchen door and into the small courtyard. Was it meant to convince them once and for all that their daughter had strayed?

Aislynn could still remember the look on Maris's face, black hair spread across her fair shoulders, her bare feet slapping against the courtyard. . . . No. There was a sour taste on the back of Aislynn's tongue. She must be remembering that wrong. How would Josetta have been able to send Maris's shoes to her parents if she hadn't been wearing them?

The sour taste grew stronger as Aislynn remembered Thackery's story about Madame Moira. How she had hacked off the toe of her former fairy godmother. And hadn't she been present the night of Maris's disappearance? Again Aislynn shook her head.

It didn't make sense. The headmistress was charged with keeping girls on the Path, not helping them stray. The Wicked Queen was known for her brutality; there was no reason to think it didn't extend to those who joined her. Willingly or not.

Looking out toward the gardens, Aislynn could only hope that Thackery would continue to evade Josetta's grasp. Her heart ached at the thought that he might be captured and there would be nothing she could do about it. Just as there was nothing to be done for poor Maris.

The moon was bright overhead as they ran. Their feet made no sound against the moss, and Aislynn knew she could run forever. Her body hurt, but it was a good kind of hurting, as if she were using parts of herself that had been long forgotten.

Out of the corner of her eye she could see the wolf, its coat like starlight. She wanted to go faster. Taking a breath so deep she thought she had inhaled the night, Aislynn ran. And the wolf ran beside her.

Chapter 25

Preparations for the ball and Linnea's wedding reached a new frenzy. With each day came baskets of lace, bolts of red satin, and an especially crabby kitchen servant. A permanent frown fixed to her face, Brigid practically snarled at any mention of the word "wedding," so Aislynn was careful to watch what she said around her.

The amount of work that needed to be done was staggering. It seemed that Aislynn's responsibility had shifted from tending to the monarch princess's daily needs to following behind her with quill and paper, recording her ideas for the celebration. Every day they seemed to go through at least five rolls of parchment, outlining everything from table decorations to music.

Of course, everything that Linnea suggested needed to be approved by Adviser Lennard, who was now staying at Elderwood so he could keep a more careful eye on the preparations and his ward.

Aislynn welcomed the distraction. If she wasn't careful, she would catch herself thinking about Thackery. Most often she worried about his safety and wondered where he was, but sometimes she allowed herself to picture him, his smile and those green eyes, and her stomach would hurt and she would usually feel so dizzy that she needed to sit down. Everything she felt now seemed sharper and often more painful.

It was his eyes she was trying not to think about when she returned to her room one evening to discover an envelope on her bed, addressed to her in her father's handwriting. Aislynn suddenly missed her family so much that it was hard to breathe.

There were two letters inside the envelope, one written in Adviser Hull's thick, blocky writing and one in her father's hand. Wanting to save her father's for last, she quickly read the adviser's terse note.

Due to a series of petitions set forth by the King and Queen of Nepeta, you have been granted permission to experience the remainder of your sixteenth year in your former position as a maiden. I will present the king with a list of potential suitors, and you will be given a formal Introduction at the autumn ball held at Nyssa Academy.

Aislynn sat there, stunned beyond words or logic. Petitions? Her former position as a maiden? Quickly she snatched up her father's letter.

Dear Daughter,

The adviser has allowed you to rejoin us for the remainder of your year. Your mother will arrive at Elderwood on the morning of the autumn ball to assist you, and I shall join you at Nyssa Academy to escort you. I have no doubt you will make a dazzling entrance.

Your loving father

Aislynn sat with the letters in her lap, unable to move.

Another chance. She was being given another chance. This was her opportunity for ever after—she should be overjoyed. Yet she felt as if she was going to faint.

Redirection was permanent, was it not? As she sat there, Aislynn realized she could not recall anything in *The Path* that explicitly declared that it was. But she also could not remember anything like this ever happening before.

What had she done to deserve it? Adviser Hull's letter mentioned petitions, but surely it couldn't be as simple as that. Aislynn's parents couldn't have been the first to want their daughter's situation reassessed.

Her head began to spin and then, suddenly, settled. Her parents. She would be able to see her family again. And Tahlia. She could go home. She would have suitors and marry and have her freedom once again. Excitement welled up inside of her.

All at once it seemed very important to see what she looked like. After all these months hidden in flowing robes and itchy fabric, avoiding mirrors and eating whatever she desired . . . Linnea would still be at dinner with Westerly. Her room would be empty. Aislynn went through their shared door and sat down at the vanity. Carefully she removed her wimple and set it to one side. She unbraided her hair. Then she looked in the mirror.

She looked tired. Her face was softer and her eyes bigger. Her hair was wild. All excitement quickly left her, and she felt, as she always had, not quite good enough. Not quite right.

Something glittered in her eyes. Something dangerous. Something Aislynn thought she recognized from paintings and tapestries. She looked like a girl who wanted things.

But what did she want? Was it the life she had been forced to leave behind? Or was it something else?

Aislynn dropped her head into her hands. When she felt a gentle touch on her shoulder, she leaped to her feet and found Linnea standing there.

"I am so sorry, Your Majesty." She snatched up her wimple and hastily pulled it over her head.

"No, wait," Linnea grabbed at her arm, her eyes bright. "The headmistress told me." When Aislynn only blinked, she continued excitedly. "About the ball. About you."

"Oh, yes. The ball."

"It's just wonderful!" Linnea was glowing with enthusiasm. "I've always wished you didn't have to hide away in the corner. Now we can go to the ball together!" Linnea turned her full attention to the mirror. "By the glass slipper," she breathed, looking at their reflections. "I never noticed how pretty you are."

"I think that's the point." Aislynn responded drily, and Linnea laughed, the bright sound lightening the mood. It had been so long since things had felt friendly and easy between them.

"Yes, I suppose you're right." Linnea sighed wistfully. "Just think how romantic it would be for your suitor . . . what was his name again?"

"Everett," said Aislynn quietly.

"Just think how awfully romantic it would be if Everett swept you off your feet!"

"Yes, it would be awfully romantic."

Aislynn told herself to be happy, but all she could think about was the girl in the mirror, the girl who no longer knew what she wanted.

Chapter 26

Adviser Lennard replaced Aislynn with a temporary fairy godmother, promising Linnea a permanent one as soon as he could manage it. The new fairy godmother was a woman nearly as unpleasant as Madame Moira, and she didn't look too kindly on Aislynn's attempts to visit Linnea. Even if she had, the monarch princess had very little free time, whereas Aislynn had entirely too much.

It didn't make sense for her to continue her fairy godmother training, and the headmistress felt that to include her in royal courses would be too distracting for the others. A few of her old dresses had been sent to Elderwood, but Aislynn chose to wear her purple robes, though without the itchy wimple.

She was no longer permitted to eat with the rest of the fairy godmothers, so she mostly kept to her room, curled up on her bed, wishing for time to pass, reciting bread recipes in her head to keep all other thoughts at bay.

The day before the autumn ball, she was called to Madame Moira's study. With the leaves on the trees falling rapidly and the air puffing soft, early warnings of winter into the face of anyone who ventured outside, the headmistress's small, dark study should have felt cozy. Instead it was cold and airless.

Several large boxes were stacked on Madame Moira's desk, each tied with a blue silk ribbon.

"Your ballgown," said the headmistress, her voice flat. "And other necessary items. They arrived this morning. One of the servants will bring them to your room."

"Thank you, Headmistress."

"Brigid will be assisting you," Madame Moira said, and Aislynn was surprised. She had assumed that Tahlia would be coming along with her parents. "Your mother will arrive in the afternoon, though it is expected that you will be dressed and your trunk packed before then."

The headmistress placed her hands on the desk and stood. "You will not be returning to Elderwood after the ball. You will return home with your parents. However, if you are not able to secure a marriage proposal by the end of the season, you will once again be Redirected." Madame Moira smiled. It was a terrible sight. "I've heard the academies in the West are always needing new teachers."

The words seemed to come from far away, and all Aislynn could do was nod. She had just begun to accept the reversal in her fortunes, being able to return home and marry, reaching ever after. Yet it could all still be undone.

"May I be excused?" she asked when it became clear that the headmistress had nothing more to say to her.

"Please," Madame Moira urged, her dark eyes unblinking.

Aislynn stumbled out the back door into a flurry of leaves, which were dancing a waltz with the gusty wind. Her purple robes billowing around her, she tucked her chin to her chest and headed toward the stables.

As she approached, she heard voices and the soft round *clop* of hooves. She wandered around to the back of the stables, where she found Brigid seated on a bale of hay, watching Ford lead a foal around in a circle. Brigid glanced up, and for the first time in days, smiled. She patted the space next to her.

Aislynn settled onto the hay and sat in silence, the air thick with unsaid things. Linnea's wedding. The headmistress's threat.

Brigid and Ford's inevitable departure. And, of course, Thackery.

Ford looped around again with the speckled foal, raising his fingers to his hat in greeting.

"Are you nervous about tomorrow?" Brigid asked.

Aislynn didn't know how to answer. "Nervous" wasn't the word she'd use to describe how she felt. She knew she should be nervous and excited and lots of other things, but she wasn't. She just felt . . . numb.

"Why should I be nervous?" Aislynn asked with false bravery. "It's only one night."

Brigid gave her a small smile and shook her head. "No, it's not." And she was right. Tomorrow changed everything.

The headmistress's words finally sank in. Everything she would regain tomorrow night could be taken from her just as quickly. Aislynn began to tremble. She could lose it all again.

Brigid reached out and took Aislynn's hand. She held on tight, and the gesture was like an anchor, tethering Aislynn to the earth.

Looking down at their hands, Aislynn noticed that Brigid's sleeve had been pulled back, revealing her wrist and the red mark that marred her skin.

Aislynn thought of her own scars, ugly and numerous. The ones on her legs would be well covered, first with stockings, then with layers of crinoline and satin—but she would be unable to hide her arms from the person sent to help her dress.

"I need to show you something," Aislynn said, removing her hand from Brigid's. She pulled back her sleeve, revealing the two scars on her arm. "They don't hurt." It seemed important to say that. "And I'm not showing you so you'll feel sorry for me," Aislynn said, letting the fabric fall back to her wrist. "I need you to help me hide them tomorrow night."

Brigid was silent for a moment. The air smelled of dust and unshed rain.

"I used to think we were so different," she finally said. "That girls like you didn't feel pain. That you never got hurt. I never even imagined you'd have scars." Her hand reached up and curled over her shoulder, where Aislynn knew Josetta's brand was burned into her skin. "And I never thought they'd look almost like mine." Brigid met Aislynn's gaze. Her eyes were sad but steady. "I wish I could heal them. I wish I could make them go away."

It was the first time Aislynn had even thought of using magic to remove her scars. For a moment she imagined herself without them. Clear and unblemished. New again.

But she shook her head. "They're a part of me now," she

said, surprised to realize it was true. She didn't want to be new. She wanted to be who she was.

Brigid took Aislynn's hands again. "No more new scars," she said. It was not a question.

"No more new scars," Aislynn agreed.

Brigid wrapped an arm around her and the two of them sat there for a long time, watching the foal gallop and the leaves fall.

Chapter 27

Aislynn's dress was tight. She could barely breathe as she was laced into it.

"You look nice," Brigid said, but she seemed to be regarding Aislynn as a stranger. And for good reason. A glance at the full-length mirror that had been delivered to her room the previous day revealed someone whom Aislynn barely recognized.

The scars on her arms were hidden under thin gauze bandages, and Brigid had sewn tiny invisible loops on the gown's sleeves, for Aislynn to hook onto her fingers so the sleeves would be unable to slip back above her wrists. Still, even with all the layers of undergarments and six petticoats,

Aislynn felt more naked then ever before. More exposed.

Brigid gave Aislynn's shoulders a comforting squeeze before fastening the last button. The room felt stuffy and hot; sweat was already beginning to form at the base of Aislynn's spine.

She knew that people would be staring at her tonight, knew that the story of her Redirection would be a popular item of gossip and that she would spend the evening being chased by whispers and giggles. Glancing again at the mirror, she decided to imagine her dress as armor, protecting her from sharp and cruel remarks. It was the only way she would survive. She took her broken locket from the dresser, and Brigid helped her with the clasp.

"Good luck," Brigid whispered.

Aislynn forced a smile and clutched her bag to her stomach. She could feel the outlines of Tahlia's mirror and letter through the satin, and they gave her some small comfort. Taking a deep breath, Aislynn headed to the drawing room to greet her mother.

The queen arrived in a flurry of perfume and unshed tears, collapsing into Aislynn's embrace. Linnea, who had insisted on being present for their reunion, stood on the other side of the room, watching the scene with delight.

"Hello, Mama," said Aislynn into her mother's shoulder, her voice muffled. She filled her senses with the familiar scent of her perfume. Orange and spices.

"You look wonderful," said the queen, dabbing gently at her eyes, her powder remaining impeccable. "Just wonderful."

Aislynn smoothed her hair self-consciously. The bandages, thin as they were, made her arms feel stiff and uncomfortable, and the dress made the rest of her feel the same way. Underneath the massive skirt and petticoats, her ankles were wobbling in shoes that pinched her toes and arched her feet. She had forgotten how to walk in them, and she felt as graceful and elegant as a bundle of sticks. The queen smiled and took Aislynn's face in her hands as if she couldn't bear to look away.

"Believe me, all eyes will be on you this evening." The queen looked at Linnea and curtsied gracefully. "On both of you."

There was a comforting little fire burning in the fireplace, and the three of them placed their bags on a corner table and settled onto the small chairs in front of the warm flames.

"You know, I met your parents at a ball once," the queen said gently, turning to Linnea.

"You did?"

Aislynn could see the yearning in the other girl's eyes.

"Indeed. Just after they were married." The queen gave a deep sigh.

Aislynn smiled—it was the sigh that meant she was about to tell a story that involved romance and drama.

"Your mother was quite a beauty. You get your hair from her, I see."

Linnea's hand went automatically to her head. "Yes, I'm often told I look like her."

"It's no small compliment, my dear. And your father, well." The look on the queen's face was wistful. "He was handsome, too. Not as handsome as *my* husband, mind you." The queen winked, and Linnea laughed. "But handsome indeed. And he would look at your mother with such devotion. For him, there was no one else in the room."

The story was a kind lie, as Aislynn was certain that her mother had never met Linnea's parents. But the monarch princess deserved to hear something good about her mother and father once in a while, and so Aislynn didn't say a thing.

There was a knock at the door, and Linnea's new fairy godmother entered.

"Your Majesties," she said with a curtsy before turning to the monarch princess. "Shall I escort you to the carriage, my lady?"

"I thought we were traveling to Nyssa Academy together?" Linnea asked, her brow wrinkled with confusion.

"You are," said the fairy godmother. "But the headmistress

would like to see Princess Aislynn. In private."

"Of course," Linnea said, grabbing her bag and giving Aislynn a quick hug before following her fairy godmother out of the room.

As soon as the door was shut, Aislynn turned to the queen. "Where is Tahlia, Mother?"

Aislynn's mother paused for a moment before giving her daughter a placid smile.

"She's gone away."

"Away?" Aislynn noticed that her mother would not quite look her in the eye. "She went away?"

Your family was the brightness of my life . . .

Was. Had this been what her fairy godmother had been trying to say in her cryptic letter? That she was leaving?

"Yes, darling, away." The queen retrieved their bags. "Don't act so alarmed, dear. It's not the first time."

"It's not?"

"Of course not." Her mother's laugh was almost lost amid the jangling of her earrings. "Why, when you were a child, she disappeared for almost a year. Don't you remember?"

But there was no time to answer. There was a brisk knock, and the headmistress entered the sitting room holding a glass jar in which a pale blue light pulsed steadily. Aislynn's loving heart.

Aislynn placed a curious hand to her chest. She had been so sure that her loving heart had already been returned to her. How could she have felt so much without it?

"Your Majesties." Madame Moira gave a low, respectful curtsy, but her expression was decidedly displeased. With a slender finger, she tapped the side of the glass. "Are you prepared?"

Without waiting for a reply, she slowly unscrewed the lid. The glowing light rose out of the jar and hovered in the air, quietly pulsing. The entire room seemed to hold its breath.

Then, with a bright flash, the little blue glow rushed straight into Aislynn's chest. If she hadn't been so surprised, she might have thrown out her hands, but she was frozen in place as it disappeared into her.

Aislynn gasped. The breath she had been holding burst out as if there was no longer room inside her lungs to contain it. Her body seemed to expand, ribs spreading, bones shifting, chest nearly bursting.

And then, suddenly, it was as if everything was brighter and closer. Whatever she had felt in the garden with Thackery was nothing compared to this moment. Every emotion, every feeling was now sharp and raw and overwhelming. It was too much, too fast. She felt as if she was burning, as if her heart was on fire. It was agony. She burst into tears.

Immediately her mother's arms were around her, guiding her to a chair and gently rubbing her back as Aislynn sobbed into her handkerchief. It wasn't until she had calmed down that Aislynn realized that the headmistress was gone.

Through her pain came the wish, unbidden, that she could give Madame Moira her own loving heart, so that she might share in the agony that came with its return. But it was such a cruel and wicked wish that Aislynn quickly pushed it away.

"Darling?" the queen whispered.

"It hurts." The admission was raw in Aislynn's throat.

The queen smoothed a hand across her cheek, but the gentle gesture only made it worse, loss and longing slamming into Aislynn like a speeding carriage. It was as if the past two seasons had been a strange dream.

But everything felt real now. And with it came the familiar feelings of inadequacy and loathing. "What if I can't do this?" she whispered. With or without her loving heart, she was still a failure. And as if to remind her what had brought her here in the first place, magic flickered in her chest. "What if I can't control it?"

"Darling, what do you mean?" Her mother's face was lined with concern.

"What if I can't control my magic?"

"Then you'll have to find a way to hide it." Her mother

took a deep breath. Slipping off her shoe, the queen carefully rolled down her own stocking.

Aislynn stifled a gasp. The bottom of her mother's foot was nearly covered with painful-looking red welts, not unlike the ones that marred Aislynn's legs.

"When I was your age," said the queen, "I could not control my occurrences. So I found a way to hide them."

"But father—"

"Your father has never seen them." The words were sharp. "No one has to know about the magic you do, my dear." Resting her forehead against Aislynn's, the queen took a deep breath. "If you are careful and quiet, you will be safe."

The fire crackled in the grate, and Aislynn was speechless—and, suddenly, flush with anger. Why had her mother kept this secret from her? If Aislynn had known that her own mother was just as weak, just as imperfect, maybe it would have kept her from feeling so broken. So lonely.

There was a knock, and Madame Moira entered again. "The carriages are waiting," she said.

The queen rose. "Are you ready, my darling?"

Aislynn shook her head. "I need a moment by myself," she said, and the queen nodded, shutting the door very quietly behind her.

In the empty room, even with the fire burning, Aislynn

felt cold and confused and so very alone. She reached out for her evening bag, for Tahlia's letter. Tahlia had believed in her, hadn't she? The writing was blurry as she wiped her tears away and began to read.

The handwriting was different. This wasn't Tahlia's letter she was holding. And why was Linnea's bag in her lap, not her own? She glanced at the bottom of the page. In beautiful script it read:

My love always,
Brigid

Chapter 28

Aislynn did not speak during the carriage ride. Her heart ached, and her head was practically brimming with secrets—first her mother's, and now Linnea's. The more she thought about Linnea and Brigid, the more it was like a puzzle, that final piece revealing the entire picture.

Aislynn had heard gossip about ladies-in-waiting, stories about friendships that had evolved past what the advisers considered acceptable, but she had never heard a whisper of such affection forming between a royal and a servant.

When they arrived at Nyssa Academy, Linnea and Aislynn were shepherded into the waiting room. It was already full of nervous and excited girls, eagerly chattering to one another.

Aislynn recognized several princesses from Nerine but said nothing to them, choosing to stay with Linnea. There were stares and murmurs, but Aislynn ignored them.

Still, she was grateful when Nyssa's headmistress stepped forward to lead them all in the prayer of gratitude. It meant that the whispering would stop, if only for a few moments.

"I am grateful for my father, who keeps me good and sweet. I am grateful for my mother, who keeps her own heart guarded and safe. I am grateful for my adviser, who keeps me protected. I am grateful for the Path, which keeps me pure. Ever after."

Standing next to Linnea, Aislynn bowed her head but did not recite the prayer. To say it would be a lie. Instead she listened as the voices blended together, surrounding her.

Surreptitiously she glanced up. Linnea's head was down, her chin nearly touching her chest, and her eyes were tightly closed. What did she feel when she recited those words? Was she filled with the same doubt, the same shame that lingered in Aislynn's heart? And what about the others? Looking around the room, Aislynn wondered how many secrets, how many lies were tucked away in each bowed head.

The faint sound of music drifted into the waiting room. The ball had begun. Aislynn obediently joined the line of girls and tried to imagine the suitors who were assembling at the bottom of the stairs, but all she could see was Thackery's face. She pushed it away. There was no use wishing for something she could not have.

When the curtains finally opened, her father was waiting for her. There was more gray in his hair than before, but otherwise he looked the same. When it was time to take his hand, she was surprised by how tightly he held on to her, as if he would never let go again.

The ballroom smelled like cider and candles. Enormous orange pumpkins, their thick stems curling up toward the ceiling, had been placed at the edge of the dance floor. Each table was heavy with yellow and red candles and a bouquet of autumn leaves.

"Adviser Hull and I have spoken about your prospects," said the king quietly. "Though the list is"—he cleared his throat—"not substantial in length, I believe it is more than exceptional in quality." He squeezed his daughter's hand. "There is one young man in particular who would be especially happy to have you as a wife."

"Does he know?" Aislynn asked, surprising herself with the bitterness that crept into her words. What kind of lies had her father told to convince this suitor that she was a favorable match?

Her father looked confused, so Aislynn continued.

"Does he know what I'm capable of?" The thought of being Redirected again made her ill, but so did the thought of a marriage based on falsehoods and the lifetime of secrets that would follow. Were these her only choices? Her hands were balled into tight fists. "The reason you're afraid of me. Why I was Redirected. Does he know?"

The king paled and quickly shook his head. "No one has to know." He ushered Aislynn out of the way of the giggling couples and happy chatter. His voice was hoarse and hurried. "We will take care of you. If you are quiet and careful, you can be safe."

It was exactly what her mother had said, but nothing about this felt safe.

"All you have to do is say yes to Everett," he murmured.

"Sir?" As if he had been conjured, Everett appeared out of the crowd. "Might I take a moment of your daughter's time?"

The king looked relieved and put Aislynn's hand in Everett's. "She would be honored," he said with an approving nod.

Everett was exactly the same. His smile was just as wide, his shoulders just as broad, and his eyes sparkled with a familiar hazy excitement. Aislynn guessed that he had probably already found the champagne. Pulling her hand, he led her through the brightly colored crowd. Staring at their entwined fingers, Aislynn waited for the giddy flutter she had felt the last time they had seen each other, the last time they had touched. Nothing happened.

"Aislynn!" Linnea came hurrying over, Westerly and his dour expression following behind. "Is this Sir Everett?" she asked after the two girls exchanged a hug.

"Your Majesty!" Everett's bow was unsteady, as if he was nervous. There was good reason to be, Aislynn reminded herself. Most monarchs would not bother to mingle with someone of his status. "It is an honor," he said, kissing the back of Linnea's hand.

The monarch princess smiled, her gaze catching Aislynn's as if to say "I approve." But Aislynn didn't smile back. Her attention was focused on the fourth finger of Westerly's hand, where Monarch King Dominick's ring gleamed.

"I've heard you're a lover of horses," Westerly said to Everett. The silver ring glinted in the light of the shining ballroom, and the white stone gave off a faint glow.

Everett seemed to go gray. "You—you have?" he stammered.

Westerly raised an eyebrow. "Everyone's heard."

Everett gripped Aislynn's arm, but she was barely aware of him. So Linnea had followed Adviser Lennard's advice and given her father's ring to her fiancé after all. Even though Aislynn had no reason to believe Linnea would have gone against her adviser's recommendation and kept the ring for herself, Aislynn was shocked at the anger that surged through her.

Her head ached. The room was full of perfume and candle smoke, and she couldn't think properly. "I need some air," she said abruptly, and without waiting for a response, she pushed through the crowded ballroom and out into the cold night.

Just as there was at Nerine and Elderwood, there was a ballroom terrace at Nyssa, and past that terrace and down the stairs, there was a secluded and mostly hidden garden.

Aislynn welcomed the crisp air. Some things would always be consistent, such as a chill in autumn and the sound of violins at a ball. She had just settled onto a terrace bench when a warm hand fell on her shoulder.

"It's a beautiful night" was all the monarch princess said. She sat down and tipped her face to the night sky, and Aislynn did the same, watching the millions of tiny stars twinkling brightly above. A full moon was rising in the west. It was a creamy yellow, just like whipped butter.

"A little cold, perhaps, but quite lovely, don't you think?" Linnea asked, scooting closer. "Can I tell you a secret?"

Even though she had heard enough secrets to last a lifetime, Aislynn nodded. "Of course."

"A part of me wishes that you could be my fairy godmother forever." Linnea sighed. "It's terribly selfish, I know, but I'm going to miss you. There are so few people in my life who have cared about me. My parents. Adviser Lennard. You." She paused. "Westerly."

"Do you really love Westerly?" It was a bold question, but a part of Aislynn wanted Linnea to confide in her about Brigid. The bag of love letters tied to the sash at her waist felt as heavy as bricks. Aislynn wanted to give it back. She didn't want to carry another secret around.

Linnea pulled away. "Of course I love him," she said.

"The way your parents loved each other?"

The monarch princess's face darkened. "That was a story, Aislynn." Then her expression cleared, and Linnea smiled a sad kind of smile. "There are many different kinds of love. I love Westerly, in a way. The way you'll love Everett." It seemed almost like a plea.

"But don't you want to be happy?"

"No." Linnea's voice was quiet and sure. "I want to be safe."

"Ladies." Westerly's voice startled them both, and Aislynn wondered how much he had heard of their conversation. He and Everett stepped out of the shadows. "We've been looking everywhere for you."

Linnea gave them a brilliant smile and held out her hand to Westerly. "I just wanted some fresh air, darling. But I'm ready to come in now."

"Lovely."

Without waiting to see if Aislynn or Everett would follow, he led the monarch princess back to the ballroom.

"Well," said Everett. He glanced around the empty terrace and out into the garden. When he looked back at Aislynn, he wore a mischievous smile. "Come on." Grabbing her hand, Everett pulled Aislynn from the bench.

She followed him, just as she had before, down the wide steps and into the garden. It was almost exactly the same as the gardens at Nerine, but the hedges were higher and the moon brighter.

Aislynn shivered. Gallantly Everett pulled off his jacket and draped it over her shoulders, looking at her with expectant eyes.

When her father had called her list of suitors insubstantial, Aislynn knew that there was only one name on that list. Once Everett had appeared, she also knew that he would ask her to marry him. But it wasn't until this moment that Aislynn realized she could not say yes.

She knew she should. Aislynn knew without a doubt that this was what her parents and Linnea would tell her to do. Say yes. Be good. Be safe. But she couldn't.

"Everett, I—"

"Please don't." All cheerfulness vanished from his face, and he took both of her hands in his. For a moment Aislynn feared he was going to get down on one knee, but he just stared at their joined hands. "Just say yes," he said. "Please." There was fear in his voice.

"I don't love you," said Aislynn. The statement was as blunt as it was true.

Everett perked up as if this was the most wonderful news. "And I don't love you either." He squeezed her hands. "Don't you see? It's perfect. I would never try to control you, and I'd never be in the way, never even bother you, really. And I'm not the jealous type, trust me."

"I don't understand." Aislynn's head was swimming, and she was having a hard time making sense of what he had just said to her. "Why do you want to marry me, then?"

"Because we belong together." This time he did lower himself to the ground, to both knees, as if he was begging. "You can save me, Aislynn. Please."

Aislynn knelt, too, not caring that the dirt and grass would stain her beautiful dress. She understood why her father had chosen him as her suitor. His situation was just as desperate as hers.

His eyes were so hopeful, his face so handsome—and for

a moment, Aislynn thought that she might submit.

"No," she said finally, taking off his jacket and handing it back to him. He stared at it, his body as limp as a doll that had lost its stuffing.

"What am I going to do?" he asked.

Aislynn had no answer.

"If only we could have loved each other, it would have fixed everything." He laughed without humor and got to his feet, slipping his jacket on. "It would have fixed everything." He didn't even bother with a bow before he left, his shoulders slumped and head low. The gate slammed behind him.

And Aislynn was alone.

Chapter 29

Far away, the clock struck midnight. Aislynn sat back on the grass heavily, her enormous gown billowing up around her. What had she done?

Get up, she ordered herself. Get up, you stupid, foolish girl and chase after him. Fall at his feet and beg him to forgive you, beg him to marry you, beg him to save you.

But she couldn't. She couldn't pull herself from the dirt, couldn't make herself go after him.

At that moment she envied Linnea's obedience. Her unwavering devotion to the Path.

Aislynn tugged at her locket, hating the heart that beat beneath it and hating the thought of losing it again.

Maybe it was better this way. Better to forget her family, forget Linnea and Brigid and Ford and Thackery. Thackery. She was overwhelmed with regret, the feeling sharp and raw. What would it have felt like to kiss him like this, completely whole?

Now she'd never know.

Aislynn drew her knees up to her chin and lifted her eyes to the moon. It stared down at her, pale and round and silent. As if it knew. Knew that she didn't deserve the second chance she had been given. Knew that she deserved to be shipped off to the Western Kingdom.

Her shiver wasn't from the cold. Who could tell what waited for her beyond the Western borders? Every season brought more royal refugees escaping from the rapidly expanding Midlands, and surely nothing could be more tempting to the Wicked Queen than a failed fairy godmother sent practically to her doorstep.

Brushing off her dress, Aislynn stood. She would not let herself get hysterical. Surely the advisers knew something she did not. They would never willingly put her in danger. Would they?

She should return to the party. But before she could move, Aislynn heard footsteps coming toward the garden, and she stilled. She began to catch snippets of a conversation. One of the voices was barely audible, the other painfully clear.

"If only I had been given a little more time," Madame Moira was saying, her voice half annoyed, half begging. "She's been trouble since the day she arrived. I'll be glad to be rid of her."

The next part of the exchange was muffled, the voice too quiet to make out. "The parents always make a fuss when they disappear," said Madame Moira.

Fear pressed against Aislynn's chest, and she could feel her pulse ticking in her neck. She no longer wanted to hear the rest of the conversation. Slowly, quietly she got to her feet.

"Make sure to take a souvenir. Sometimes it's the only way to convince them that their daughter isn't coming back. A lock of hair will do." The headmistress let out a low chuckle. "Or a toe."

Aislynn took a step back. And another.

Then, before she could move any farther, someone reached out of the darkness behind her and slid a hand over her lips.

Chapter 30

Aislynn tried to scream, but the sound was muffled by the leather glove pressing against her mouth. She felt a warm breath on her cheek and started to struggle.

"Shhh," Ford whispered.

Aislynn stilled, and he let go. She spun around to face him, her heart racing. What was he doing here?

"Did you hear something?" Madame Moira asked. It sounded as though she was just a few yards away.

Taking her hand, Ford pointed to the other side of the garden, where Aislynn could make out the shape of another gate. This one was open.

"Go!" he urged hoarsely.

Gathering her skirts in her hands, Aislynn rushed toward it, Ford close on her heels. Her dress caught on the latch, but she freed herself with one sharp yank and tumbled out of the garden doorway onto a dusty path. Scrambling to her feet, she glanced frantically around. They were surrounded by hedges.

"This way." Ford pointed to a break in the foliage.

Aislynn could hear the headmistress in the garden. "Is someone there?"

Stumbling on the uneven ground, Aislynn's feet slid painfully in her too-tight shoes, but she did not slow. Ford's breath and his footsteps were heavy behind her as they raced through the hedge maze.

Suddenly it ended. Aislynn skittered to a stop at the edge of a road. There was the forest, dark and waiting. "You just be careful of the woods," Aislynn remembered Ford telling Thackery once. "They're dangerous." That night seemed so long ago.

Ford's footsteps came crashing behind her. "Don't stop!" he wheezed.

Heels clicking on the stone road, Aislynn sprinted into the trees, the darkness swallowing her immediately.

Her feet hit the forest floor, breaking through the twigs and leaves that were strewn across the ground. The faraway sounds of the party, of the world, faded as she ran. Every muscle burned, and she was sure her feet were bleeding. Her corseted lungs screamed for air.

With dense branches above, there was hardly any moonlight now to guide her way, so she didn't see the thick tree trunk until it was too late. Aislynn slammed against the ground. It was muddy and slick. Spots swam in front of her eyes as if someone had boxed her ears, and she struggled to pull herself up, her hands and knees unsteady.

Somewhere behind her, a branch snapped. Footsteps. "Ford?" she whispered, still out of breath. The footsteps came closer and faster.

Suddenly a hooded figure burst through the trees in front of her. Aislynn scrambled backward, her hands and knees slipping in the muck.

"Where is it?" The stranger yanked her to her feet. "Where is it? Where is the mirror?" he thundered.

Aislynn kicked him. His grip loosened, but before she could pull away, his other hand was around her throat.

"Don't try to run," he hissed, his hood and the dark masking his features. Tangling his fingers in her necklace, he gave it a yank, and the delicate chain broke. When he held it up to examine it, Aislynn saw that he was wearing a large silver ring. A silver ring with a white stone. It began to glow.

"Where's the mirror?" Westerly demanded, his hand on her neck tightening.

Her magic gave a strange lurch, as if it was being pulled from inside her. As if there was a hand sliding up through her ribs, stripping the magic away from her very core. As if she was being turned inside out and scraped clean.

Then, suddenly, the feeling stopped. Aislynn dropped to the ground, gasping. Westerly was backing away from her, his hands raised. The ring was no longer glowing.

Something brushed against her arm.

A wolf was standing next to her. Aislynn jerked back, startled, but the animal didn't seem to notice. It snarled at Westerly, sharp white teeth gleaming.

It was the animal from her dreams. With a shaking hand, Aislynn reached out and touched its silvery fur. It was soft and warm. The wolf turned and gave her chin a gentle nudge.

With an angry cry, Westerly lunged toward them.

Aislynn's magic returned with a burning rush. She slammed her hand into the grass and from the ground burst a wall of fire, the power of it blowing Westerly off his feet. Through the flames, Aislynn saw him hit the forest floor several yards away. He did not get up.

Without hesitation, the smell of smoke and flame in her nose, Aislynn pulled herself to her feet and took off, deeper into the trees, the wolf racing beside her.

Chapter 31

Her legs were warm, but the rest of her was cold. The blanket must have slipped to the end of the bed, Aislynn thought hazily as she reached out for it. But instead of wool, her fingers found a soft, thick handful of fur.

Aislynn's eyes snapped open. The silver wolf was lying on her legs, and she was sitting up against a tree.

"Oi, you!" A girl's voice broke through her confused haze. "Get up!" There were two figures standing nearby, silhouetted by the sun.

Aislynn scrambled to her feet. Her first instinct was to bolt, but her knees buckled and she collapsed next to the wolf, which licked her face.

"Whoa there," a male voice said. He stepped forward but paused at the wolf's growl. "We're not going to hurt you," he said.

"Who are you?" Aislynn's voice was hoarse.

"Who are *you?*" asked the girl, stepping closer. She was around Aislynn's age, and like the boy, she had a blade at her side, a quiver of arrows across her back, and a bow in her hand. Their clothes, colorful and worn, indicated that they were peasants. The girl's dark hair was braided and pinned around the crown of her head, her face covered in freckles.

Kneeling down, the boy reached out to the wolf, which approached cautiously. Aislynn watched as she sniffed the extended hand and gave it a lick, her tail wagging.

"I was attacked," Aislynn said, the rest of the evening coming back to her in a painful jumble. The headmistress's threat. Ford. The glowing ring. Westerly's hand around her throat. The mirror.

The mirror . . .

Aislynn fumbled for the bag at her waist, but instead of the familiar curved edge, she felt only the soft crunch of paper.

"No," she whispered, her insides turning to ice. She and Linnea had never switched their bags back. The wolf let out a quiet whine. "No, no, no, no." Tears began to fill Aislynn's eyes. She was exhausted and everything hurt.

The boy and girl exchanged a nervous look.

"We can't leave her here," the boy said, but the girl looked unconvinced. He knelt down next to Aislynn. "What's your name?"

Tahlia had trusted her with that mirror, and Aislynn had left it behind. She touched a hand to her throat. The skin was raw. What would Westerly do if he discovered the mirror was with Linnea?

"Aislynn," she finally said. The boy's eyebrows shot up.

"Thackery's Aislynn?" he asked.

Somehow, despite the fear and exhaustion, Aislynn still managed to blush. "I—"

But he was already standing, wiping his hand on his trousers before offering it. "I'm Rhys," he said. "And this is Elanor."

Realization dawned on her. "You're Orphans, aren't you?" A tiny bit of hope blossomed in her chest.

Rhys nodded as he helped her off the ground. Every muscle in her body was in agony, and even though she couldn't see them beneath the ruined hem of her gown, she knew her feet were swollen and bleeding.

"What are we going to do with her?" Elanor whispered to Rhys. They both looked concerned. "She looks like she's about to collapse or go insane or both."

"We could take her to Muriel's," he suggested. "It's not too far."

Elanor glanced at Aislynn. "Can you walk?" she asked.

Gritting her teeth, Aislynn nodded. She wanted to be out of the forest as soon as possible.

The other girl narrowed her eyes suspiciously but didn't question her.

"Fine," she said. "Let's go."

Sunlight filtered through the orange and red leaves, creating a stained-glass canopy. Elanor led their small party, with Rhys bringing up the rear and Aislynn hobbling between them, the wolf at her side. Each step felt as if she was wearing red-hot irons on her feet, but she bit her lip and tried to keep up.

She had attempted to explain to Elanor and Rhys how she had ended up in the woods with a wolf and a torn ballgown, but they seemed unconvinced and confused. She didn't blame them. None of it made sense to her either.

Everything inside her felt numb. Why would Westerly want a hand mirror that Aislynn's fairy godmother had given her? How did he even know about it? Tahlia had told Aislynn to keep the mirror close, which meant it was important.

Which meant that Aislynn had to get it back.

The wolf gave her hand a gentle nudge, and Aislynn started. Looking down, she realized how pale those eyes were in the sunlight, and how the fur behind her ears was marked with streaks of carroty red. The wolf had saved her life last night. Her dreams had never shown her that. Had they ever been dreams, or were they something more?

The snap of a branch made her jump.

"Sorry." Rhys had come up behind her. He was holding out a hunk of cheese. "I thought you might need something to eat."

Aislynn realized that she hadn't eaten since yesterday. But as hungry as she was, and as good as the cheese smelled, it tasted like dust in her mouth.

Elanor was nowhere to be seen. "She's scouting ahead," Rhys said before she could ask. He stooped to feed the wolf a piece of cheese. "Does she have a name?"

"Cinnamon," Aislynn said, the name coming without hesitation.

"Cinnamon." Rhys gave the wolf a good scratch behind her carroty ears. Someone had broken the boy's nose. Not recently, but it looked crooked, in a familiar way. "You know"—he gave Aislynn a sideways glance—"Thackery described you perfectly. Minus the wolf, of course."

"Thackery." Aislynn blushed again. "Does he . . ." She

stopped, knowing that Rhys wouldn't have the answer to the question she really wanted to ask. "Is he okay?"

Rhys nodded, still kneeling to scratch Cinnamon. "Hasn't been his usual pleasant self since he returned to camp, but I bet that'll change soon," he said with a wink.

Suddenly Elanor appeared, her face serious, and the smile dropped from Rhys's lips. He stood.

"Any sign of them?" he asked, his tensed shoulders relaxing when Elanor shook her head.

"Best to keep moving, though," she said.

Once again Elanor took the lead, but instead of following behind her, Rhys matched Aislynn's labored stride. It was getting harder and harder for her to hide her limp.

"Here," he said, offering his arm. "M'lady." Even though his tone was playful, Aislynn could see that his smile was strained. Cinnamon padded silently behind them.

"Do you think we're being followed?" she finally asked.

A muscle in his jaw twitched. "It's nothing we can't handle," he said. The fear must have been evident on her face—Rhys's expression softened, and he patted her hand comfortingly. "Today's not the day we get captured by Josetta's huntsmen."

Elanor appeared in front of them. "We're almost there," she said.

With a nod, Rhys dropped Aislynn's hand and slipped off into the trees.

Elanor turned to Aislynn. "Follow me," she said, heading off in the opposite direction.

Her footsteps barely made a sound on the forest floor, and Aislynn did her best to walk quietly through the mud and leaves. She was so tired, and it almost seemed as though they were walking in circles.

Suddenly the trees ended and a huge mountain towered over them. Nestled at its foot, between a craggy cliff and a grove of trees, was a cheery yellow house. Rhys was standing on the porch, and Cinnamon raced to join him.

"How did he—" Aislynn was confused.

"He cleared our tracks while we took a detour," Elanor explained as they climbed the cottage steps. She rapped sharply on the door.

"Muriel?" Rhys called. "It's us. And we have a guest."

The door opened, and out stepped a round, redheaded woman. She was followed by the scent of sugar and cinnamon and flour. Bookbinder bread, Aislynn thought . . . just before everything went dark.

Chapter 32

When Aislynn came to, she was sitting in a soft chair with a blanket over her lap and a bundle of herbs under her nose. She coughed and pushed the lavender away.

"You gave us quite the scare," the redheaded woman said, handing Aislynn a plate. "Eat this."

It was the bread Aislynn had smelled before she fainted. Her stomach growled, and this time, when she took a bite, she tasted every crystal of sugar, every dollop of butter. It was like bookbinder bread, but different somehow, the recipe just slightly altered. The redheaded woman smiled, the expression adding wrinkles to her already creased face. She was short and swathed in delicate, colorful scarves. Muriel.

Aislynn glanced around the small cottage. The walls were painted a quiet blue, and they curved up toward one another, meeting in a dome in the ceiling, which had exposed beams of gnarled, well-worn wood. A stone fireplace, crackling and popping with a cheery fire, took up most of one wall, with a door on either side of it. There was a kitchen visible through an open archway, and Aislynn caught a glimpse of a small stove and wooden counters, sparkling clean. Hanging from the two windows in the front were beautiful, glittering glass shards, which threw colored light across the wooden floor. Resting on Aislynn's lap was an old quilt, pieced together out of yellow and gray squares, soft underneath her fingers. The scent of spicy herbs and flowers drifted through an open window, and Aislynn thought that if she closed her eyes she could sleep for days.

Rhys and Elanor were sharing a bench against the wall, each devouring their own plate of bread. Cinnamon curled up at Aislynn's feet, and she fed the wolf a piece. Next to the fire was a small chair, where Muriel had perched.

"So tell me, Aislynn, what brings you to my cottage today?"

The question caught Aislynn by surprise. She glanced at Rhys and Elanor. Had they not told Muriel what had happened?

"You were kind of babbling the first time," Elanor said. "We only got bits and pieces."

"I think you need to tell us again," Rhys added gently.

And so Aislynn did. Slowly this time, and starting at the beginning, she told them about her Redirection and how she had been sent to Elderwood to become a fairy godmother to Linnea. She told them how she had met Thackery and Brigid and Ford and how the monarch princess had become engaged to Westerly. She told them about Maris's disappearance and Josetta's army, about the headmistress, and the mirror and Westerly's attempt to take it from her. Her words were a waterfall, and when she was finished, she felt wrung dry.

For a moment no one said a word.

"A grown man strangling a maiden? Sounds like a royal to me." Rhys glanced up at Aislynn. "No offense."

"He didn't just strangle me. He . . ." She searched for the words to describe how she had felt when he attacked her—as if her magic was being pried from her bones. "It was like he was pulling the magic from inside me."

"That's impossible," said Elanor, her arms crossed.

"Shush, Elanor," Muriel chided her. "Let her speak."

"I don't know how he did it," said Aislynn, holding a hand to her head, which had begun to ache.

It didn't matter. All that mattered was getting the mirror back. It was important and dangerous and Tahlia had entrusted it to her. Aislynn could not leave it with Linnea. She took a deep breath. "I have to go back."

Chapter 33

"I'm sorry?" Elanor sputtered, a look of disbelief plastered across her face. "You've just told us that you were attacked in the forest by a lunatic royal who tried to"—she shuddered—"rip magic from your bones, and now you want to go back?"

"I *need* to go back," Aislynn corrected. There was no time to be annoyed that Elanor didn't believe her. She knew what she had to do. "The mirror is my responsibility."

Suddenly Muriel, who had gotten up to clear away the dishes, collapsed against the doorway, her face white as parchment. Rhys darted up from his seat to grab her before she fell to the floor.

"I think you need to lie down for a moment," Rhys said gently, leading her to the bedroom.

Muriel looked confused, as if she didn't recognize him. Then she nodded. "Yes, I think you're right, Dominick."

"That's Rhys," said Elanor, but Muriel didn't seem to hear her. The two girls sat in silence until Rhys returned, shutting the door behind him.

"She's resting," he said as he settled back on the bench. He looked at Aislynn. "She has a tendency to act strange on occasion. Forgets where she is, forgets who you are. It always passes, though. Do you know who Dominick is?" he asked Elanor, who shook her head.

"She called me Lia once." From the floor, Cinnamon let out a low whine.

"Who's Lia?" Aislynn asked.

Elanor shrugged. "I don't know. Muriel had a life before she came to these woods, a life that she won't talk about. I try not to pry. Everyone has things they'd prefer not to remember." Elanor let out a huff of breath. "Now, let's discuss your foolish mission."

"It's not—"

"There are other things happening in these woods and in the places beyond them that are far more important," Elanor said. "We can't just drop everything to help you retrieve a mirror that you think is special."

"You needn't bother yourself with my foolish mission," Aislynn snapped. "I'm not asking for your help."

"Well, we're offering it," said Rhys, sending a glare in Elanor's direction. "The woods are dangerous." He let out a deep sigh. "That fancy gown of yours is not the first we've seen out here. It's just the first we've seen with someone still in it."

For a moment, Aislynn didn't understand. Then she glanced down at the tattered remains of her dress and shivered. "I still have to go," she said stubbornly.

"First let us go back to camp and send word to Ford. See if he learned anything else that evening."

If he got away, thought Aislynn regretfully, but she remained quiet as Rhys continued. "Elanor is right—there is a lot of danger and dissent brewing, especially throughout the Midlands. It's not safe to try to do this alone. We'll do what we can to help."

"Thank you," said Aislynn.

"All for a stupid mirror," said Elanor, but her voice had lost its contempt.

"It's not just a mirror—"

"Whatever." Elanor threw the word over her shoulder like a handful of salt as she headed into the kitchen.

Rhys lingered a moment. "Just . . . just think about what you're doing," he said. "There are some things you can never return from. Some things you can never undo."

Aislynn nodded. She was beginning to learn all about the kinds of decisions you couldn't undo.

Chapter 34

Vines had grown over the windows, blocking out the light. Aislynn's nose was filled with dust; the floor and furniture were covered in it. Dead leaves crunched under her bare feet as she wandered the halls of her parents' home.

It was silent, as if everyone was asleep. Even the fireplace was slumbering and filled with nothing but ash.

"Mama? Papa?" Aislynn called out, but she heard only echoes. Suddenly the front door burst open, carrying with it a cold wind and a whisper. "Come home," it said. "Come home."

Aislynn woke in a strange bed in a strange nightgown. It took her a moment to remember where she was and how she had arrived there. Pulling the blankets back, she swung her feet off the bed. When they touched the floor, she realized with a start that they no longer hurt. She straightened her legs to look at them, expecting swelling and sores from the previous day, but they were completely healed.

Her ruined ballgown was gone, but there was a pile of cotton dresses next to the bed. The smell of porridge came wafting through the bedroom door, and Aislynn hastily dressed.

Muriel was alone in the kitchen, making breakfast.

"They left early this morning," she said when Aislynn asked where Rhys and Elanor were. Even though she knew they had planned on departing as soon as possible, Aislynn was still disappointed that she had been left behind so quickly.

She did her best to keep busy. She weeded the garden, swept the house, and washed the dishes. Then she dusted the bookcases, cleaned out the fireplace, and swept the floor again—anything to keep from thinking.

Part of her agreed with Elanor, that it was foolish to risk so much for something she knew so little about. There was a part of her that wanted to stay hidden in this little house forever, her past forgotten, her future unknown.

But the mirror was *her* burden, not Linnea's, and Aislynn could not leave such a dangerous item in the monarch princess's hands. Besides, Tahlia had trusted her to keep it safe. She wouldn't let her fairy godmother down.

As she cleaned the windows, Aislynn could hear Muriel in the kitchen, talking to herself. Or, more accurately, talking to Cinnamon. Though Muriel had been kind and welcoming to Aislynn, it seemed that she preferred the company of the wolf. She even directed questions at the animal, clearly expecting answers.

"I always measure twice," she was saying as Aislynn peeked into the kitchen to see her pouring a perfectly even cup of flour back into the bag before spooning it out exactly as she had done before. "And make sure your herbs are fresh." Cinnamon, lying on the floor with her head on her front paws, whined. "I know you prefer dried herbs, but in this case you're simply incorrect."

Aislynn smiled when Cinnamon let out a sharp bark. "Mother always said sweet bread was for when your life was bitter and savory bread was for when your life was bland," said Muriel, checking the oven. Wiping her floury hands on her skirt, she smiled down at Cinnamon. "Though your life is hardly dull these days, is it?"

Feeling as if she was intruding on a private conversation, Aislynn quietly slipped away from the kitchen and out onto the front steps. The sun was just disappearing behind the dense grove of trees, and the sky was smeared with red and orange.

Settling onto the warped wooden step, Aislynn stared out at the forest. The wind kicked the fallen autumn leaves, blowing them up into her face and hair, but still she didn't go back inside. She felt so useless. Useless and helpless.

Adviser Hull had always praised her mother for her strength, reminding Aislynn that "While all women are wicked, not all are weak." To Adviser Hull, the queen was the ideal royal woman, pure and unwavering in her loyalty to the Path. Yet she had secrets and scars just as Aislynn did.

The more she learned about herself, about her mother, and about Linnea, the more Aislynn doubted that such an ideal woman existed.

Cinnamon nudged the door open and settled on the stoop, resting her chin on Aislynn's lap. It was growing cold; the sun was completely gone, and stars beginning to appear above. Aislynn shivered in her borrowed dress. It was worn thin, with neatly stitched patches along the elbows, the seams thick with mending. And though she was grateful for it, Aislynn couldn't help wishing the sleeves were a little longer or the fabric were something other than an itchy beanstalk green.

It was a silly thing to think about, but as Aislynn rubbed Cinnamon's head, she imagined the kind of dress she'd choose if she had a choice. It wouldn't be blue or purple. It wouldn't need a corset or a wimple. No, what she wanted was a dress the color of Thackery's eyes, one that was soft and warm and fit her perfectly. She wished.

Like a morning glory opening its face to the sky, her magic revealed itself, strong and steady. At first she wanted to push it away, to swallow it down, but she closed her eyes and forced herself to relax. To let it wash over her. The air crackled and warmed around her. She felt at peace, clear-headed and new as if she had slept for days. Opening her eyes, she found that the sturdily patched dress had been replaced by soft linen in the deepest green. She spread her arms wide. The sleeves now draped past her wrists, and the waist nipped in around her ribs and hips. Standing, much to Cinnamon's annoyance, she discovered that the skirt skimmed the ground perfectly, and that embroidered along the hem was a curling vine with tiny thorns. Twirling, she ended up facing the door of the cottage, where Muriel was now standing.

"Impressive," she said, and this time she was not speaking to Cinnamon.

"Thank you."

"You have quite the natural ability."

"It doesn't usually do what I want," Aislynn said, and Muriel smiled.

"Yes, there is that tendency, isn't there? You just need practice. And a good teacher." With a sigh, Muriel looked up at the stars now filling the sky. "But those days are gone."

"Those days?" asked Aislynn.

"Maybe things will change," Muriel said to Cinnamon, who whined and tilted her head. "I know, I know, they don't just change on their own. But maybe . . ." She looked at Aislynn. "Maybe they'll be strong enough."

"Who? And strong enough for what?"

But Muriel had already entered the cottage and closed the door, leaving Aislynn and her unanswered questions outside in the autumn night.

Chapter 35

Elanor and Rhys returned early the next morning. Their arguing reached the cottage before they did. Aislynn was in the kitchen, cooking breakfast, her hands and apron covered in flour, when their voices floated in through the window.

"I don't like the plan," Elanor was saying.

"Then make it better," said Rhys, and Aislynn could practically hear Elanor glare.

"I would if I could," she retorted, "but we don't have the time."

"It's too dangerous."

Brigid! Racing to the door, Aislynn flung it open. Four

pairs of tired eyes looked up at her. "She's braver than you think," said Thackery with a smile.

Aislynn's heart somersaulted into her throat.

"Hello," he said.

Aislynn wanted to throw herself into his arms, but before she could do or say anything, Brigid grabbed her and started weeping.

"Ford's dead," she whispered, and everything inside Aislynn stopped.

"What . . . what happened?" she asked. The words felt as if they were coming from someone else.

"Let's go inside," Rhys said gently, leading Brigid up the steps.

Muriel was waiting with hot cups of tea and a tray of bookbinder bread, as if she had been expecting them. Brigid was helped to the overstuffed chair, while Aislynn joined Thackery on the bench. Rhys hitched his shoulder up against the wall, and Elanor paced in the doorway. No one ate.

"They found him halfway down the road." Everyone in the room jumped as Elanor threw her fist into the wall. "Stabbed in the heart and wrapped in briars." Elanor hit the wall again. Aislynn could see the blood on her knuckles.

"Josetta must have been sending a message," said Aislynn, swallowing her guilt. "That's her signature."

"It wasn't Josetta," Elanor's voice was flat.

"Josetta would have taken him back to the Midlands," said Thackery softly, running a finger over his own knuckles. "She would have made an example out of him and shown her people what she does to those who run away."

"But the brambles—"

"The brambles?" Rhys sounded confused.

"It's what Josetta does," insisted Aislynn. "She marks her victims with briars from her forest. Like she did with Maris's shoe. . . ." But as Elanor and Rhys continued to look at her with the same doubting expression, Aislynn realized that they didn't think Josetta was involved at all.

"The royals do believe that," said Brigid, her eyes red but dry. "They also believe that Josetta is responsible for any girl who strays from the Path."

"She recruits them to be a part of her army," said Aislynn lamely. She felt so foolish.

"There is no army," said Rhys. "Not that kind, at least."

"Josetta fears outsiders," Elanor interjected. "After her husband was killed, she barricaded herself in a tower of her castle where only her most trusted subjects can go. None of us have seen her in years. She'd never allow royals inside the palace, let alone recruit them." Tracing an imaginary pattern on the wall, Elanor shrugged. "And if there were maidens emerging from the forest to serve her, trust me, I'd know."

Horror rattled through Aislynn. Maris wasn't the first girl to be dismissed as a stray, and it seemed unlikely that she would be the last. "Then where did they all go?"

There was no answer.

If Josetta wasn't behind this, then who was going to the trouble of convincing others that she was? And what were they doing to the girls that everyone believed had strayed?

Aislynn remembered the conversation she had overheard in the garden. She had thought once before that Madame Moira might have been working with Josetta, but if the Wicked Queen wasn't to blame, how did the headmistress fit in? And why was Westerly involved? None of it made sense.

"It could be connected to the mirror," said Brigid, but even she seemed doubtful. "But until we know more, the only thing we can do is help you get it back."

"What about Linnea? Has there been any new information about her?"

"She'll be married next week," said Brigid softly, and Aislynn shuddered. She couldn't just leave the monarch princess at the mercy of someone like Westerly. Linnea had no idea how dangerous he was.

It wasn't until Thackery gently uncurled her fingers that

Aislynn realized she was clenching her fists. Half moons from her nails marked her palms.

"Well," she said with false confidence, "I guess I should leave right away."

"We," Thackery corrected, linking his fingers with hers. His hand was surprisingly soft, but strong and warm. "*We* should leave right away."

"No." Aislynn rose. "I can't ask you to help me."

"So don't ask." Thackery stood as well, his hand still entwined with hers.

"You've helped us," Brigid reminded her. "Let us return the favor."

"Don't go." The plea came from Muriel, who was standing in the doorway to the kitchen. Her skin was as white as milk. "Bad things are coming."

"Come on, Muriel." Rhys placed his arms around her shoulders. "I think that's enough excitement for today." Her head bobbing like a child's toy, she allowed herself to be led from the room.

It wasn't until Rhys returned that Elanor leaned toward Aislynn and said, "Thackery says you're braver than we think. Are you?"

Chapter 36

Rhys unrolled a map along the floor. It was far more detailed than the map Aislynn had seen at Nerine Academy—the Midlands and Josetta's castle were both clearly labeled. Kneeling on the floor next to him, Aislynn studied it closely.

Rhys pointed to a spot near the border of the Eastern and Northern Kingdoms. "That's where we are." He then dragged his finger to Erysimum, in the Eastern Kingdom. "That's where Linnea will be in a month."

Brigid nodded. "She'll be attending the winter ball there."

"And why can't we just go to her home?" Elanor asked.

"She's a monarch princess," Aislynn explained. "The palace in Eremurus will be well guarded, with her fairy godmother, adviser, and Westerly all watching her carefully."

"A ball is not as carefully protected," Brigid added. "There's a greater chance she'll be able to sneak away, if only for a moment."

Aislynn looked at the map. She found Nepeta and, without thinking, placed her fingers over it. Her parents. They must be heartbroken, convinced she had strayed. Her own heart ached thinking about it.

"What's there?" Thackery asked, kneeling down next to her.

"Nothing important," she said, pulling her hand away. Shaking her head, she tried to focus her attention on the distance between Muriel's home and Erysimum. A week? Maybe two?

But Thackery persisted. "Your home?"

"It was," she admitted, thinking of all the afternoons she had spent in the garden with her father, walking with him as he identified roses for her. Or sitting in the bedroom as her mother got dressed, hoping that one day she would be just as graceful. Or those mornings with Tahlia, covered in flour, safe in the warmth of the kitchen.

"Come home . . ." came a whisper from the back of her mind. "Come home." Aislynn's dream returned to her. The overgrown windows, the dusty floors, the sleeping palace.

Cinnamon was curled up in front of the fire. What if this dream was like the others? Not truly a dream, but a premonition. A command.

Suddenly it was very clear. She was supposed to go home.

"I should go to Nepeta," said Aislynn.

The others, who had been engaged in a conversation of their own, paused to stare at her.

"Why would we do that?" asked Elanor, looking down at the map. "That would add at least two days to the journey, maybe more."

"It's her home," said Thackery, but Aislynn shook her head.

"No. I mean, it is." Aislynn could still smell the dust on the furniture, could still feel the wind through the house, could still hear the whispers. "But I think I'm supposed to go there."

If her parents allowed her inside. Aislynn tried to imagine what they would think when they saw her. She was a stray. They were no longer allowed to acknowledge her at all.

"From Nepeta, we could get to Erysimum in a day," Brigid pointed out. "Less if we found some horses."

"Fine!" Elanor threw up her hands. "Make the trip longer. Linnea is your concern, not mine. I still don't know how we're going to get Aislynn into the ball undetected."

"I don't have to go inside," said Aislynn. "I just have to get to the balcony without anyone seeing me." She swallowed, wishing she could forget the feeling of Westerly's hand around her throat. "And find a way to get Linnea outside." For the first time, a terrible thought crossed her mind. "How can we make sure she brings the mirror?" Surely Linnea would have discovered the mirror by now, and she would have no reason to bring it to the ball. Hopefully she had hidden it away in a drawer somewhere, maybe even forgotten about it.

"I can take care of that," offered Brigid. Her hands were crossed in her lap primly.

"How?" asked Elanor.

"I'll send her a letter." Her easy solution drew blank stares from everyone.

"What if Westerly finds it?" asked Aislynn.

"It won't be the first letter that Linnea has hidden from him," said Brigid drily. "I know how to be discreet."

Elanor cleared her throat. "So you'll make sure she knows to be on the balcony with the mirror?"

"I can't guarantee that she'll be there." Brigid turned to Aislynn. "But I can ask."

No doubt the monarch princess had been informed that Aislynn had strayed. There was no way to know how she'd react to Brigid's request. Aislynn wanted to hope that she would help, but she also remembered how Linnea had reacted when Aislynn suggested that she go against Adviser Lennard's order to give her father's ring to Westerly. Linnea might be unwilling to help a stray, even one who had once been a friend.

Chapter 37

The straps of her pack dug into her shoulders. Aislynn tried to adjust it but did not complain. Everything on her back was necessary: enough food and water for the journey, something to sleep on, and several extra handkerchiefs. All the others were carrying similar bags, as well as their weapons, and no one else seemed bothered by the load. Shifting awkwardly, she struggled to find a comfortable place for it to rest against her body.

"Would you like some help?" asked Brigid as she approached with Elanor.

Aislynn nodded, and Elanor slid her fingers under the straps of Aislynn's bag. She winced at the weight.

"I think she overpacked," she said to Brigid.

"Just think of feathers," Brigid replied.

Elanor rolled her eyes, then squeezed them shut, her forehead wrinkled with concentration. Nothing happened, and Elanor let out a snort of frustration. Aislynn watched with confusion as Elanor shook out her arms and rolled her head from side to side before placing her hands on Aislynn's shoulders again. There was a soft hum of magic, barely perceptible. It pulsed a few times before settling around Aislynn. All of a sudden, the weight of the bag was gone.

Looking over her shoulder, Aislynn half expected her pack to have disappeared. But it was still there, still piled high, only now she could barely feel it. It weighed as much as a light coat.

She let out a sigh of relief. "Thank you."

"Mm-hmm." Elanor waved off the gratitude and walked away.

"She can make a sword out of shackles and shoot a date out of a bird's mouth, but, well . . ." Brigid sighed. "Magic's different for everyone. I would have done it myself, but I'm a little limited these days." She studied the marks around her wrists wistfully.

"Can the custody spell be undone?" asked Aislynn, watching Thackery kneel to pet Cinnamon. He smiled when the wolf licked his face.

"It can, but it's not easy. Far beyond Elanor's abilities. And yours," Brigid quickly added.

"Are we ready?" Elanor called out. "We should leave before the sun gets too high." She looked regretfully back at the cottage.

From the porch, Muriel had been watching the preparations in a panic, running her wrinkled hands through her hair and creating a wild red halo around her head. She was muttering and pacing back and forth on the squeaking steps, her eyes never leaving the small party.

"It's not safe," she said. "It's not safe out there."

Cinnamon gave a low, mournful howl, as if she agreed. Elanor had prepared Aislynn for this moment, warning her that no matter how many times people came and went from Muriel's home, she was always convinced they would never return. Today that fear seemed very much alive in her. When Aislynn approached to say good-bye, Muriel latched her surprisingly strong fingers onto Aislynn's arm and refused to let go.

Then Cinnamon trotted over, and Muriel's grip loosened. "Wondrous things, aren't they?" Her eyes seemed to focus for a moment as she stared down at the wolf, which cocked her head and stared right back. "Just as feared as we are."

"Don't worry about us, Muriel," said Aislynn. "We'll be all right."

Muriel knelt down, her hands flat on the step. "You remember, don't you?" she whispered to Cinnamon as the wolf let out another soft whine. "We trusted them, and they took everything. Took it all." Struggling to her feet, she gave the wolf a final pat and, without saying another word, walked back into the cottage.

After two days of trekking through the thick, rambling forest, Aislynn realized exactly how foolish it would have been to undertake this journey on her own. She would have been hopelessly lost in an hour. Thackery, Rhys, Brigid, and Elanor took turns navigating, and Aislynn was endlessly grateful that they had agreed to help her. It was clear that Thackery had needed to convince the others, especially Elanor, who wore her distrust like a badge. Aislynn couldn't blame her.

Her thoughts turned to the mirror. What had Tahlia given her? Aislynn knew Tahlia loved her and wouldn't deliberately put her in harm's way, but she couldn't help feeling anxious that she knew so little about what she was meant to protect.

Finally Elanor called for a halt in a small clearing, and Aislynn happily slipped off her pack. It may not have been heavier than a coat, but it was still more than she was used to carrying.

"Spun straw for your thoughts," said Thackery, coming up behind her. Aislynn jumped.

"Sorry." There was a sheepish smile offered along with his apology.

She managed a small smile of her own, her palms suddenly damp. "I'm sorry to have pulled you into my troubles," she said.

"I didn't have anything better to do," he joked. "Besides, I like your troubles." Giving a strand of her hair a tug, he caught her eyes and held them. "I do."

Rhys let out a laugh at the other end of the clearing, startling them both. Thackery dropped his hand.

"Elanor wants us to come back to the mountains when we've found your mirror," he said.

"Is that where you were after you left Elderwood?" Aislynn asked.

Thackery nodded. "Brigid and I were going to start looking for a new academy to use as a safe house. Someplace where we could hide those who are escaping Josetta." He looked ahead at Elanor, who was examining the map with Rhys. "But Elanor says she needs us at camp for now. She's convinced a war is coming." He smiled. "Rhys is convinced she's trying to start it."

"What's in the mountains?"

"It's where the main Orphan camp is. It's where Elanor and Rhys are headed—once they leave us. They'll continue through the Northern Kingdom and eventually reach the base of the Midland Mountains. Follow that, and you'll find our home." He grinned. "Well, you won't exactly find it, but the chances are someone will find you. Better hope it's the Orphans and not Josetta's huntsmen."

"You consider that your home?"

"I was born there. My mother." Thackery plucked a smooth rock from the ground. "She fought in the First Rebellion." He heaved the stone into the trees, and Aislynn could hear it breaking through the bare branches as it fell. "Died in it, too."

"What was she like?"

Rubbing the back of his neck, Thackery shrugged. "I don't really remember her. I was only a kid when she died. Those who survived like to tell me how brave and clever she was." He smiled. "Kind of like you, I bet."

Aislynn blushed and looked away. "And your father?"

"Died before I was born." He took a deep breath. "Must be awful to die that way. Not knowing if you made any difference." Picking up another rock, he weighed it in his palm. "The one thing I remember about my mother is how she made rainbows, even in the dark." Holding the stone between his fingers, he held it up to the light. "We had all these pieces of glass, like the ones in Muriel's house, hanging in the windows. I remember our house being full of rainbows, even when we had the shutters closed. I later realized that she had been using magic to make the glass sparkle, but when I was little, it just felt like it was a part of my mother, like she was made of light and color."

He tossed the smooth stone up in the air, but before it could land in his palm, Aislynn caught it. The magic inside her had built to a simmer, tapping against her heart. She watched as the slate-gray stone in her hand was replaced by crystal.

The trees around them rustled and shifted, branches parting to let the sunlight in. Beams of light broke through the foliage and bounced off the crystal in Aislynn's palm, reflecting brilliant rainbows all around them. She looked up through the sparkling colors and found Thackery staring at her with such intensity that it nearly knocked her off her feet.

Elanor's furious voice burst through the clearing.

"What are you doing?" she demanded.

Aislynn dropped the stone. It landed in the dirt, once again gray and smooth.

"Are you mad?" Elanor fumed. "Why don't you just send out a warning flare telling everyone where we are?"

Suddenly Cinnamon began to howl.

Chapter 38

The wolf's howl was both mournful and chilling. Everyone froze except Aislynn, who darted forward and wrapped her arms around Cinnamon's shaggy neck.

Elanor stalked toward them. "You need to quiet that animal before someone—" She stumbled back, hand flying to the arrow that seemed to have grown from her shoulder.

"Ellie!" Rhys ran forward, catching her before she hit the ground. She shook him off, gritted her teeth, and snapped the wooden shaft in half.

"I hate it when you call me that!" Elanor grabbed her bow and struggled to her feet as a dozen soldiers crashed through the trees in front of them and into the clearing.

Elanor let loose an arrow, hitting their archer. He fell forward at Aislynn's feet, dead. The soldier behind him charged with his sword raised.

Before she could even scream, a pair of strong hands grabbed Aislynn's shoulders and pushed her aside. She hit the ground, hard. In an instant Thackery was standing over a second lifeless body, bloodstained sword at his side.

He didn't see the ax that was headed straight for his head.

"Thackery!" Aislynn cried, throwing her hand up as magic surged through her. The deadly weapon froze in midair and quivered there as if unsure where to go next. Then, with a jolt, it shot backward, plunging into the chest of the man who had thrown it. He crumpled to the ground.

Pain ripped through Aislynn. She clutched at her chest, expecting to find a dagger or sword there, as it felt as if she had been run through. But there was nothing. No injury, no wound. And just as quickly as the pain had arrived, it disappeared.

Aislynn struggled to her feet, slipping on the wet grass. A hand reached out to help her.

"That's what happens when you use magic to kill someone," Elanor said, hoisting her off the ground. "It's why I prefer an arrow."

The skirmish was over, and the clearing was littered with

uniformed bodies. As everything came into focus, Aislynn was shocked to realize that some of them were women, all wearing matching crests on their chests: a dark circle with a shield in its center. Identical to the mark on Thackery's shoulder.

Brigid was cleaning a dagger while Elanor fended off Rhys's attempts to check the arrow still in her shoulder.

Aislynn stared down at the ax and the man it was buried in. He had very blond hair, and blue eyes opened wide in shock. A chill spread through her, and her knees began to shake. This was her doing. He had been alive a few minutes ago, and now he was dead because of her. She raised her hands, expecting to find her palms blackened or bloody, but aside from a few smears of dirt, they looked exactly as they always did. She felt sick. With frantic swipes, she rubbed her hands against her hips, trying desperately to cleanse them. A gentle hand settled on her shoulder.

Thackery.

She turned and, without hesitation, wrapped her arms around him and held him tight. She could feel his heartbeat against her cheek as he squeezed her back.

"Is everyone all right?" asked Rhys.

He was rewarded with a series of muttered confirmations.

"Cinnamon?"

Pulling away from Thackery, Aislynn looked around for

the wolf. Her heart stopped. Then she heard a sharp bark, followed by the rustle of leaves. "Cinnamon!"

Bursting through the trees, the wolf bounded into the clearing, her tail wagging furiously. Aislynn dropped to her knees, pressing her face into the wolf's thick coat.

There was a piece of parchment between Cinnamon's teeth, and Aislynn removed it carefully. The others gathered around. Crudely drawn in ink were a series of portraits—Rhys and Elanor were there, as were Thackery and Brigid. And Ford. A sum of money was listed below the portraits, as a reward for their capture or death.

"Yet another unflattering artist's rendition," said Rhys. "My chin doesn't look like that, does it?" He tilted his head toward Elanor.

She snatched the paper away and scanned it quickly before tossing it aside. "They've never sent this many after us before," she said.

"They weren't looking for us," Thackery said. "They were looking for Aislynn. They came right at her."

"What?" Aislynn scrambled to her feet. "That's absurd. My likeness isn't included."

"They did attack you first." Rhys scratched at his chin.

"No." Aislynn gestured to Elanor. "They shot at her first."

"It doesn't matter," Elanor declared. "They're widening their search, that's all we need to know. I've never seen Josetta's huntsmen this far north before."

"Do you think something has happened?" Rhys adjusted the bandage wrapped around his head.

"Or is about to," said Elanor. Her expression was grim. "I can't go any farther with you, Aislynn."

"Elanor . . ."

"Josetta has a plan, Rhys," she snapped. "She would never risk so many huntsmen so far beyond her borders unless she's planning something. We need to find out what it is, and we need to find out now." Turning to the others, her glare softened, but only a bit. "You'll have to go on without me."

Rhys sighed. "And me."

Brigid and Thackery nodded, but Aislynn was concerned by how much blood was soaking through the dressing on Elanor's shoulder.

"Let me . . . maybe I could heal you—" Aislynn offered, to her own surprise. She reached out, but Elanor pushed her hand away with a painful grunt.

"I'll be fine," she said.

"We've seen far worse," Rhys said. With a hand to his own head, he managed a faint smile.

"You'll return to the mountains when you're done with

this . . . mission," Elanor said to Brigid and Thackery. It was more of a statement than a question. They nodded. "You're welcome to join, as well," she added gruffly, looking at Aislynn.

Aislynn hadn't thought about what she was going to do once she had retrieved the mirror. If she retrieved it. But before she could respond, Elanor had already grabbed her pack and stomped off into the woods.

"She likes you," said Rhys, and the bewildered look on Aislynn's face made him laugh. "No, it's true. You impressed her." His smile faded. "Not a lot of people do that." He pulled his pack onto his shoulders and gave a graceful bow before disappearing into the trees, headed west.

Chapter 39

Wanting to put the attack and the clearing full of bodies as far behind them as possible, Aislynn, Thackery, and Brigid headed north immediately. They kept to the safety of the trees, doing their best to avoid roads and other travelers. A trio of dusty servants looking for work might not draw suspicion, but Aislynn's unmarked wrists and the wolf traveling at her heels would.

The ambush had changed the mood and pace of their journey. They no longer stopped to eat, and they moved as silently and quickly as possible. They slept in brief shifts, their bedrolls in a triangle, and every night Aislynn dreamed of her home, asleep under dust and vines.

Each day brought them closer to Nepeta, and with each day Aislynn's fear grew. She wanted to believe that her parents would still open their door to her, but she couldn't shake the horrible doubt that clung to her like wood sap. There was no knowing what they had been told.

After a few days, the landscape began to look familiar. From the safety of the woods, Aislynn began to recognize buildings and landmarks from when she was a child, places she had seen when her parents had taken her on carriage rides.

And suddenly there it was. Castle Nepeta, its elaborate wrought-iron gates and cobblestone drive, with its tallest tower reaching up into the clouds.

They waited until dusk, Aislynn's nervousness vibrating in her fingertips. The last time she had been here, she had been drowning in her own tears.

"Please, Mama," she had begged. "Papa, please don't make me go. I'm sorry, I'm so sorry; I didn't mean to do it. I promise I'll never do it again." Even though she had no idea how she had been able to turn the books into ash, she knew that it had been horrible and wrong. "Please." The tears that slid down her mother's cheeks had only made Aislynn cry harder.

"It's time to go." Adviser Hull had gestured to Tahlia, who smoothed back Aislynn's hair and hugged her. Her embrace was warm, and Aislynn had stopped crying, but only for a moment. As soon as she realized that Tahlia was not getting into the carriage with her, she began weeping anew, her fingers scrambling for the carriage door. When she had realized that it was locked, her crying became a wail, the sound filling the courtyard. Adviser Hull had led her parents back into the castle as the carriage pulled away.

The setting sun painted the sky with orange and red. Aislynn waited until the color was gone, the world now gray and still, before she emerged from the forest, Thackery and Brigid following behind her. She was home again.

It was quiet, and it wasn't until they had passed through the open gates that Aislynn realized how strange that was. Where were all the servants?

A trickle of fear slid down her back, and unable to help herself, she broke into a run, Cinnamon at her heels.

There were no vines covering the windows, but the castle seemed as hushed and deserted as it had been in her dream. She lifted the heavy iron door knocker and held her breath. The sound it made when it fell resonated through her.

She was just about to try another entrance when she heard the soft patter of feet. Cinnamon's tail swished against the stone step.

The door swung open, but instead of a footman, it was her mother standing there. The queen gasped and pulled Aislynn into a fast, fierce hug.

"My dearest, my darling girl." Aislynn let herself be held as if she were still a child. When the queen finally pulled back, her eyes searched Aislynn's face, looking for answers to questions she had not yet asked. "Are you all right?" she finally said.

"Yes, Mama," Aislynn said. "I'm all right."

"Darling?" her father's voice came from inside the darkened receiving room. "I heard someone knocking. Who is it?"

"Hello, Papa," Aislynn said as he appeared behind her mother in the doorway.

His eyes met hers and didn't falter. "You're here," he said, sweeping her into his arms. A rumble of laughter rose in his chest as he held her tight. "You're here, and you're safe."

Chapter 40

The queen kept a tight grip on Aislynn as they all followed the king into the castle. Everything was covered with a thin layer of dust, though it was nowhere near the disarray Aislynn had seen in her dreams. But it was quiet, so very quiet.

The sound of Cinnamon's nails against the stone floor echoed in the foyer. If either of Aislynn's parents minded a wild animal entering their home, they made no mention of it. Aislynn could only imagine how surreal this experience must be for them, and she squeezed her mother's hand.

"Where is everyone?" she asked, now noticing how gaunt her parents had become.

"They've all gone," said the queen.

They followed the king into the library, where the furniture was also dusty and neglected. Cinnamon sneezed.

"I suspect we all have questions," said the king. "Please." He gestured for them all to sit.

Sharing nervous looks, Thackery and Brigid each took one of the two chairs by the window, while Aislynn's mother produced a small plate of cheese and stale bread. She offered the tray to Thackery, who hesitated.

"There's not much left," the queen said, clearly embarrassed.

Brigid quickly elbowed Thackery in the side. He took a slice of cheese, his face red.

"Thank you, Your Majesty," he said.

"Thank *you*," the king replied. "For bringing Aislynn to us."

Thackery nodded, his face still red, but some of the tension eased from the room.

Aislynn perched between her parents on the couch. She could feel Cinnamon's breath on her ankles as the wolf curled up at her feet.

"What happened that night?" the king finally asked and when Aislynn turned to him, she could see the dark circles under his eyes.

"We thought we'd never see you again," said her mother.

So Aislynn told her parents what had happened, careful

not to mention the incident in the forest where she had nearly been strangled or the ambush in the clearing. There was no need to upset them more. But when she finished, her mother started crying quietly.

"What happened to Everett?" her father asked, his voice unsteady.

"Everett?" Aislynn repeated, not understanding. "What do you mean?"

"He disappeared during the ball as well," said the king. "Adviser Hull told us that you had seduced him and convinced him to abandon his family and the Path."

Aislynn nearly choked on the bread she was chewing. Across the room, Thackery's eyebrows rose in surprise.

The king continued. "Adviser Hull demanded we offer our condolences to Everett's parents in their time of grief." He laughed harshly. "There was no grief. They were more concerned over the loss of one of their stable hands than they were with the disappearance of their only son."

"These condolences were in the form of servants and livery," the queen said quietly. "We were told that if we did not publicly denounce you as a stray, all commerce in our commonwealth would be sent to more deserving followers of the Path."

"You refused?" Aislynn asked, some pieces falling into place.

Her parents nodded.

"Everett's family has been given a manor in the county just to the west of us. They are gleefully profiting from our pain." Aislynn had never heard her mother sound so angry before.

"And a few days ago, this arrived." The king reached into his pocket and pulled out Aislynn's locket. The last time she had seen it was in Westerly's hand. "It was tangled in a briar," the king said.

Aislynn glanced at Thackery and Brigid. "Someone wanted you to believe that I was with Josetta," she said slowly, still not fully convinced that the Wicked Queen was not involved. "Mama, I need to look in Tahlia's room. To see if she left anything that could help us."

The queen nodded. "I'll go with you," she said, rising from the couch.

As Brigid and Thackery scrambled awkwardly to their feet, Aislynn realized that this whole situation must be as strange for the two of them as it was for her parents. And though the king and queen seemed as unmindful of Brigid and Thackery's status as they were of Cinnamon's presence, Aislynn imagined her friends could not help but feel uncomfortable and out of place.

Thackery stepped forward and bowed stiffly. "Your Majesty, if you'd like, I could chop more wood for the fireplace."

"And I could make supper," Brigid chimed in quickly. "Your Majesty," she added hastily, with a curtsy.

Aislynn's father shook his head. "Nonsense," he said. "You are guests in our home and will be treated as such."

"Maybe our guests would like to see the rest of the castle," Aislynn's mother suggested.

"That would be lovely," said Brigid, smiling as Aislynn's father offered her his arm.

"Come with me, young lady. Young sir." He gestured at Thackery, who looked beyond amused to be addressed in such a manner. Winking at Aislynn, he followed the king into the dining room.

"He seems very nice," said the queen.

Aislynn blushed. "He is," she said.

They climbed the stairs to Tahlia's room, Cinnamon padding quietly behind them.

Even though there was only one window and, like the rest of the castle, everything was dark and covered with dust, Tahlia's room felt cheery and warm. Instead of curtains, the window was decorated with hanging bundles of dried herbs. The bed was neatly made, with a pair of shoes still peeking out from beneath it. Pulling open the drawers, Aislynn was surprised to find them full. After frowning at herself in the mirror above the dresser, she began yanking the purple robes from the dresser, hoping to find something tucked in their folds. Cinnamon sniffed at the carpet.

"You were only ten when you did this." Aislynn's mother was staring at the opposite wall, where nearly a dozen stitching samples were carefully pinned. The queen was looking at an awkwardly embroidered square in particular.

Aislynn crossed the tiny room and looked over her mother's shoulder. In uneven letters, she had stitched A PURE HEART IS YOUR ONLY COMPASS.

"You loved that verse," the queen said.

The sampler was familiar to Aislynn. It was the first one she had completed, and she had been so proud to give it to Tahlia. How silly and amateurish it looked now.

She traced the words with her finger. It had all seemed so easy then. Just be good and pure, and everything would be fine. As if wanting to be something was the same as actually achieving it.

"Mama, you told me that Tahlia had disappeared once before," said Aislynn.

Her mother nodded and took a seat on the bed. "You were only three. One morning she was simply gone. Your grandmother sent my former fairy godmother to help—I didn't know how to take care of a child on my own."

Cinnamon, who had been curled up on the rug, rose and rested her furry chin on the queen's lap. To Aislynn's surprise, her mother began stroking the wolf's ears.

"When Adviser Hull came to visit, I expected he would request a new fairy godmother for me, but he didn't even notice she was gone. I don't think he's ever actually looked at Tahlia." Aislynn's mother frowned. "And when she returned, she was so distraught that I couldn't turn her away. You loved her so much."

The queen stood, and Cinnamon whined. "I will leave you to your search, darling," she said, lingering at the door. "Do you think Tahlia's in danger?" she asked, her forehead creased with worry.

Aislynn didn't want to lie to her. "I don't know," she said.

The queen nodded. "I'll check on the others," she said, leaving Aislynn alone with Cinnamon and a dresser full of abandoned robes.

Aislynn shook each uniform again, hoping she had missed something. She checked each pocket and found nothing. There was nothing under the bed, nothing in the bedside table, nothing behind the dresser. She lifted the mattress, pulled the bedding apart, and even checked behind each sampler. Nothing.

She was about to give up and head downstairs when Cinnamon began scratching at the dresser. Curious, Aislynn watched as the wolf leaned against the heavy wood, furiously pushing all her weight against it. Then she jumped up on her hind legs and pressed her front paws into the top drawer, causing the entire piece to fall back and hit the wall.

The impact shook the mirror free, and before Aislynn could grab it, it fell from its frame and shattered into a dozen jagged pieces.

"Cinnamon!" Aislynn scolded.

There was a note stuck in the now-empty frame.

Excitement charging through her, Aislynn snatched the parchment and unfolded it to find Tahlia's familiar handwriting.

Dear Aislynn,

My dear girl, you are so brave. One day I'll be with you again, but until then keep the mirror near—it will give you strength. If you are ever in any true danger, I will send someone to watch over you.

Beware the storyteller, for his truth is born of lies.

Love always,

Tahlia

Chapter 41

Aislynn folded the note carefully and knelt next to Cinnamon.

"Tahlia sent you?" she whispered, a warm happiness spreading through her. Cinnamon cocked her head. But the only answer she gave was a set of wet kisses across Aislynn's cheek.

"Come on, girl," Aislynn said with a soft laugh. "Let's go find the others."

No one was in the library or the dining room or even the kitchen. The enormous castle was quiet and dark. It made Aislynn sick to think of her parents abandoned here.

She headed out toward the gardens with Cinnamon. The moon was bright in the sky above her.

At the gate, she stopped short. Everything was dying. Brown and dying. The ground was dry and covered in sad, discarded leaves that broke under her feet. Thick vines, knotty and covered in thorns, had wrapped themselves around the trellis.

She glanced back at the castle. Only a few of the windows were illuminated. Her home was falling apart, destined to become overgrown and forgotten. What would happen to her parents without someone to chop wood and stock their pantry? If only . . .

The Orphans. Didn't they need a safe house, somewhere to hide those fleeing from Josetta? What better place than this, a castle that was shrouded in shadow and purposefully ignored? No. Her parents would never agree. Aislynn tried to push the idea away, but it was stuck like a log in a stream.

It was part selfishness that allowed her even to entertain such a thought. Even though autumn was nearly over and the wind was swirling around her, Aislynn wasn't cold. Her skin seemed to burn with anticipation, an eagerness to charge forward. She was no longer a girl wishing for a pure heart to guide her. She knew exactly where she wanted to go.

She wanted to be with Brigid and Elanor and Rhys and Thackery. She wanted to help the Orphans. It was a decision that felt so sure and so right that Aislynn wanted to shout it out loud.

There was a noise behind her, and she spun around. Her father was walking along the crumbling path.

"I've been looking for you," he said, leaning down to pet Cinnamon. "Your friends are resting, and I thought you might be tired as well."

But Aislynn was practically buzzing with excitement. "I think I'll stay here a little longer," she said, holding out her hand. "Would you like to join me, Papa?"

He stared at her extended hand for the longest time before grasping it tightly. His skin was cold, his face ashen.

"What is it?" she asked.

The king took a deep breath. "At the ball, you said I was afraid of you. Of what you had done." He squeezed Aislynn's hand. "I *was* afraid," he confessed. His dark hair was peppered with more gray than had been there before, and it gleamed in the moonlight. "But I've come to realize I was afraid *for* you. Your powers were so strong, and you were so young. I blamed myself. I was afraid of what would happen if we didn't send you away, if you didn't learn to control your abilities."

"You thought you were doing the right thing, Papa," said Aislynn. "You didn't know."

"I should have. I should have been more wary when they took you from us when you were a child." There was a pained look on the king's face. "And then when you were Redirected,

Adviser Hull told me to pretend you had never existed. As if it would make the separation more bearable." He hung his head. "I was so focused on following the Path that I didn't realize how far away it was taking me from the people I love." His fingers tightened before he released her hands. "I *was* afraid. But not of you, my dear. Never of you."

Aislynn closed her eyes. Deep in her chest, she felt the magic unfold. Nothing about it felt wrong or wicked. She felt powerful and extraordinary. She felt herself expand, felt the magic rushing through her.

The sad, untended garden seemed to sigh and shimmer. Smooth green vines uncurled across the trellis and gate, passing sweetly opening flowers as they climbed. With her father's hand in hers, Aislynn concentrated on the sagging brown shrubbery, and soon it exploded in vibrant green, dotted with perfect white flowers. The rosebushes were last, each blossom taking its time to unfurl soft petals and open its face toward the autumn moon.

"Beautiful," said Aislynn's father, but when she glanced up at him, she realized that he wasn't looking at the garden at all. He was looking at her.

Chapter 42

Aislynn frowned at her reflection. She looked every inch the princess, from her shimmering curls to her rouged and powdered face. But it was just a facade. If she looked closely, she could still see glimmers of her true self beneath her armor.

With Brigid's help, Aislynn had transformed an old dress of her mother's into a suitable ballgown. The dark blue dress was simple, with the long sleeves and rigid high collar of the Northern Kingdom. Modest, demure. Since she would be riding, there were no stiff petticoats to navigate, and Aislynn had refused to wear a corset. A cloak was attached at her shoulders. It had a hood that she could pull up to obscure her face. She would be almost invisible.

Beneath the embroidered rose on her chest, her heart gave a nervous lurch. It was almost time to leave. The academy was over half a day's ride away, and Linnea would be expecting her at midnight, or so Brigid had said.

It was Brigid who would be remaining behind with Aislynn's parents for the time being, with Cinnamon as protection. Aislynn was grateful but guilty. She had been careful when she told her parents about her plans. They knew she would not be returning tonight and that she would be gone for a while. Aislynn touched her throat. They did not know that there was a chance that she might never come back at all.

Reaching for her tea, Aislynn felt a rush of magic jolt through her. When she lifted the cup to her lips, it was full of sand. Annoyed, she put it back on the tray. Things like that had been happening all week—she had turned her dress three different colors before finally asking Brigid to fix it. Short, uncontrollable bursts of magic when she least expected it, and nothing when she consciously attempted to use it.

It was unacceptable. She needed to be prepared. She thought of the wall of fire she had created that night in the forest, and how she had made the soldier's ax fly back at him. She needed to be ready.

There was a knock at the door.

"Come in," said Aislynn and Thackery entered, stopping midstep as she turned to face him.

"You look . . . nice." His smile faltered. "Like a princess."

"I'm not a princess," Aislynn corrected him.

He raised an eyebrow.

"I'm a baker."

"The *best* baker," he said, and Aislynn laughed.

"The best baker," she agreed.

Thackery smoothed a lock of hair away from her face, and for a moment everything was the way it was meant to be. Then, far away, the afternoon bell sounded, and Aislynn was brought back to reality.

"Your Majesty?" Thackery extended an arm. "The ball awaits."

When they reached Erysimum Academy, it was very nearly midnight. They had been riding all day, but Aislynn had thought of nothing but the mirror and Linnea, causing the miles to speed by. The only indication of the long journey was how stiff her fingers felt when she finally uncurled them from the reins. She never thought she would be so grateful for the riding lessons she had taken as a princess.

Thackery found a grove of trees next to the road where he and the horses could remain hidden. Aislynn allowed him to help her down from her horse, her insides knotted up like a basket of hair ribbons. Every part of her was shaking, from her hands to her knees.

"I can't do it," she whispered, almost to herself.

"You'll be fine." Thackery's voice was close to her ear, his hand resting at the small of her back. "You're very brave."

"I don't feel brave," she said, turning to face him.

"You don't have to feel brave to be brave," he said, but her hands had already gone numb, and she was afraid that her legs would be next.

All her carefully made plans seemed ridiculous and impossible. What was she thinking, putting herself and her friends back in danger for a silly hand mirror? The world began to spin, and she reached out for Thackery.

Suddenly everything was still and solid again.

"You don't have to feel brave to be brave," she whispered. But as she curled her fingers around his neck, as she lifted herself on her tiptoes, as she brought his lips to hers, she felt brave. She felt strong and beautiful and wonderful.

Through the moonlight, a clock bell echoed. It was midnight.

"I'm late," she told him. Her fear was gone, replaced by a wonderful brightness.

"Don't be long," he said, looking a bit dazed.

"I won't," she promised, stealing another kiss. Then she stepped out of the safety of his embrace and into the shadows.

Chapter 43

The music was always the same, Aislynn thought as she crept through the garden. It was the violins that reached her first, followed by the golden strum of the harp. Giving thanks for the winter wind that cooled her hot skin and the clouds that kept her in shadow, Aislynn walked up the stairs leading to the ballroom terrace.

At the top, waiting for her, was Linnea.

"Aislynn," the monarch princess breathed, wrapping them both in the warmth of her red fur cape. She looked around quickly. "I don't think anyone realizes I'm out here," Linnea said. "Yet." She removed the mirror from her small bag.

A wave of relief broke over Aislynn as she took the mirror and slid it into the simple pouch tied at her waist. "Thank you," she said.

The monarch princess smiled and then threw herself into Aislynn's arms. "I've missed you so much!"

"I've missed you, too." Linnea was ice cold and trembling, and Aislynn knew that she could not leave her here.

"They told me you strayed." The monarch princess's eyes were darting nervously around.

"They lied." Aislynn pulled back, using the edge of her cloak to dab at her friend's tearful face. "Linnea, you need to come with me. It's not safe for you here—"

"Not safe?" asked Westerly, emerging from the shadows, his red suit opulent and bright. Aislynn bit her tongue as he bowed mockingly. "Please don't let me interrupt the tremendous lie you are currently constructing."

Swallowing her fear, Aislynn ignored him and tried to tug the monarch princess toward the stairs. But Linnea seemed rooted to the ground, looking from Westerly to Aislynn and back again.

"Darling?" Lifting a hand to her head, Linnea seemed to be struggling against her own thoughts.

"Go back inside, true love," he said.

Linnea hesitated for the briefest moment, then gently

pulled away from Aislynn and walked stiffly across the terrace and back into the ballroom.

"Linnea," Aislynn pleaded, but the other girl didn't even look back.

Suddenly Westerly's hand shot out, and with a strength belying his slender frame, he gripped Aislynn's arm painfully.

"Linnea!" Aislynn managed once more before a gloved hand was slapped over her mouth, muffling her cries. Aislynn fought him, twisting and squirming as he hauled her down the stairs and dragged her around the side of the academy. He headed with astounding speed toward one of the side entrances, crying out when Aislynn bit his hand.

"You stupid little stray," he spat, grabbing her cloak and pulling her the rest of the way. She scratched and kicked, but his grip only tightened. As he yanked her inside, Aislynn threw her heels against the floor, slowing him down—but only for a moment. Roughly, he grabbed the back of her neck and lifted her off her feet as though she was an animal.

With a great heave, he tossed her to the floor of the darkened library. She heard a loud rip and landed hard on her hands and knees. Panic rose in her throat. She needed her magic. Westerly came after her again, but before he could touch her, Aislynn punched him. Hard. There was a *crack*, and blood spiraled down from his nose in ribbons, staining his suit. Mewing like an injured cat, he swiped at her once before a voice interrupted them.

"Aislynn! How nice of you to join us." Madame Moira stepped out of a dark corner. She walked the perimeter of the carpet, the expression on her face both curious and cruel. "We've been looking for you, my dear. How kind of you to come to us."

Aislynn said nothing, ignoring the pain that shot through her legs when she stood. Where was her magic? The room was large, but the book-filled walls felt as if they were pushing up against her.

Jerking her head in Westerly's direction, Madame Moira dismissed the bleeding prince, who hurried out a second door, leaving them alone.

Madame Moira shook her head slowly. "My dear Aislynn. What are we going to do with you? I assume you have the mirror."

In spite of herself, Aislynn glanced down at her waist, where the pouch was concealed by her cloak.

The headmistress smiled and held out her hand. "It's time to give it to me."

"I'm not afraid of you," Aislynn said, finally feeling the familiar hum of magic vibrating through her. It felt stronger, more powerful than ever before. She stood up straighter and unfolded her hand.

"My dear child," said Madame Moira, "I will do my best to remedy that."

The air around Aislynn seemed to crystalize and she thrust her hands forward. A cold wind roared and the icy gust flung the headmistress to the other side of the room. The fire in the fireplace went out. Aislynn turned to run but in an instant felt the headmistress's magic slamming into her, shoving her to the ground. She slid across the floor, and before she even came to a stop, she was yanked up by her hair.

"Shall I tell you your problem, my dear girl?" Madame Moira's voice was a hiss in her ear.

"Please," Aislynn managed through clenched teeth.

"You never listened. You never *listened*. How many times did I tell you to remain with your own kind? I hope you know"—the breath she sucked in was full of pleasure—"that your friend Ford is dead because of you. And your other friends, the maid and the gardener, they'll suffer as he did. All because you don't listen."

Swallowing the bile that was rising in her throat, Aislynn willed herself to remain silent. The headmistress continued, "You're not mine to deal with, of course, but that doesn't mean I can't have some fun with you first."

She forced Aislynn's head back. "You remember my spindle, don't you, Princess?" she asked, pressing the sharp point to Aislynn's exposed throat. "You remember how I drew blood from your fingertips? Now give me the mirror, or we'll see how much blood I can draw from your pretty little neck."

Aislynn let her entire body go limp, and Madame Moira pitched forward, sending both Aislynn and the spindle crashing to the floor.

On her hands and knees, Aislynn scrambled for the needle. Just as her fingers closed around it, Aislynn felt Madame Moira's hand grabbing her cloak. She tore away and struggled to her feet. Madame Moira lunged, and Aislynn thrust the spindle forward.

"Don't. Move," Aislynn warned.

The spindle's sharp point was pressed against the embroidered rose on Madame Moira's uniform. Right over her heart.

"You wouldn't dare," said Madame Moira. She gasped when Aislynn gave the spindle a push, hard enough to pierce the uniform's fabric.

"Test me," Aislynn said, gritting her teeth. "Please."

The headmistress narrowed her eyes but didn't move.

"I'm going to leave," said Aislynn. "And if you follow me,

I'll make sure this finds its way right to your heart." The magic inside her was steady, and Aislynn knew that if she needed to, she could send the spindle into the headmistress—the same way she had sent the ax at the soldier in the forest.

Aislynn began to back away. She had taken only a few steps when the headmistress leaped forward. Aislynn threw up her hand, but instead of the spindle, she released a terrible wish. A wicked, horrible wish that she had made once before—a wish that burst from her before she could take it back.

There was a bright flash of light. When it cleared, a glowing blue orb hovered in the air between them. Madame Moira screamed as her loving heart shot straight toward her chest. She stumbled back.

Aislynn could still remember the pain that had filled her when her own loving heart had been returned to her. The agony. The headmistress sank to the floor.

For a moment, everything was still . . . and then Madame Moira's shoulders gave a great heave. When she finally lifted her head, Aislynn was shocked to see tears streaming down her face. Madame Moira raised her hands, staring at them with astonishment.

"They're warm," she said, her voice both joyous and hesitant. Slowly she pressed a palm against her cheek, closing her eyes. Then she reached up and pulled the wimple from her head. Her long braid fell over her shoulder, thick and curly with gentle lines of gray.

Suddenly there were footsteps in the corridor outside the library door. Aislynn froze, and Madame Moira's face went colorless.

"He's coming," she said.

The door opened.

"Good evening, Princess."

Standing in the doorway, his teeth as white as his suit, his smile as wide as it was loathsome, was Adviser Hull.

Aislynn's feet were as heavy as blocks of ice. She couldn't move.

Raising his arm, he made a dramatic bow. On his lifted hand was a familiar silver ring.

"It was you . . ." said Aislynn slowly. "In the forest. Not Westerly, you."

He smoothed his thumb over his knuckles, over the ring's white stone, and she flinched.

"Very good, Aislynn." Admiring the ring in the light, he said, "A kind gift from a generous prince, don't you think?" He took a step toward her, but before he could take another, Madame Moira rose and moved in front of him.

"She doesn't have it," the headmistress said, but her voice quavered. "The mirror. She doesn't have it."

"Is that so?" Adviser Hull regarded Aislynn thoughtfully. He smiled. Then, without warning, his hand shot out and closed around the headmistress's throat. She gasped.

"Why would you lie to me?" he asked, pulling her close. "Why would you be so foolish?" He looked at Aislynn. "But you really should give me the mirror, my dear girl. It is mine, after all." Aislynn backed away, fear freezing the magic inside of her. The spindle dropped from her fingers.

"Don't you want me to punish her?" he asked Aislynn, his fingers tightening around the headmistress's neck. "After all she's done to you. To your friends."

Aislynn's heart pounded in her ears. "No."

"Pity." Adviser Hull stared down at Madame Moira's terrified face and seemed to loosen his grip. "You're useless to me now, Moira. You couldn't even find a tiny little hand mirror when it was right under your nose." He glanced back at Aislynn. "Shall I show you what I do to girls like you? Girls who stray."

"I didn't stray," said Aislynn, her voice even.

Adviser Hull smiled. "It doesn't really matter, does it? You have no idea how easy it is to convince others of the wickedness of a girl like you. Almost as easy as convincing someone of their own wickedness. You know . . ." He tilted his head to the side. "You remind me of someone. She's serving her purpose quite well, I think. All we need to do is send a message once in a while on her behalf. A toe or a necklace." He winked, and Aislynn felt sick. "A couple of brambles—that's usually enough to breath new life into that story."

"Josetta," said Aislynn slowly. Was Hull the storyteller Tahlia had warned her about?

Adviser Hull looked pleased. "It was my idea to call her the Wicked Queen," he said. "More entitlement than she deserves." He sniffed, looking at the ring on his hand. "But isn't that the case with all you women anyway? Always taking what isn't yours. Like your dear, darling fairy godmother . . . what is she calling herself these days?"

Aislynn could see all of his teeth as his smile widened.

"Ah, yes, Tahlia. She really shouldn't have dragged you into this mess." He placed his hand on his cheek in mock concern. "She should never have given you that mirror." He shook his head pityingly. "But it's too late for that now.

"I was going to show you something, wasn't I?" The adviser looked down at the headmistress. Her eyes were closed, a single tear sliding down her cheek. "Ah, yes. I was going to show you what I do to those who don't follow the Path." He looked up at Aislynn. "And what I'm going to do to you."

The stone on his ring began to glow, a bright, blinding white, just as it had in the forest. With a grunt, Adviser Hull pressed his thumb into Madame Moira's neck. Her eyes flew open.

Aislynn watched in horror as the headmistress's eyes rolled back in her head.

"Give me the mirror, Aislynn," said Adviser Hull. "Can't you see it belongs to me?"

Aislynn looked down and gasped. The mirror was glowing. Through the layers of fabric, she could see an eerie blue light. She dug it out frantically. The blue stone in its handle was now pulsing as white and bright as the stone in Adviser Hull's ring.

"Very good, my dear," he said, sweat beading on his forehead. He flicked his fingers, and Aislynn felt her feet take a step toward him. Not of her own accord. But by magic. His magic.

It was impossible. Men were unable to do magic.

Madame Moira had gone limp, but Hull kept one hand tight around her neck. The streaks of gray in her hair seemed to be multiplying, and her face looked as if it was aging right before Aislynn's eyes.

"You don't deserve it. None of you do," Adviser Hull sneered.

Aislynn struggled to stop, to turn around. She couldn't breathe. He reached out for her. He was so close.

Suddenly magic burst from Aislynn like a gasp of air, the force of it knocking Hull back. He released Madame Moira, who collapsed on the floor, her breathing barely visible. The fire burst to life in the fireplace, spitting embers and smoke, and the entire room began to shake, the ground cracking and splintering. Books tumbled to the floor, their pages fluttering as a hot wind swept through the library. The ash bucket overturned, and the air was thick with soot. It filled Aislynn's lungs, settling around her like dark snow.

Adviser Hull stumbled as he stood. And although the sneer was still plastered across his face, Aislynn could see a shimmer of fear in his eyes as he glared at her.

But she was not afraid anymore. She was angry. She was furious. And she despised him. Hated him with every wicked, wild part of her being.

With an outraged roar, he charged toward her. But Aislynn barely noticed. Magic crackled all around her. It no longer felt like a kettle threatening to erupt without her control. Instead, her body felt like an instrument. Like a harp. Her strings hummed. She pressed the mirror against her chest. The stone glowed. It was no longer white, but blue, a deep, bright blue.

Adviser Hull lunged, and Aislynn let herself fall, unafraid, into her magic's embrace. It seemed to wrap its arms around her and, with a gentle tug, the room and Hull's face—now twisted with fury and confusion—disappeared. She fell from a high distance, but when she hit the ground, it was like landing on a featherbed.

"Aislynn?" Thackery's face was contorted with worry as he knelt next to her.

She was lying in the middle of the road. Scrambling to her feet, she shook the soot from her gown and looked back at the castle, its silhouette bathed in moonlight.

Thackery was staring at the mirror. "Is that . . . ?" he asked, and Aislynn nodded, handing it to him. Carefully he turned it over in his hand. The stone had already returned to a polished white. "It looks so ordinary," he said.

There was so much to tell him, but it would have to wait.

"We need to go." Aislynn knew that it wouldn't be long before Adviser Hull came after her.

With a sharp nod, Thackery retrieved the horses from their hiding place behind the trees.

Looking back at the academy again, Aislynn felt a sharp twinge of regret—almost panic—knowing that she was leaving Linnea behind. But that didn't mean that Aislynn would forget about her. That she wouldn't try again to protect her. To rescue her.

On the side of the road was a wild rose bush. Aislynn thought of all the times she had been warned that magic would cause briars to grow in her heart. She had always been afraid of briars, afraid of what they meant. It was a fear that had been planted and carefully nurtured by Adviser Hull and by others. She knelt and pressed her hand into the dusty road. She felt the ground quake.

He would try to follow her, but she would do her best to slow him down. The road split, and the rose bush's thick vine emerged from the dirt, sliding like a snake toward the castle. It climbed over the gate, tendrils twisting back the iron, and moved quickly in the direction of the ballroom. Aislynn imagined brambles growing, thick and sharp, across every window and door. It was time for Adviser Hull to be afraid of thorns.

"Do you think he'll come after you?"

She turned to find Thackery holding the reins for her horse, eyes wide. She nodded as she stood. "I have something that he wants."

If the ring gave him magic, then perhaps the mirror could as well. And Aislynn imagined there was nothing Adviser Hull wouldn't do to obtain it.

She swung herself onto her horse's back. Clicking her tongue, she took the lead, turning in the direction of the mountains. She knew exactly where they were going.

As they headed down the road, Aislynn took one last look at the world she was leaving behind. She was no longer safe.

The thought should have frightened her, but it didn't. She hadn't been safe for a long time.

Instead of fear, something else was simmering inside of her, as warm and powerful as magic, steady and absolute, almost like courage, but more reckless and wild.

She smiled and whispered to herself, "I will accept the path I am taking. . . ."

Tahlia's Cinnamon Bookbinder Bread

(makes one loaf)

Aislynn's favorite bread. Best made with one's fairy godmother, or someone with baking experience.

INGREDIENTS

For the dough:

2¾ cups all-purpose flour *plus* 2 tablespoons for handling the dough and preparing the pan

¼ cup granulated sugar

2¼ teaspoons active dry yeast

½ teaspoon salt

2 large eggs, at room temperature

⅓ cup whole milk

¼ cup unsalted butter *plus* extra for greasing the pan

¼ cup water

1 teaspoon pure vanilla extract

For the filling:

1 cup granulated sugar

2 teaspoons ground cinnamon

¼ cup unsalted butter

DIRECTIONS

Make the dough:

1. In a large bowl, whisk together 2 cups of flour, the sugar, yeast, and salt. Set aside.

2. In a small bowl, whisk eggs together. Set aside.

3. In a small saucepan, heat milk and butter together until butter has melted, stirring constantly—do not let the mixture boil. Remove from heat, then mix in water and vanilla extract. Let cool until mixture is warm but not hot.

4. Slowly fold the milk mixture into the dry ingredients.

5. Add eggs and mix until smooth, then work in the remaining ¾ cup of flour with your fingers. (The dough will be sticky.) Place the dough in a large greased bowl and cover with a kitchen towel. Put the covered bowl in a warm place and let it sit until the dough has doubled in size, about one hour.

Make the filling:

Do this when the dough has doubled and you are ready to start constructing the bread.

1. Mix the sugar and cinnamon together. Set aside.

2. In a small saucepan, melt the butter until it is just starting to turn brown. Set aside.

Construct the loaf:

1. Butter a 9 x 5–inch loaf pan and dust it with flour. Set aside.

2. Knead the dough. As you work, add the last 2 tablespoons of flour as needed to make the dough easier to handle. Shape the dough into a smooth ball, then cover it with a kitchen towel and let it rest for five minutes.

3. Working on a floured surface, roll out the dough. Try to make a square that is about 18 inches on each side and about ¼ of an inch thick.

4. Add filling: brush the melted butter across the dough. Then sprinkle on the sugar and cinnamon mixture.

5. Slice the dough into six long strips, each about 3 x 18 inches. Then stack the strips on top of each other. This will give you a tall, thin pile of layers.

6. Slice down into the pile to make four sections. Each section will be about 3 x 4½ inches.

7. Working with one section at a time, place each section in the pan on its side (the long side). Keep them together as much as possible. There will be extra room in the pan, but the dough will expand to fill the space.

8. Preheat oven to 350 degrees.

9. Cover loaf pan with a kitchen towel and let dough rise for about 45 minutes. There should still be some room in the pan; the dough will rise more in the oven.

10. Bake loaf for 30 to 35 minutes, until the top is golden brown.

11. Let cool for a few minutes. The bread is best when it is still warm and can be pulled apart and eaten in chunks.

Those Who Must Be Thanked

My family. My parents, who filled our house with books and never let us go to bed without a story. My mom, who gave me my love of baking, and my dad, who gave me the tenacity I needed to write a whole damn book. Adam and Abra, for indulging the creative whims of their bossy older sister, even when it led to the creation of many embarrassing home movies. And Bubbe, who took me to see *Into the Woods* when I was young and impressionable.

My agent Samantha, who pulled *Stray* from the slush, cleaned it off and found it a home.

My editor Virginia, who had all the right questions and made sure that Aislynn never got too weepy.

Tu Anh, Preeti, Gina, Martha, and everyone at Greenwillow Books and HarperCollins for giving *Stray* a place among your collection of wonderful stories.

My friends. My actual, real-life Fairy Godfather Shephard, who bolstered me with tea and Chinese food. My nerd-in-arms Tal, for her wise words and limitless love of YA. And everyone who read a version of *Stray* and helped shape it into the book it has become: Greg, David, Rachel, Sally, Sean, and Kate.

John, for reading the first draft in one sitting. I love you, fella. Like, a lot.

Basil, my constant companion. You're a dog and you're awesome.

Turn the page to start reading *Burn*,
a companion to *Stray*.

Burn

*Magic always
leaves its mark*

THE COMPANION TO *STRAY*
ELISSA SUSSMAN

Chapter 1

Elanor's shoulder was bleeding. The wound pulsed like a second heartbeat, blazing hot beneath her jacket before turning heavy and cold, blood soaking the bandage. Rhys had removed the arrowhead days ago, but his hands had been shaking. For someone so proficient with a sword, he wasn't very fond of the sight of blood.

They should stop. Elanor looked over in Rhys's direction. They hadn't spoken since sundown, moving at a punishing pace through the forest, and in the moonlight she could see him slumping under the weight of his pack, his chin dipping toward his chest.

He was exhausted. They both were, but these woods weren't

safe for those who needed a place to rest. There were wolves and bears and other beasts, but mostly there were huntsmen. Josetta's huntsmen. And nothing ceased their searching.

Elanor knew they wouldn't be safe until they were past the barrier. Until they were home. The queen had sought out their hidden camp for years, filling the woods with spies and soldiers. And if not for the magical barricade constructed by the Elders and for the Orphans' constant, watchful eye, Josetta would have found them many times over. Only the Mountain was safe, and Elanor had learned long ago not to trust the world beyond it.

They were close. Elanor could smell it. Fire and iron. Home. Her face tingled in the chilled air. Snow was on its way. That, too, she could smell, fresh and clear and sharp.

To keep herself awake, Elanor assessed her injuries. There was her shoulder, of course, but there was a host of other pains that would need to be healed. Her legs ached, and she couldn't remember when she had last removed her shoes. Every inch of her exposed skin was cold and stiff. Her face, her ears, her fingers. Winter had come fast during their journey; neither of them had been prepared. Elanor's hood lay limply against her neck. Pulling it up over her head might warm her, but it would also restrict her sight and hearing. With exhaustion already threatening her senses, she couldn't risk another distraction. There had been too many of those already.

Elanor swallowed the bitter taste that came with the memory of the ambush. She should have been paying attention. She should have heard the huntsmen coming. Instead she had let herself be distracted by the princess and her magic. By the trees rustling and the welcoming sunlight and the bright slash of rainbows dancing across Aislynn's and Thackery's faces.

And when Elanor had finally come to her senses, it had been too late. Even now, Cinnamon's howl echoed in her ears— the low, mournful call of trouble. Why hadn't her bow been drawn? Why hadn't she reached for one of her many knives? Why had she just stood there until an arrow cut through the air and through her shoulder?

She had stumbled, might even have fallen if it hadn't been for Rhys.

"Ellie!" he had said.

How she hated that nickname.

The pain was nothing. She'd had much worse, but it was the shame of getting caught that stung. Of being surprised by a group of huntsmen so large that a deaf boar would have heard them coming.

It was later, when she was wiping her weapons clean, that Elanor realized how truly unnerving the attack had been in the first place. The others seemed mainly concerned about who the huntsmen were looking for, but Elanor knew that wasn't what really mattered.

"I've never seen Josetta's huntsmen this far north before," she had said, knowing she had to turn back. The Elders needed to know what had happened.

That had been several days ago. Rhys had not questioned the pace Elanor set for them, and now they were close.

Suddenly Elanor's skin tingled with the sensation of magic. It was a bittersweet feeling, one she missed the moment it was gone. Like forgetting thirst until drinking a single drop of sweet, cold water and then thinking of nothing but your parched tongue. That was how magic always felt to her. She heard Rhys let out a sigh of relief. They had reached the barrier.

Wide-awake now, Elanor sped up. Rhys matched her strides and they moved through the trees together, the surroundings familiar even in the dark. The branches above them began to thin, sending soft beams of moonlight onto the forest floor. Then Elanor saw it. The Mountain. The scent of it, of fire and iron and cedar and stone, filled her senses. For a moment she lost herself in it. But not enough to miss the rustle of footsteps behind her.

Quickly she spun around, her knife finding the man's throat. Ioan grinned, his teeth gleaming in the light of the moon.

Chapter 2

"I could have killed you," Elanor said to her brother, quickly regretting how her voice echoed. This was neither the time nor the place for conversation. She returned her knife to her belt, frowning.

Ioan's smile only deepened, showing all his dimples. He shared that grin with Rhys, who could only shake his head. Without another word, Ioan squeezed Elanor's arm, stepping out of the shaft of moonlight and back into the darkness.

He wouldn't be the only person on guard tonight. At all times there were at least half a dozen well-armed Orphans protecting the expanse of land around the Mountain's entrance. Because even though they were inside the barrier, even though it was past midnight, even though it was winter, the Orphans took no chances when it came to protecting their home.

The energy that had carried Elanor this far began to flag as she followed Rhys toward the Mountain's only point of entry. To the ignorant eye it might look like any other felled trunk, resting on the rock face at the edge of the forest. It looked like a dead end, nowhere to go but back. Elanor had once questioned the wisdom of living so close to the queen's palace, but it wasn't long before she realized that the Mountain's impenetrable sides and single, well-guarded entrance provided more strategic protection than any distance could offer them.

In the clearing between the Mountain and the forest, the stars and moon shimmered in the satin blue sky above them. The last leg of their journey illuminated, they made their way toward the tree, its twisted roots facing them, spread like outstretched fingers. Elanor stepped inside the trunk, her hand finding the familiar ridges in the bark. Even though she knew that following the cuts on the wall would lead her inside the Mountain, to its warm, inviting glow, Elanor still hesitated before stepping into the complete blackness of the tunnel. How she hated the dark.

But in she went. Twelve steps straight ahead and then twenty-two down into the earth. When she reached the bottom, Elanor could see the faintest hint of illumination ahead. Two dozen steps more and then twenty up and into the light.

The entryway was quiet except for the soft echo of faraway water and the crackle of magic-lit candles melting into the rock ledges. Everything around her seemed to hum with magic, and the chill left her skin. For the first time in weeks, Elanor felt safe.

Carved into the entryway was an altar to honor the Four Sisters. Once upon a time, they had been legendary warriors who gave their lives in battle. As a reward for their bravery, they were allowed to remain in this life, but in different forms.

They had each thought carefully about what they would become. One of the sisters, known for her cunning, chose to become a fox. Another, known for her wisdom, asked to be an owl. The bravest of the sisters was transformed into a noble wolf, while the gentlest of the four became a swan.

Captured forever in stone, the Four Sisters were seated together, each wearing a mask that depicted the animal they had become. Each Orphan had a sister that they pledged their loyalty toward. Kissing his fingers, Rhys touched the carving of Sister Swan, and then brought his hand back to his forehead. Elanor did the same to the statue of Sister Fox.

Behind the altar was a series of four tunnels. It was late,

but Elanor knew Bronwyn would still be awake. She looked over at Rhys, who was doing his best to keep steady on his feet. In the candlelight she could see for the first time how truly exhausted he looked.

"You should have Dimia look at your head," she told him, though his bandage showed no signs of continued bleeding.

"Only after she looks at your shoulder."

In the excitement of returning home, Elanor had pushed aside her pain, but now it came back, roaring like an angry giant. She shook her head.

"I need to speak to Bronwyn," she said.

"I'll go with you."

"I can manage on my own," Elanor said firmly. "Go to the infirmary." When he hesitated, she drew herself up to her full height, still a head and a half shorter than him. "Go see Dimia and then head immediately to the mineral pools. You stink."

Rhys smiled then, the expression softening the hard lines of weariness on his face. He bowed. "Yes, Your Majesty," he said.

Elanor watched him head down the second tunnel to the left, where the infirmary and most of the sleeping quarters were. When he was out of sight, she gritted her teeth, adjusted her pack, and took the tunnel farthest to the right, toward the kitchen, dining cavern, and lodging for the Elders.

Elanor could hear an argument as she approached Bronwyn's quarters. She paused just beyond the threshold.

"You're being selfish," Wren was saying. Elanor could hear her annoyance.

"I could say the same thing about you," Heck answered, calm as always.

Then Bronwyn called out. "It's rude to hover," she said. "Come in if you have something to say."

Her neck hot with embarrassment, Elanor pushed aside the curtain and entered the room. Wren was standing with her arms crossed, while Heck leaned casually on his crutches, one pant leg pinned neatly beneath his knee. The air was tense, the argument lingering in Wren's flushed face and Heck's frown. Only Bronwyn, seated in her chair, remained impassive, as usual.

"Next time you want to spy," she said, "avoid casting a shadow in my doorway."

"I didn't mean to eavesdrop," Elanor said.

Bronwyn waved Elanor's apology aside. "You've returned."

"Yes, Elder," Elanor said. Her pack was like a bag of rocks on her back, her feet and shoulder aching. "We came across a large party of huntsmen. Near the northern border."

"How close to the border?" Wren interrupted, shoving a

hand through her short, brilliant blond hair.

"Less than a day away."

"How large was the group?"

"Nearly a dozen," said Elanor. She didn't need to point out that this was more than double the usual size for one of Josetta's patrols.

"This is good news," said Heck.

Elanor was sure she had heard him wrong.

"You and I have a very different understanding of what good news looks like," Wren said, echoing Elanor's thoughts.

"If you would stop being stubborn and look at it from a different perspective, you might understand what I see," Heck responded.

"I understand exactly what you see. I still think you're wrong," Wren snapped, glaring at him.

"What do you think it means?" Bronwyn stood, directing her question toward Elanor.

"That Josetta wants to expand her rule beyond the Midlands. Beyond the western kingdom."

"What would you recommend we do?"

Elanor was startled by the question. That was not something she was usually asked. That was the job of Orphans like Wren and Heck, who were both several years older than Elanor and offered counsel to the Elders.

"I think we should find out how far the patrols are now going," she said.

"It doesn't matter how far they're going," said Wren.

"It doesn't?" Heck asked, one dark eyebrow raised. "I think it matters quite a lot."

"It matters to you," she shot back.

"Both of you can leave," Bronwyn said abruptly. "I have heard what you have to say. I will discuss it with the other Elders."

Heck and Wren bowed their heads respectfully and made their exit, continuing their argument the moment the curtain fell behind them.

As their voices faded, Elanor turned back to Bronwyn, who had returned to her chair. Her twisted gray dreadlocks were up and circling her head, exposing a graceful neck scarred by age and war. Her hands were clasped in her lap, nearly disguising her missing fingers, two from her left hand and one from her right. She never referred to them, except once in a rare instance of humor, when she had joked that she should cut off one more to make it even. She had been drinking. No one had laughed.

"Did you at least retrieve what you intended to retrieve?" Bronwyn asked. The Elders had not been pleased when they learned that four able-bodied soldiers had intended to help one royal. But they had done nothing. Orphans were free to make their own decisions, something that set them apart not just from Josetta's followers, but from other commoners who were at the mercy of royal commands.

"Rhys and I departed before the mission could be completed," Elanor said.

"I assume the others are still with the princess?" Bronwyn's disapproval was evident.

"Yes, Elder."

"We lost two Orphans during your absence," said Bronwyn. "Two more were injured."

If Bronwyn's intention was to make Elanor feel guilty, she had succeeded.